The Block Party

by

NICOLE PYLAND

The Block Party

Holiday Series Book #2

Talon Mitchell had gotten a job right out of college, had her own coffee mug at the office that no one else could use, and planned to keep her job as sales manager for a long time because she had practically grown up working for this company. She was content and not looking for anything when a new sales director showed up and changed everything.

Emerson Bagley just got a new job, and while she felt ready for the next step, when she sees someone she recognizes from a holiday party working on the same team, she can't believe her luck, both good and bad. Good, because Talon Mitchell was very attractive, very smart, and seemingly, very interested in Emerson, too. Bad, because she couldn't date someone who worked for her, especially in her brand-new job.

Feeling the simmering heat begin to boil over, the two women decide to at least take one step and deal with the rest later. When neither of them had been prepared to seek out love, they managed to find it where they least expected it.

To contact the author or for any additional information, visit: **https://nicolepyland.com**

ISBN-13: 978-1-949308-81-5 Paperback

ISBN-13: 978-1-949308-82-2 eBook

BY THE AUTHOR

Stand-alone books:

- The Fire
- The Moments
- The Disappeared
- Reality Check
- Love Forged
- The Show Must Go On

Chicago Series:

- Introduction – Fresh Start
- Book #1 – The Best Lines
- Book #2 – Just Tell Her
- Book #3 – Love Walked into The Lantern
- Series Finale – What Happened After

San Francisco Series:

- Book #1 – Checking the Right Box
- Book #2 – Macon's Heart
- Book #3 – This Above All
- Series Finale – What Happened After

Tahoe Series:

- Book #1 – Keep Tahoe Blue
- Book #2 – Time of Day
- Book #3 – The Perfect View
- Book #4 – Begin Again
- Series Finale – What Happened After

Sports Series:

- Book #1 – Always More
- Book #2 – A Shot at Gold
- Book #3 – The Unexpected Dream
- Book #4 – Finding a Keeper

Celebrities Series:

- Book #1 – No After You
- Book #2 – All the Love Songs
- Book #3 – Midnight Tradition
- Book #4 – Path Forward
- Series Finale – What Happened After

Boston Series:

- Book #1 – Let Go
- Book #2 – The Right Fit
- Book #3 – All Good Plans
- Book #4 – Around the World
- Series Finale – What Happened After

CONTENTS

CHAPTER 1

"How are you doing there, Champ?" Talon asked before pulling her long brown hair back up into a ponytail, using her teeth to hold on to the plastic champagne flute.

"Not all that great. If this is how my year is going to start, I can't imagine the rest of it is going to go well," Weston said.

"Technically, it's how last year *ended* for you. So, think of it like that. Maybe this year will be great," Talon replied after finishing the champagne and placing the cup on the table behind them. "Sorry, by the way."

Talon watched as Aria and Eleanor joined their ranks, holding on to their own champagne flutes and, likely, also coming over to help console Weston.

"What exactly happened?" Aria asked.

"I honestly have no idea," Weston said.

"She just dumped you?" Ellie asked, her brown eyes flittering at Weston in sympathy.

"She said we fight too much. I offered to get her a drink, and she said she wasn't drinking because she's been fasting since Christmas to try to lose the holiday weight before the new year."

"She's been fasting?" Aria asked. "*Before* the new year? Who does that? That's kind of weird."

"Hey, maybe she was just hangry, and that's why she ended things?" Talon suggested. "If we shove some food into her, maybe she'll think straight."

"Why bother?" Paisley Hill said, walking over from the

food table with her perfectly coifed red hair and gorgeous green eyes, staring back at Weston with her patented *I told you so* look. "She's not good enough for you anyway, Wes."

"You say that about everyone I date, Pais," Weston remarked.

"And it's been true every time," Paisley replied, sipping her red wine because she always had to be different.

"Senior-year Sarah was fine," Aria said, moving to stand next to Paisley now.

"What about junior-year Celine?" Talon asked.

"Celine was sophomore year. Remember, she was only in the US for the semester, and then she went back to France," Ellie corrected her.

"Oh, right. Weston dated her first. Then, it was Beth."

"Beth was junior year, yes," Weston said.

"Beth? From college?" Scarlet Campbell chimed in as she walked over.

There they all stood, the six of them. They'd known each other for so long now, it was one of the most common sights Talon knew; the six of them standing around or sitting in a bar booth sharing stories from the past or catching up on their weeks or things they missed because life kept pulling them in all sorts of directions these days. Talon could track meeting them all the way back to freshman orientation at a tiny liberal arts college that she'd been lucky enough to get a scholarship to attend. *A lot she'd done with that degree*, she thought to herself now. They'd all been relatively inseparable ever since. This party was an annual tradition, while they all still lived somewhat close to one another. Talon wondered how long that would last. Paisley owned her own company, and it was doing well. She could move wherever she wanted because she traveled for work all the time anyway. Weston was a writer who lived off a trust fund, and while the woman didn't flaunt that, she owned her own modest home and a cabin that she loved in the woods, and it wouldn't surprise Talon if she relocated there permanently one day. It was only about an hour and a half away from Weston's house now, but an hour and a half when Talon was used to driving for fifteen minutes and hanging out with Weston after a long day at work, would make a difference.

Then, there was Aria, who was the third of their well-off friends. Talon remembered the college had named a building after Aria's grandfather, who'd paid for the thing. The Bancroft Art Building had been finished just before they had all arrived on campus. Aria now edited academic journals for a living but did so freelance and only when she felt like it. The rest of her time was usually spent traveling to exotic locations and finding women to sleep with. Such a far cry from Talon's own life, but it didn't matter. No matter how different they all were, it somehow still worked.

Every year, this party was thrown by someone in the group's ex-girlfriend, who was now married to her wife and had a shitload of money to throw massive holiday parties at event halls like this. Talon couldn't even remember which of her friends had dated this woman at this point, but they were all still always invited, and they all still showed up. Now, they were all standing around Weston, forming an army of support, as they'd always done for one another, because her girlfriend of about six months had just dumped her.

"And we all know who freshman-year was," Aria said, smirking in Talon and Weston's direction.

"It was two months!" Talon and Weston said in unison, just like every other time people brought up the fact that Weston and Talon dated when they were nineteen.

"Two months of hot and heavy sex," Paisley joked.

"In a twin bed," Talon said. "So, not the sexiest thing in the world."

"Hey," Weston said, chuckling at her friends. "*You* two dated, too." She pointed to Aria and Eleanor.

And Talon was happy to have the subject changed away from her and Weston being a very short-term couple who did enjoy having sex. It had been new to Talon back then. In fact, the amount of times she wanted sex when they'd been dating, had been part of the reason Weston had ended things, which was a good thing because they were way better off as friends. Weston hadn't been a virgin when she'd arrived at college, and Talon had been so taken by her. Weston was artsy and creative. She was smart and funny. She was also clearly rich but didn't act like it. Weston had always made Talon feel like she'd belonged anywhere they went, even when Talon often felt like the scholarship kid who also had to do work-study and babysit to make enough money to live off of just to go to school.

When they'd gone on their first date, Talon knew she liked Weston, but it wasn't long after that that they'd had sex for the first time, and since Talon hadn't had a real girlfriend before, she kind of thought they should always just be having sex. It was dumb and naïve, but the sex they had was amazing to her at nineteen, and she wanted it as often as she could get it. Once Weston brought up that they hardly ever left their dorm rooms, Talon started to realize that they weren't really dating anymore – they were just sleeping together. Not long after that, it was over, they were back to being friends, and they had been ever since. It came up in conversation a lot within this group, and sometimes, it was Talon's own fault, but as much as she could joke about it, it also still took her back to when she didn't understand how adult relationships could and should work, which made her feel like an idiot.

"One date," Aria replied. "Not the same thing."

"It still happened," Talon said, poking fun at Aria and Eleanor's one date.

"Barely. I didn't even get a goodnight kiss," Ellie said, looking away from Aria with a mock-scowl.

"Want one now?" Aria joked, moving closer to her. "I'm tipsy. It's the New Year."

"I don't want your pity kiss," Eleanor said, laughing and pushing at Aria to move away.

"You two never dated within the group." Weston

pointed at Paisley and Scarlet. "How'd you manage to avoid it all this time?"

"I don't like clichés," Paisley said.

"She dated that guy from bio for, like, two years when we first got to college – that's how. Once we all got through freshman year, we found other people – or, no one at all, in my case," Scarlet explained. "Paisley avoided all of the initial time we all spent trying to figure out if we liked each other as friends or as more than friends."

"That's right. What was his name?" Talon asked, laughing.

"Milo," Paisley replied.

"Of the *Cape Cod* Milos," Talon mocked in her hoity-toity rich person voice.

"Of the *Manhattan* Potters. Milo *Potter*, you asshole," Paisley said, laughing at Talon. "Milo worked for me back then." She shrugged a shoulder. "He knew I was bi, didn't seem to have a problem with it, and–"

"Went to school three states away, boned every girl on campus, and didn't care if you did the same?" Weston interjected.

Talon laughed.

"We're almost thirty... Do we have to say *boned*?" Paisley asked. "And we didn't cheat; we were both *allowed* to do what we wanted. We knew what it was: our parents forcing us to try before we could tell them we gave it two years, and it wasn't working – which, it didn't. And now, here I am."

"Still single," Aria said.

"But on purpose; I don't want anyone. I just want to focus on my company and my work. I don't have this need to find someone and settle down," Paisley explained.

"Well, *I* do," Eleanor replied, sitting down in a chair in front of the table. "God, where is she, guys? I feel like I've been waiting forever to find her."

"Get in line," Aria said, sitting down next to her.

"At least, you're getting laid," Talon said.

"Hookups help, but it's not a relationship," Aria stated.

Talon stared at her confusing friend. Aria waffled about whether she wanted to just hook up with the women she met or if she wanted a real relationship. Talon often got whiplash trying to keep up with Aria's moods and thoughts on the subject.

"You're better off without a relationship anyway," Paisley said, convincing no one, as usual.

"I'm ready for a new one," Talon said. "I dated Leigh for a year, and when I said, '*Pass the gravy,*' at Thanksgiving, she said, '*It's over, Talon,*' and that was the end of that. What's with us getting dumped on holidays?" she asked Weston.

"No idea. I thought we were good. Yeah, we fought a lot, but–"

"All the time," Aria and Scarlet said at the same time.

"Like, literally every day," Eleanor added.

"Like I said, she's not good enough for you," Paisley said, finishing her wine.

Weston sat in an empty chair next to the rest of them now. Talon felt bad for her, and she could empathize. Her ex hadn't exactly dumped her at the table while passing the gravy, but it had been on Thanksgiving, the first holiday they'd decided to share with family. Talon had invited her to spend the day with her family since Leigh's parents weren't huge fans of her being gay and didn't welcome Talon to their holiday dinner. They hadn't been fighting that morning, but by the time dinner came around, Leigh was angry with Talon about something, which caused every argument they'd ever had to spill out of her mouth. That was it. Leigh declared them over, ordered herself a ride-share, and went back home, which thankfully, wasn't *also* Talon's home because they'd yet to move in together.

"I think, this is the first time that we've all been single at the same time," Talon commented, realizing it at that moment.

"Yeah, I think it is," Ellie added. "I don't want to go into my thirties unattached, though. I'm trying that new dating app for lesbians only."

"Really, Ellie?" Aria asked.

"You're having regular sex with a slew of women you meet on apps – you can't judge," Talon told her.

"First of all, it's not a slew." Aria held up a finger. "Second of all, that's not the same thing. It's sex; I'm not looking for the love of my life in an app."

"Well, I haven't met her anywhere else," Eleanor replied. "And I've *been* everywhere. I go to the gay bars, the straight bars, the bookstores that still exist, stalk the produce aisle at the grocery store, hang out at the cafes – it's not happening."

"Oh, speaking of… Have you guys seen there's a new bakery popping up over on sixth?" Aria asked the group.

"How is that a *speaking of?*" Talon asked.

"She said café. It made me think of pastries, which made me think of bakeries, which–"

"Okay. We're there," Talon interrupted.

"We need a new bakery. We only have cafés, and their stuff is frozen and delivered," Aria stated.

"When does it open?" Weston asked.

"No idea. I just saw a permit in the window, so… a while, probably."

"Well, now I want fresh-baked goods, and I can't have them. So, thanks, Aria," Paisley said.

"Oh, you know what would be great right now?" Scarlet asked.

"The rolls from *Domingos,*" all of them said at the same time, recalling the off-campus restaurant that was open all the time and had the best buttered rolls in the world.

"You know they sell them in the grocery store now," Weston said.

"What? They do?" Talon asked.

Paisley pulled out her phone.

"What are you doing?" Aria asked her.

"Finding a grocery store that's open right now so we can pick some up and go to Weston's place, since it's the closest, to eat them."

"I wish we had the coffee from the union. That stuff was turbo-powered," Aria added.

"You know that's just ground coffee beans and water, right?" Ellie asked. "I know the brand; I'm sure we could find it."

"Shit. You worked at the union for a semester; I forgot," Aria said.

"Coffee and rolls at Weston's?" Talon asked the group, hoping they all say yes because she wasn't ready to go home to her lonely apartment just yet.

"Only if my coffee can have booze in it," Weston said. "Broken heart and all."

"I think we can *all* have booze in our coffee as long as we can crash at your place," Scarlet suggested.

"Deal," Weston said.

"Adult sleepover," Ellie said rather loudly.

"You know that means something completely different than what you just said, right?" Aria said, nudging her shoulder.

Talon laughed when Ellie rolled her eyes at Aria, and then they all took off. Paisley had the store. Eleanor remembered the brand of the coffee. All six of them went into the only open grocery store, probably, in the tri-state area. Weston and Talon grabbed a couple of bottles of alcohol Weston was missing at her place. Scarlet and Aria got the snacks, knowing exactly what everyone in the group loved and hated. Eleanor got two huge bags of coffee. Paisley got four bags of rolls, since they only had six to a bag and that would give each of them a few. Talon then went back and saw there were still two more bags in the freezer, so she grabbed those too just in case. Paisley rolled her eyes at first but then nodded, knowing they could finish them easily.

An hour later, they had *Domingos'* warm buttered rolls, union coffee that tasted almost how they remembered it, chips, dips, candy, rum, Kahlúa, and bottles of water all around Weston's living room. Two hours after that, most of them were asleep on the floor or on Weston's furniture. Talon looked around at her friends, silently laughing because they used to be able to stay up all night without a problem the next morning, and now, she could predict the hangovers and grizzly bears she'd encounter in a few hours.

CHAPTER 2

Emerson hadn't wanted to come to this party in general, but she definitely didn't want to come to a New Year's Eve party on a third date with a woman she'd started seeing two weeks ago. They'd met through a friend, and their first date had been great. She'd liked Miranda enough to ask her out for a second date, which had been the previous weekend. That date hadn't been as good, in Emerson's opinion, but when they'd kissed goodnight at Emerson's door and Miranda suggested they do this again, Emerson hadn't wanted to be rude, so she accepted. Now, she was at someone's holiday party on a third date, feeling a bit like an outsider because she didn't know anyone.

"Are you okay?" Miranda asked.

"Yeah. Why?" Emerson lied, taking a drink of the sparkling water she'd managed to find earlier.

"You're just kind of staring."

"Oh, I don't know anyone here, so I'm trying to get my bearings."

"Aren't you in sales?" Miranda asked, knowing the answer already.

"Yeah. Why?"

"Shouldn't you be able to mingle with the best of them?"

"Not everyone in sales is extroverted or the life of the party, Miranda," she replied, not meaning to sound as harsh as it came out.

"I just meant that meeting people isn't usually hard for

salespeople because they have to put themselves out there to get the sale."

"This isn't work, though. It's a party," Emerson replied.

Miranda nodded and said, "Should we not have come here?"

"No, it's fine. I'm sorry," Emerson said, sighing. "I've never been on a date on New Year's Eve with someone I just started seeing."

"Neither have I," Miranda replied with a smile. "I just thought it would be fun for us. You could meet some of my friends, but not in some awkward, arranged way. They're here, but it's a party."

Emerson held back that she thought a third date was a little soon to be introducing her to Miranda's friends.

"Yeah, I get it. I think I'm going to grab a snack or something. I'll be right back."

"I can get it for you," Miranda volunteered.

"No, I'm okay. Can I get *you* anything?"

"I'm good. I'm going to go talk to my friend over there. Meet me when you're ready?"

Emerson nodded and walked off toward where she'd seen the food earlier, hoping to find something she could occupy herself with for a bit. Though there were caterers making rounds with trays of food, and there had been a light buffet, the party organizers had thought to add a table of more standard party food like fruit and veggie trays over in one corner. Emerson was grateful for that now because she needed a break from Miranda.

"Can you believe that?" a woman asked.

"No, it's New Year's Eve. What kind of person breaks up with someone on New Year's Eve?" another woman asked back.

Emerson looked up from the table and noticed a woman who looked to be a little younger than her, with long brown hair and beautiful brown eyes standing on the other side of the table, grabbing a carrot stick.

"Wes deserves better than her anyway," the first woman said.

"I feel like she dates women who won't ever be the one," the brown-eyed woman said as she crunched on her carrot. "She chooses women who don't get her and is then surprised when things end."

"She does the best she can, just like the rest of us, Talon," the first woman said.

"I know. I'm going to go console her if I can."

"I'll be there in a minute."

Emerson watched as the brown-eyed woman walked over to another woman who had short brown hair. The other woman joined them later, as did a few more, but Emerson had a hard time taking her eyes off the one with long brown hair. When she laughed, Emerson smiled and then pulled it back, wondering where in the hell that smile had come from.

"Hey, here you are," Miranda said.

Emerson turned to see Miranda standing next to her.

"Oh, hi."

"You've been standing here for a while now. Did you find something to eat?"

"Yeah," she lied. "Sorry, I got caught up talking to someone."

"Who?" Miranda looked around.

"Oh, I don't know. I didn't get their name. We were just chatting, and she got pulled away."

"Well, a few of my friends are over there and want to meet you if that's okay," Miranda said.

"Sure. Let's go." Emerson put on the face she didn't really have the energy to put on tonight.

As they walked, Emerson's head turned on its own to look at the woman again. She wasn't sure she'd heard right before, but it sounded like her name might be Talon, which was such an interesting name and, she guessed, had an interesting story to it. Emerson met Miranda's friends and noticed that Miranda got very touchy-feely around them with her. She held her hand, touched Emerson's elbow, lower back, pulled her into a hug, and gave her a quick kiss as she introduced Emerson to friend after friend. Emerson was attracted to Miranda; she had been since they met. But she hadn't prepared for quite this much PDA and meeting the friends on only a third date. She played along, though; figured it was just one night, and Miranda had mentioned she'd been single for a while. Maybe she just needed to show off the fact that she had a date at all.

When the countdown began, Emerson felt Miranda's hand tug on her own to get Emerson to turn to her for the traditional kiss at midnight. As Emerson turned, she caught sight of the woman named Talon, who was standing around a couple of the same women as before, and she wondered if any of them would be her kissing partner tonight.

"Happy New Year," Miranda said and wrapped her arms around Emerson's neck.

It wasn't their first kiss; that had been at the end of their second date on Emerson's stoop. That kiss had been good. It was long, and Emerson had considered asking Miranda inside, but she'd decided it was too early for that. Tonight, she'd expected a peck on the lips since they were surrounded by people, but Miranda went for it. Her tongue slipped into Emerson's mouth and Emerson, again, felt unprepared for this type of affection. She kissed her back but pulled away after a minute or so and smiled at her.

"Your place after this?" Miranda asked, pulling Emerson in for a hug.

"Sure," Emerson replied.

Miranda had driven them, so they had to go to her place, but it was the third date, and it had been a while since Emerson had had sex, so if Miranda was interested in that tonight, Emerson wouldn't mind starting off her year with an orgasm given to her by someone else and not her trusty vibrator. It was only a little past midnight when Miranda tugged on her arm yet again and asked if she was ready to go. Emerson hadn't wanted to attend in the first place, so she was definitely ready to go. As they walked to the door, though, she saw that Talon woman again and wondered still who had kissed her at midnight.

***

Emerson let Miranda inside the house, which she hadn't yet seen. Miranda dropped her purse and keys onto the kitchen island and had her arms around Emerson quickly after. Emerson wrapped her arms around the shorter woman's waist, and as their lips connected, they were off. Miranda lifted herself up and sat on the island, spreading her legs for Emerson to stand between. When Emerson did, Miranda moaned. That turned Emerson on, and her hands moved under Miranda's dress, resting on her thighs. Miranda moaned again, and Emerson kissed her harder. Miranda *was* a great kisser. She was sexy in her little black dress tonight, too. Emerson had been proud to have her on her arm. She just had this feeling she couldn't quite shake, and it had started before midnight.

"Bedroom?" Miranda asked as Emerson moved her lips to Miranda's neck. "Or, I'm okay here, if you want–"

Emerson moved her hand to Miranda's center, noting the thong that was probably see-through or close to it. Miranda gasped and kissed her hard. Then, Emerson thought about Talon kissing someone. She wasn't even sure she'd heard right. Was her name even Talon? Had it been Fallon or Kallon? Was Kallon a name? Maybe she'd heard wrong entirely, and it was something else. Either way, she thought about the woman with the long brown hair and those brown eyes that were light and dark at the same time, and she removed her hand from Miranda's sex.

"No, please don't stop," Miranda said, moving Emerson's hand back to where it was and rocking her hips against Emerson's palm while she kissed Emerson again.

"I…" Emerson pulled back, removing her hands from Miranda entirely now.

"What's wrong?" Miranda asked with swollen lips, breathing hard.

"Nothing. I just…"

"Too fast? Do you want to slow down? We can go to your bedroom."

"No, it's not that. I want to, but I…" Emerson ran her hand through hair that wasn't really there anymore.

She'd cut it into a pixie cut not all that long ago and still hadn't adjusted to the fact that her hair was now much shorter than it used to be.

"Emerson, what's going on?" Miranda asked, sliding her legs together now.

"I don't know that I'm ready."

"You had your hand on my pussy just a second ago," Miranda said. "Come on, baby. It's New Year's Eve. Let's celebrate." Miranda put her arms on Emerson's shoulders and pulled Emerson back to her, spreading her legs again.

Emerson moved into her, feeling the heat between them and wanting to touch Miranda, wanting to hear her come and feel her clench. Emerson was horny; that much, she knew. What she didn't know yet was whether or not she wanted to sleep with Miranda or just someone, and that wasn't Emerson's style.

"I don't think we should have sex for the first time just because it's a holiday," Emerson said.

"Okay. Can we just have sex because we want to have sex, then?" Miranda asked, looking confused.

"I don't think so. Not tonight," Emerson said.

"What happened? We were…"

"Nothing. I thought I was ready, but I'm not. It's not you, though."

"It's not me; it's you? Really, Emerson?" Miranda asked.

"Sorry. Can we maybe just sleep tonight?"

"Sleep?"

"Yeah. You can still stay over, but we'll just sleep. I can hold you tonight," Emerson said, placing her hands on

Miranda's thighs.

"I don't want to just sleep, Emerson. I came over because I wanted us to take this relationship to the next level. I gave you, like, a million signals tonight."

"I'm not ready, Miranda."

"Okay. That's fine." Miranda hopped off the island, forcing Emerson to back up to allow her some space. "It is," she added. "I don't want to pressure you. I just thought we were both on the same page, but it's fine." She reached for her purse and her keys. "I think I'll just head home, though. I need to cool off, if you know what I mean."

"You don't want to stay?"

"I do. I just don't want to sleep," Miranda replied.

"I'm sorry if I led you on or teased–"

"You did, but it's okay. You're not ready. I'm not looking to convince a woman to sleep with me."

"It's not like that. I want to. I–"

"You're not ready." Miranda nodded. "It's our third date, Emerson; it's fine. I'll call you tomorrow, and maybe we can set up date number four for some time this week."

"Sure," Emerson said, feeling like she said that a lot to this woman.

Miranda kissed Emerson's cheek.

"I'll call you."

"Yeah," Emerson said.

CHAPTER 3

"She's here," Weston said.

"Who's here?" Talon asked.

"Annie."

"Annie, the agent you're crushing on?" Talon asked, looking around the restaurant.

"I'm not crushing on her."

"Oh, please…" Talon wasn't having it. "You just got out of a six-month relationship with a woman you supposedly loved, and you can't stop talking about this Annie woman. I don't even know if you remember your ex-girlfriend's name at this point."

"Kind of hard to remember it when my friends all just called her 'the bitch' and kept telling me I deserved better," Weston argued.

"Well, you do. Is Annie it?"

"What? No. She's my agent," Weston said. "And she's here on a date, I think."

Talon followed Weston's gaze until it landed on two women who were seated at the bar and had glasses of wine in front of them. Talon rolled her eyes at her best friend. It had been less than two weeks since Weston had been dumped, but Talon had heard her talk more about Annie Halifax, her new literary agent, than the girlfriend she'd had for more than six months. Talon knew that her friend was more than smitten.

"I don't think so," Talon said, realizing something.

"Huh?"

"I don't think it's a date," Talon clarified. "They look a lot alike – I'm going with sisters or, at least, cousins or something."

Talon's hypothesis was based on the fact that the women had the same color hair and similar bone structure.

"What?" Talon asked.

"I didn't say anything," Weston replied, turning back to Talon.

"Your face did. You *want* them to be sisters, don't you?" Talon smirked. "It would mean you still have a chance."

"No, I just… I don't need a chance. She's my agent." Weston looked over again at the two women. "She's really pretty, though, isn't she?"

"Annie or the other woman?"

"Talon, I'm serious…"

"Yes, Annie is very pretty from what I can see from thirty feet away. The other one is hot, too, though. I might be praying they're sisters as well."

Talon checked out the woman she knew her friend wasn't interested in, and if that woman was Annie's sister, cousin, or related in other ways, Talon would like that because the other woman was even more attractive, in Talon's opinion.

"Seriously?" Weston asked.

"What?" Talon exclaimed. "I'm single, too. Think if they're sisters, it's likely the other one is also into women?"

She doubted it. It so rarely worked out that way, but it might be worth a shot.

"Oh, my God." Weston paused. "And she's spotted me staring at her. Perfect," Weston said.

"Just go say hello and we can get on with dinner," Talon suggested, wanting to eat sometime tonight.

"Will you come with me?"

"If it'll get me an intro to the *other* Annie, definitely," Talon replied, only half-joking.

"Do *not* embarrass me," Weston said as she stood.

Talon followed Weston, curious to see just how this would go.

"Hey. Fancy meeting you here," Annie said to Weston.

"I just saw you and thought I should come over and say hi," Weston replied. "Don't want to interrupt anything."

"You aren't," Annie said. "Weston White, this is my sister, Aubrey Halifax. Aubrey, this is Weston, a new client."

Sister? Talon smiled.

"Oh, *you're* the writer of that ridiculously good manuscript?" Aubrey said.

"I don't–"

"How do you know about that?" Annie asked Aubrey, taking a long gulp of her wine.

"I read it," Aubrey replied.

"You read it?" Annie and Weston asked at the same time.

"Oh, I work for the agency, so you don't need to worry about a leak or anything," Aubrey said to Weston, turning in her swivel chair to face her a bit more, which, of course she did. "My dad sent it to me. I read it instead of doing the work I probably should have been doing."

"If you work for the agency, isn't reading manuscripts part of your job, though?" Talon said.

"Oh, sorry. This is my friend Talon," Weston said, introducing Talon to Annie and Aubrey.

"Nice to meet you," Annie said, finishing her wine.

"Let me get you another," Weston said, smiling softly at Annie.

Her friend was adorable at times. Talon looked at Aubrey, who was definitely even more attractive up close.

"Weston, the book is going to be a bestseller," Aubrey said. "And to answer your question, Talon, I'm only recently getting into the family business. I ran off to run my own company for a bit, and I currently work at an online magazine, but I'll be leaving there to help Annie run the agency now."

"She's the prodigal daughter," Annie said softly.

"Cool," Talon said to Aubrey.

"You're running the agency?" Weston asked Annie.

"Our father is retiring," Aubrey said. "Annie and I will

be taking it over soon, but don't worry, Annie will still be your agent. Of course, you'll get a deal in no time for that book of yours, and I have a feeling you'll be pretty easy work for Annie here since you're not likely one of those writers we'll have to beg to keep working so we can keep getting you great deals."

"I've finished one book in, like, five years, so you might want to hold that thought," Weston said.

"So, you'll be the manager or head of something?" Talon asked Aubrey.

"We haven't worked that part out yet, but we'll both be involved in some capacity. So what is it that you do, Talon?" Aubrey asked her, definitely showing some interest now that Weston seemed more concerned with Annie.

"I'm a sales manager at a software company. It's not glamorous, but there's free food," she said.

"Weston, what do you do?" Aubrey asked.

Damn it. She was back to Weston now.

"Write," Weston said.

"Nothing else?" Aubrey asked.

"No," Weston replied.

"Weston is one of my wealthier friends," Talon said.

"Talon!"

"What? It's true. I have a few of you." Talon sat in the chair next to Aubrey. "We all met in college. We went to this super small liberal arts school that no one has ever heard of, but it attracts a certain group of people to which Weston belongs. I did *not* belong, but they offered scholarships, and I managed to wrangle one."

"Talon sells herself short. She's incredibly smart. She's worked her way up at that company from an entry-level sales rep to now managing a team there," Weston said. "All I've managed to do is write one book in that time."

"One really good book," Aubrey said.

"She gets it, Aubrey; you like her book," Annie said, turning back to them now. "Weston isn't a huge fan of compliments, or can't you tell?"

"Sorry, I can't help myself," Aubrey said, leaning toward Weston a bit and placing a hand on Weston's forearm.

And with that, Talon thought about giving up. Aubrey was flirting, but she was flirting with Weston, which wasn't uncommon. Weston was the creative, loner-writer type. Talon managed a sales team and didn't know how to make that sound as cool as writing a potential bestseller.

"Annie, who's likely to pick it up?" Aubrey asked her sister.

"What?" Annie asked.

"Which publisher?"

"I don't know yet. They all have it."

"You don't have an idea yet?" Aubrey asked, lowering the hand on Weston's arm.

"Not yet, no. And I don't really like to make assumptions, either," Annie said.

"I appreciate that," Weston said. "I don't want to get my hopes up."

Annie took a long drink of her wine and then motioned to the bartender for the check. Talon guessed she was leaving.

"So, sales manager?" Aubrey said to Talon.

"Yeah, I'm in charge of the wrangling," Talon replied.

Aubrey laughed and said, "*All* kinds of wrangling?"

Talon lifted an eyebrow. Then, she moved her arm over the bar behind Aubrey, thinking she'd shoot her shot.

"What's your favorite book, Talon?" Aubrey asked her as Talon leaned in a bit.

"I don't have one."

"Not a big reader?" Aubrey asked.

"No, I read all the time. One of my best friends is a writer. She's always reading and recommending books to all of us, but I don't have a favorite. I like pretty much anything."

"Oh, really?" Aubrey asked flirtatiously. "Weston, what about you?"

And now she's back to Weston? What the hell was this woman up to?

"What *about* me?" Weston asked, looking distracted as she tried to focus on Annie, who was clearly trying to leave, but kept getting asked questions by Aubrey.

"What's the writer's favorite book?"

"*Fight Club*," Weston said.

"What? That's a movie," Aubrey replied, chuckling at her.

"It's a book, too," Annie said, signing her check. "By Chuck Palahniuk."

"Yeah," Weston replied.

"*That's* your favorite book?" Aubrey asked.

"She loves that guy," Talon said, trying to bring the attention back to herself.

"He just writes what he wants, and it's interesting, genre-bending, and makes you think," Weston said.

"I'll have to check out the book," Aubrey said.

"You'd hate it," Annie said without looking at them. "It's not your thing."

"How do *you* know what my thing is?" Aubrey asked.

"Trust me; I do," Annie said, grabbing her purse. "I think I'm going to call it a night."

"We were having a drink," Aubrey said.

"I had two. I'm good now."

"Annie, you're being rude. We're talking to Weston and Talon."

"I'm sorry, Weston. It's nice seeing you again. I should get going, though. Talon, it was great to meet you," Annie said.

"You too," Talon said somewhat questioningly.

"Annie-"

"I'm getting a car. Don't worry; I'm not driving," she said to her sister.

Then, she walked through the bar and out the door.

"Sorry about that. I'm not sure what happened there," Aubrey said. "But what were we talking about?"

"Talon, I'll be right back. I'm going to…" Weston started and pointed toward the door.

"Yeah, go." Talon nodded knowingly at her. "I'm good here."

Weston nodded back at her and followed Annie outside.

"I'm sorry about that. We were just supposed to have a sisterly drink," Aubrey said.

"It's okay. Maybe she just doesn't feel well. Weston will make sure she's okay," Talon replied.

"I should go after her," Aubrey said, sighing loudly. "She might be pissed about what happened at work today."

"Sure. No problem," Talon said, removing her arm from behind the bar.

"Can I ask you something?" Aubrey said.

"Yeah." Talon shrugged a shoulder.

"Weston is into my sister, right?"

"Oh, definitely," Talon confirmed.

"I thought so," Aubrey said. "And you were flirting with me?"

"Oh, definitely," Talon repeated. "You were flirting with both of us, yeah?"

"A little. I have no shame," Aubrey stated.

"So… You and your sister?"

"Annie's gay. I'm bi."

"Got it," Talon replied.

"Problem with bisexuals?"

"Nope." Talon shook her head.

"And you don't mind that I was flirting with both of you?"

"I do, but that's because I'm used to it," Talon said.

"Used to…"

"Oh, people flirting with Weston when we're out. It happens all the time. It's like once women hear she's a writer, they fawn all over her. Plus, she's hot."

"You think she's hot? Have a thing for her?" Aubrey laughed.

"Been there; done that. Better as friends," Talon replied, picking the wine glass up off the bar behind Aubrey and taking a sip.

"Ah… so, you two?"

"When we were much, much younger."

"You don't look all that old now," Aubrey said.

"Old enough," Talon replied.

"Hey, I'm going to go. I don't feel much like dinner anymore," Weston said.

And Talon turned, realizing her friend was standing there all of a sudden, breaking up the fun banter between her and Aubrey.

"Okay. No problem," she told Weston.

"Is Annie okay?" Aubrey asked, looking concerned.

"I don't know," Weston said. "But she's on her way home."

Aubrey took her wine glass from Talon and sipped. Talon lifted an eyebrow in Weston's direction, trying to silently tell her to go.

"Okay. You're good to get home?"

"Yup. All good," Talon replied. "I'll call you later."

"It was nice to meet you, Aubrey," Weston said, but Talon could tell she didn't mean it.

"You too," Aubrey said with a smile.

Then, Weston left the restaurant again.

"So, want to get out of here?" Aubrey asked.

"Oh, definitely," Talon said once again.

***

Talon kept replaying the night over and over in her head as she used her key to get into Weston's place the following day. Aubrey Halifax had been bad in bed. Was that unfair? Maybe it was just the two of them together; Talon didn't know for sure. She did kind of hate herself for giving in to the woman's charms and putting her own charms, or whatever she had, out there because they'd left the restaurant and went to Aubrey's hotel. On the way to the hotel, they'd talked because they didn't want to make out in the back seat of a ride-share. They talked about their exes, and when Aubrey's hand moved to Talon's thigh, Aubrey mentioned that sometimes, the best way to get over an ex was to get under someone else. There wasn't much talking after that. Kissing started the moment they hit the elevator up to Aubrey's floor, and the kissing had been good; Talon had been hopeful. Then, the rest followed the kissing, and it was probably the worst sex Talon had ever had. Now, she was mad because she didn't want one-night stands. Talon hadn't really ever been a one-night stand kind of woman. Aria loved her one-night stands, but Talon had always wanted more. She'd never found it, though, and thinking about Wes being into Annie and seeing Aubrey show *her* some interest, had led Talon to make a bad decision. Why had she gone through with it?

"Hey," Talon said, walking into the office. "I let myself in."

"Obviously," Weston replied. "Grab a thing and help me with this."

"Manual labor – not really my thing," Talon replied, noting the paint rollers and the fact that Weston was painting yet another dry-erase wall in her weird writer's office.

"I asked you to come over to help me finish this," Weston said.

"I know. And I planned on supervising and providing moral support. You're doing great, by the way." She gave Weston a teasing thumbs-up.

"You're useless," Weston said, laughing. "Why did you come all the way over here if you're not going to help?" She bent down to place the roller in the tray.

"I came here to confess something in person because I know you're going to be pissed, and I'd rather just get it over with."

"Confess to what?" Weston stood up and looked at

her inquisitively. "No, Talon. You didn't..."

"I did." Talon squeezed her eyes shut.

"You slept with Annie's sister?"

"Yeah," she said, opening her eyes again. "After you left us there at the restaurant, we got to talking, and she's really hot. I talked about my ex. She talked about hers. We both talked about how sometimes certain *things* can help you get over someone, and we went to her hotel down the street."

"Wait. She's staying in a hotel?"

"She didn't want to stay with her parents or at her sister's place, I guess. Anyway, not the point."

"I'm avoiding *the point* because I kind of want to kick your ass right now," Weston said.

"I know. If it makes you feel any better, it wasn't that good. It took her, like, forty-five minutes to get me there once, and it was only okay. If her sounds and comments were to be believed, I got her there, like, five times before I left."

"You slept with my agent's sister, who I'll probably have to see because she's working there too now," Weston said, crossing her arms over her chest.

"One time. It won't happen again. I just felt like it last night. It's been a while since I've had sex, Wes. And she offered and seemed to really enjoy herself, which gives me a nice ego boost."

"You said you wanted to find someone, not hook up with a woman you just met."

"And I still do. But until she gets here, or I go find her, I still need to... you know... every so often. And Aubrey was there and into it."

"I thought you were leaving right after me," Weston commented.

"I was, but then I didn't. And despite how lackluster the sex was, the woman can kiss."

"Shit, Talon. What if Annie finds out?"

"I'm sure she will. Aubrey doesn't exactly seem the

type to kiss and not tell."

"You know I like her."

"Annie, yeah. Not Aubrey," Talon remarked.

"But I like Annie, and Aubrey is her sister."

"Who is probably already looking for her next hookup. She told me she's in that phase in her life and doesn't want anything serious. She'll have someone new to tell Annie about soon enough," Talon concluded.

"You couldn't keep it in your pants for me?"

"I did keep it in my pants for you; we were in college. We made out for hours upon hours before you said you were ready for more than that with me, despite the fact that you'd already done that, and I hadn't."

"Low blow," Weston said when Talon brought up their brief relationship in college.

"What? It's true. You wanted to wait. I waited. I was very patient. You were super hot back then, Wes. I wanted to sleep with you on the first date, but I waited."

"Then we never stopped having sex, I remember."

"It was good, though," Talon replied with a wink. "And you're still super hot, by the way."

Weston laughed and said, "Thanks, I guess. Oh, and you're finishing this wall for me."

"What? No way."

"You fucked my agent's sister, Talon."

"It's not like Annie's your boss. Oh, that would be interesting, dating your boss. Hot."

"Isn't your boss a guy?" Weston asked.

"Yeah, he's gross, too," Talon said. "Anyway, I'm not proud of myself, Wes. I didn't plan it or anything, but it happened. If it makes you feel better, I'll paint the damn wall for you, but I'm not exactly happy with myself this morning. It's why I came over here to confess."

Weston's phone rang from the living room.

"Why don't you ever just have your phone in here?" Talon asked.

"It's distracting when I'm writing," Weston said as she

headed to the living room. "Pick up the roller, Talon!"

"Fine. Fine," Talon picked up the roller reluctantly and pretended to paint the wall.

She tried not to eavesdrop, but she could tell from Weston's tone on the phone call that something was wrong. Annie was on the phone. Shit. Talon closed her eyes and walked out to face the music.

"Talon, if you fucked this up for me, I'm going to be so pissed."

CHAPTER 4

Days later, and Talon was still thinking about how Aubrey had gone down on her because her fingers weren't getting Talon there.

"Do you want my mouth?" she'd asked, sounding like she wasn't frustrated at all when Talon had been about to tell Aubrey she thought she should just go.

"Yes," Talon had said because she'd hoped that all that direct clit pressure would finally push her over the edge.

It had taken several more minutes. Finally, the smallest orgasm in the world, something Talon would have missed entirely had she not had her brain focused so intently on finding the tell-tale signs of it, happened. She was much louder than she normally would have been to let Aubrey know she could stop. Aubrey had, and that had been the end of Aubrey trying to make her come, thankfully. Aubrey was sexy in her clothing and even more so out of it, so Talon had no problem rolling them over and working Aubrey up again until the woman came once more. At least, Talon thought she had. With women, it could be hard to tell, but Aubrey's moans, gasps, and emitted expletives made it sound like she'd come.

Now, Talon was sitting in the parking garage at her work building, wishing she'd never gone back to that hotel. She didn't want this. One-night stands were definitely more Aria's thing than Talon's and sometimes even Paisley's, but after the break-up, Talon had been thinking that maybe just having a rebound fling or one night with a woman would help her move on so she could find someone new that she could be with long-term. She hadn't made a plan to act on it and had actually convinced herself it was a bad idea until she'd seen Aubrey. She rolled her eyes at herself, turned off the car, and climbed out, grabbing her backpack, which held her laptop, water bottle, and everything else a woman would normally carry in a purse. Yes, she was a woman in her late twenties who still carried a backpack, but it made sense to Talon. She needed the protective sleeve for her laptop and didn't like messenger bags like the one Weston always carried. Plus, Talon could fit more in the backpack than a purse, so this enabled her to pack her compact, a slightly larger mirror, hairbrush, a toothbrush for after lunch if necessary, gum, mints, lipstick, mascara, pens, a small notebook she never used but always felt she needed, and an actual notebook that she used for work and carried to and from the office daily and more. Since the office had a gym that the employees could use for free, some days, she even fit a towel and a change of clothes in there. More times than not, though, the towel went home dry and the clothes unused.

"Talon, hey," her boss, Nick, greeted her when she walked past the kitchen to get to her desk.

"Morning," she replied.

Nick was four years younger than her, but he'd earned himself an MBA online, which somehow meant he was ready to be a senior manager in the sales department over Talon, who had worked her way up in this company after college and was only a manager. Nick had a total of three managers, including Talon, underneath him. Those teams were responsible for one product of the four the company sold, and Talon used to take great pride in the fact that her team of account executives were generally always at the top of every metric and won nearly all the awards, of which, in sales, there were many. Now, though, Talon didn't much care for the trophies and manager-of-the-month lunches she had won. In fact, she'd lost her interest in motivating her team and herself when Nick came into the company above her. She *did* take great satisfaction in the fact that when the company had lost the director of sales a month ago to another competing tech start-up, they hadn't promoted Nick. They hadn't promoted the other three senior managers, either. They'd gone external for the role, and that gave her enough motivation to get through each day in hopes that Nick's lackluster performance with his other two teams might mean he wouldn't be here much longer. Sales was a ruthless profession. If the quota wasn't met a few times, a rep didn't last beyond it. If a manager's team missed the quota, the manager didn't last long, either. And quotas were always going up while the customers were getting smarter and more knowledgeable about products thanks to the Internet and social media than ever before.

Talon could remember being twenty-two and talking to an executive prospect who hadn't heard of the product, her company, or anything like what they offered. It gave her an opportunity to explain so much more about what they did and how the product would help their company improve efficiencies. Now, her reps were up against educated executives who conduct a Google search, check out reviews on trusted sites, and conduct internal RFPs, comparing three to five products before they reach out to sales reps themselves. Those requests for proposals, and departments built around software purchasing inside companies, made cold-calling that much more difficult.

"End of month numbers finally got finalized," Nick said before Talon could even reach for her coffee mug, which she stored in a cabinet no one really used so it wouldn't be touched by anyone else.

As one of the more tenured employees, she could get away with that. Even though all of the existing employees knew not to touch her mug, she stored it in the cabinet out of sight from some of the newer, and likely, less respectful employees who might try to use it themselves and leave it dirty in the kitchen sink for her to have to clean and sanitize later.

"Yeah?"

"Your team came in first again," he said, eating Hot Cheetos with chopsticks at eight-thirty in the morning.

"Yeah, I figured we would," she said, never needing the VP of Sales to finalize numbers to understand that her team was coming out on top for the month.

She set her mug in the coffee machine and pressed the buttons to get her a strong cup of coffee like she did most mornings.

"Well, I'm due in a meeting," Nick said, unsolicited.

Talon nodded and gave him a forced smile. He nodded back and walked off down the hall. She'd never really liked the guy but had to put up with him, so she'd perfected the art of the forced smile.

"New recruit day," Brittany said, noticing Talon in the kitchen.

"Again?" Talon replied, taking her now full cup from the machine.

"Every month, Talon," Brittany replied.

Brittany was the office manager and kept things running smoothly. Talon was convinced her main responsibility was to keep Nick in Hot Cheetos.

"Just always forget it's been a month. How many this time?"

"Ten," Brittany said, refilling the sugar packets in the caddy on the counter. "They're all about to arrive from downstairs, so I need to refill this stuff quick."

"And I should get out of here quick," Talon said.

Brittany laughed and said, "You don't want to meet ten new hires all at once?"

"Not even a little bit," Talon replied, smiling at kind Brittany and walking off toward her desk.

Not long after she'd sat down and gotten her reports pulled up to review the previous day's numbers, it was time for her morning stand-up meeting with her team, which she always held in the sales pit, as it was called. Her desk was on one side of a very large open space of desks. Her team's desks were on the other side, so she grabbed her notebook, which she used for stand-ups, and walked past the wall of conference rooms, which had glass walls and doors, enabling everyone to see inside. The new hires were already in their orientation session, and as Talon went to walk to join her team, someone pushed a cart of new laptops toward her, forcing her to pause to let them pass.

She turned her head, checking out the new people, remembering that the sales team had at least four of them in there. Then, she remembered something else. One of them was the new director they'd just hired. Talon hadn't interviewed her, but she'd heard that the woman was competent and had good experience. Talon wondered which one she could be, but there were four younger-looking people, likely her entry-level salespeople, and six people who looked to be around Talon's age or older – four women and two men. She slowly moved her eyes over each of the possible directors and settled on one woman.

The cart moved past Talon, which meant she could continue walking to her team now, but she didn't. Her feet were frozen to the floor. The woman had brown hair and green eyes that reminded Talon only slightly of Weston's dazzlers, but these eyes were brighter and had flecks of gold and maybe silver in there, too; Talon couldn't tell for sure because the woman wasn't looking in her direction. She was staring at the trainer at the front of the room.

"Talon, you coming?" one of the guys on her team yelled over the rest of the pit because a sales team was nothing if not loud.

"Yeah," she said, shaking herself out of it.

***

Three meetings and a lunch with one of the other managers later, Talon was already exhausted. Part of the job of being a sales manager was all motivation. There were always competitions going on, gong banging on the sales floor when someone sold a huge deal, and so many high-fives that Talon's hand sometimes hurt by the time she left for the day. It didn't usually bother her, but it did drain her energy on the particularly loud days. Sometimes, she'd stare over at the sales operations team and wonder. That team was quiet. They were in charge of the processes, policies, and systems the sales team used. It was a small group of desks grouped together, with people staring at their computer screens and wearing noise-canceling headphones to drown out the sounds of the rest of the floor in order to focus on their work. Talon envied those ears in those headphones some days.

Then, it was time for the afternoon all-sales meeting that took place in the pit. There were too many of them to fit into a conference room, so the VP had everyone block thirty minutes one day a week to go over department-level things. They would all put their headsets back on and get to their next call when it was over. Talon liked that she got to sit at her desk on one side of the floor because the VP typically spoke from the other side of the floor, near the reps, even though his office was behind her and the other managers' desks.

"Okay. Headsets down, or continue your calls in a call booth," he said like he always did.

The few reps that were still on calls had already begun heading to the call booths that resembled old phone booths that Talon doubted any of *them* knew about. Hell, she'd probably only seen one phone booth in *her* life.

"Before we get into the numbers and some process changes, I want to introduce our new director of sales, Emerson Bagley. Emerson will be stepping into Felix's old role and managing the teams that reported to him. She comes from *TechYes*, with ten years of sales experience there. We're excited and happy to have her join the team. Emerson, would you like to say anything to the teams?"

Talon swallowed. The woman she'd basically checked out earlier was the new director of sales. There were two of those here, and Felix had managed Nick, which meant Emerson would be managing Nick. That meant she was Talon's boss's boss. *God, she was hot,* Talon thought to herself. Emerson was far away, but she looked to be maybe a few inches taller than Talon's 5'6". That would make her at least 5'8" or maybe 5'9". Was she in heels? Talon couldn't tell from where she was sitting, but Emerson didn't look like a woman who would wear heels. She looked like the kind of woman who might wear tennis shoes and her hat to the back in the lesbian bar, but Talon shouldn't be thinking about that right now because Emerson was talking. Emerson? That was a pretty name. Talon wondered where it came from.

"Hi, everyone. I look forward to getting a chance to know all of you, not just the ones on my team. I'm excited to see how we can all work together," Emerson said.

Basic speech, but that smile that came at the end of it, was anything but basic. Were Emerson's teeth actually perfect? Did she use whitening strips, or was she just born with shiny, white teeth that made it look like she'd been in a hundred toothpaste commercials?

Talon didn't pay much attention to the rest of the meeting. The VP, Emerson, and the other director were all standing while the rest of them were sitting, which allowed Talon to hide behind her laptop. She used the opportunity to hop on LinkedIn and check out Emerson Bagley's profile. It was private. She tried Facebook, Instagram, and Twitter and then gave up. Emerson was a private person, apparently, so Talon's social media stalking would have to wait until Emerson requested to connect with her on LinkedIn, which would happen because sales were all about networking.

Her final meeting of the day now held a lot more meaning to Talon. The VP wanted to introduce all of the sales managers to Emerson in a conference room after ending the all-team meeting. Talon headed into the room with her notebook while everyone else brought their laptops. That was pretty normal. She preferred to write meeting action items down by hand while everyone else liked to type theirs out. The moment she sat down,

Emerson entered the room, followed by Nick and the other senior managers. Talon watched as Emerson sat down near the head of the table next to the VP. Talon was on the same side but at the other end. When the VP began talking about Emerson's role, Talon leaned back in her chair to get more comfortable and turned her head toward the VP.

She couldn't see him, though, because Emerson Bagley was also leaning back in her chair and was staring at Talon with all sorts of intensity in those eyes – with, yes, gold *and* silver flecks in them. Was that even possible? Talon swallowed hard and stared back, unable to take her eyes off of Emerson but wondering why Emerson couldn't seem to take *her* eyes off of Talon. Did Talon have food on her face from lunch or something? She'd had mustard on her sandwich. Was it on her chin? She stared at Emerson, who was only a few feet away from her and making direct eye contact with Talon until Talon couldn't take it anymore. She had to look away. When she finally did, she wiped at imaginary mustard on her chin just to be safe.

CHAPTER 5

Emerson had an office for the first time in her life. The other director shared the same office, but it was at least an office. The sales operations director got his own office, but he needed more quiet, she guessed. He also had a small conference table in there, where she could see his tiny team working while he wrote things down on the dry-erase board he also had in there. She wasn't jealous. Okay. She *was* jealous. She shouldn't be, though. She had an office, after all, and her counterpart director didn't seem to be in here very often. It was her second day on the job, and she'd only seen him in here a few times. He seemed to like to reserve conference rooms and spent a lot of the rest of his time out in the pit with his team. That was fine with Emerson, and she hoped it continued.

"How's day two? Have we scared you off yet?" Nick, one of her new direct reports, asked as he stuck his head inside her open office door.

"No," Emerson said, laughing at the joke she'd heard about ten times so far. "Just getting my bearings on a few things."

"Need any help?" he asked, walking inside now.

"Not yet. You guys… I mean, we," she corrected. "Use a different system than I'm used to. I'm getting up to speed on how we progress from opportunity to a closed deal, but it's kind of a mess."

"Yeah, sales ops have been meaning to help with that for a while now, but they keep getting pulled in other directions. Whenever month and quarter close comes up, they get pulled off of every other project and put on compiling the numbers for the teams."

"We don't have anyone that just does projects?" Emerson asked.

He shook his head and said, "No. It usually falls to the senior managers like me, or we pick someone from the management team to help."

Emerson thought of Talon. She turned her head to where she could see Talon from behind, and the woman appeared to be marking a deal closed from what Emerson could see over her shoulder, and the rep standing next to Talon offered his hand for a high-five. Emerson rolled her eyes internally.

"Managers?" she asked, returning her attention to Nick.

"Yeah, they all sit out there with us," he said, pointing to the row of desks. "I've got three. There's Ruben, Dimitri, and Talon. All of them have helped out from time to time, but Talon's probably my best when it comes to projects. She's got a knack for it, I guess."

"Talon?" Emerson asked, pretending as if she'd never heard the name before.

"Yeah, she's been here forever, I think. She started from the bottom."

"In sales?"

"Yup. She still holds a few records, and she hasn't been a rep in a while."

"And she's a manager now?"

"Yeah, her team is the top-performing team consistently."

"That's rare," Emerson said, looking out at Talon again. "Mostly, people are good reps or good managers of reps. You don't always find people who can do both."

"Tell me about it. We'll have to talk about Dimitri soon. His team is usually at the bottom, and he's got some performance issues of his own that I've already let HR know about."

Emerson was *not* ready to talk about people issues. It was her second day here. She wanted to get to know the systems and processes and some of the people before she had to make decisions about hiring and firing. She also wanted to stare at the back of Talon's head as often as possible. Talon's hair looked extra soft and shiny, and the woman in Emerson wanted to know what kind of shampoo Talon used until she remembered – she had shorter hair now and didn't really need to worry about making her hair shinier or softer. Of course, the lesbian in her wanted to stare at Talon for an entirely different reason, and she had the previous day.

She'd sat down and thought she'd seen a ghost when she noticed the woman from the New Year's Eve party sitting at the table just a few feet away. When her eyes had met Talon's, Emerson had tried to pull her own away. She was pretty sure that if Talon had wanted to, she'd have a good claim for sexual harassment because there could *not* have been any other way of taking how Emerson had stared at her. She'd loved Talon's light-brown eyes and cute little button nose. Those full lips with just a bit of color had almost been Emerson's undoing, and she'd regretted not having sex with Miranda now because she was just horny. That was all it was; Emerson just needed to get laid.

Miranda had called a few days after the whole kitchen debacle, and they'd gone out one more time, but it was clear that Miranda was still mad about what had happened that night, and Emerson didn't want or need any unnecessary drama in her life. So, they'd ended things, and now Emerson couldn't stop staring at the beautiful woman who was technically this pimply-faced mid-twenties-looking guy's subordinate, which meant she was also under Emerson.

Oh, that gave her all sorts of thoughts she shouldn't be having. Where was this coming from? Emerson hadn't ever lusted after a woman like this. Even when she'd just discovered her sexuality and had her first girlfriend, she hadn't wanted sex this much. It wasn't just sex, either – it was sex with the woman who was currently turning around in her chair, which meant that Emerson needed to stop looking at her. She cleared her throat and returned her gaze to Nick, who was still standing in her office for some reason.

"Right. We can talk about him during our meeting," she said, reminding him that they'd have their first official meeting tomorrow.

"Cool. Thanks. Want anything from the kitchen? I'm going to grab some Hot Cheetos."

"No, I'm good for now. Thanks," she said.

Nick, thankfully, left the office, and Emerson turned to look at Talon before she could even stop herself. Talon was sitting in her rolling chair, facing and talking to someone else. Then, she stood up and walked over to a dry-erase wall, and Emerson watched as she drew up a square and an arrow downward. She wrote words Emerson couldn't quite make out from where she was sitting, but Talon was explaining something to the person she was talking to, and it looked like a process. The person nodded and gave Talon a high-five before they walked off. Talon turned to go back to her desk, which meant she was facing Emerson's office now, so Emerson looked down at her computer, blushing.

***

"So, you've been in sales for a while?"

"Yes, about ten years," Emerson said to Dimitri, who had decided to join her for lunch at one of the communal tables in the kitchen.

"Cool. I've only been doing it for a couple of years, but I'm learning. I've got some brand-new guys that I'm trying to whip into shape," he said.

Emerson nodded. She wanted to get to know her new team, but she didn't like when managers talked about their people like they were animals. She'd been that employee with that kind of manager. That felt like so long ago now. Growing up dirt-poor and having to take care of her three siblings meant she didn't get to just go to college at eighteen like everyone else. Her mom had been a single parent, and Emerson had been the oldest. It was her responsibility to help with the others, so she'd lived at home until the youngest left the house. Then, she'd moved into a tiny studio and had waited tables for a long time before she'd gotten an entry-level job in sales. She'd started putting herself through college at night and worked her way up from the trenches as a rep to a manager and then to a senior manager at her old company.

When they'd decided to hire externally for the director role at *TechYes* and hadn't even explained why she wasn't a good candidate, she'd started looking for something else. After applying for a few jobs on her own, a recruiter had reached out to her to tell her about this job. Emerson thought it a bit hypocritical that she'd be the outside hire here and had left her old place for the same reason, but she'd been assured that no one here was ready for the director role and that she'd be a good fit. After meeting Nick, she had confidence in the decision to go outside the company for the role.

Emerson had always felt a little behind everyone else. It likely had to do with the fact that she kind of *was* behind everyone else, but when they'd hired the director at *TechYes*, and the guy was at least seven years younger than her thirty-two, she wondered what he'd had that she hadn't, so she'd looked him up. He'd gotten his MBA by the time he was twenty-four. Emerson had a business degree, too, but it was a Bachelor's, and despite all the studies saying that experience matters more than a college degree, people still cared about that stuff. Maybe she should consider settling in here and then going to graduate school or something.

"Oh, Talon. Can you do three instead of two for our meeting today?" Dimitri yelled.

Emerson looked up to see that Talon was standing at the coffee maker on the other side of the kitchen. Talon turned to see Dimitri, and then her eyes met Emerson's. Emerson swallowed and then nearly choked because she hadn't realized she had a potato chip in her mouth.

"You okay?" Dimitri asked her.

"Yup. I'm good," she said, coughing a little and reaching for her water.

"I can do three," Talon said.

"Cool. Thanks," he said back to her.

"I need a refill," Emerson said of her water. "I'll talk to you later, Dimitri?"

"Sure," he said. "I have a meeting now anyway."

Emerson waited for him to walk off. Then, she took her water bottle over to the water cooler, which just so happened to be next to the coffee maker.

"So, I'm Emerson," she said.

"Talon."

"I've heard a lot about you so far," Emerson said.

Please don't say that stupid 'All good, I hope' thing people always say when they hear that, Emerson thought to herself as she filled her bottle.

"Yeah?" Talon asked, turning with a full coffee cup to face Emerson head-on.

This was the closest they'd been. Even at the party, Talon had been on the other side of a table. Now, she was standing right in front of Emerson. She was a couple of inches shorter than Emerson, and that t-shirt with the company logo on it did nothing for the likely sexy figure beneath, but Talon looked comfortable, and there was something sexy about that, too.

"Yeah, all good," Emerson said, capping her bottle after filling it. "I hear you're a great manager."

"I've got a great team," Talon replied.

Emerson smiled.

"I hear that, too," she said.

"I should probably let you get back to your lunch," Talon replied, nodding to the table where Emerson's unfinished food still sat.

"Yeah, sure," Emerson said. "Actually, there are two coffee makers in this kitchen. They're not the same, either. Can you tell me which one makes the best coffee?"

"Oh, I don't know that there's much of a difference.

This one makes regular coffee pretty well, but don't use it for espresso stuff. Use the other one for that."

"The other one?"

"The one with the pods," Talon said, placing her cup on the counter and taking a few steps over. "Do you like a light or dark roast?"

"I don't know that I really have a preference," Emerson said, moving to stand next to her.

Talon smelled amazing. That shampoo she used had something in it that Emerson didn't recognize, but it was good; she knew that much. Talon smelled good.

"Okay. Well, this one is a little trickier than the other one, but not that hard. Just put the pod in that you want. Brittany does a good job stocking everything, but if it's ever empty, there are more in the cabinets. Just press this thing down – there are a couple of options you have to choose from – and then press to start."

"Seems easy enough," Emerson said, reaching for a blue-colored pod just as Talon reached for the one right next to it.

Their hands brushed, and Emerson didn't pull away. *For fuck's sake, Emerson. Get it together*, she silently told herself.

"Sorry," Talon said, pulling back before Emerson did.

"No problem," Emerson said. "So, the blue one is good?"

"It's my favorite: bold."

Emerson stared into Talon's apparently endless eyes and wasn't sure if Talon was talking about the coffee or about Emerson's near attempt to take her hand a moment ago.

"I like bold," she replied, licking her lips.

Oh, fuck... She needed to find a good lawyer. Emerson was definitely going to get sued.

"Yeah?" Talon asked, licking her lips then, too.

"Sometimes, you *need* bold," Emerson said without paying attention.

She'd managed to put the blue pod in, close the lid, and press some buttons without even noticing. She'd also managed to forget to put a cup under the dispenser.

"Oh, shit," she said, finally looking down and away from Talon.

Hot coffee was spurting out and onto the counter because it had no cup to go into. Surprisingly, Talon didn't laugh. She simultaneously reached for the paper towels and a paper cup, which she placed to collect the rest of the espresso and gave Emerson the paper towels.

"I hope you like it," she said, probably about the coffee, but Emerson was too busy trying to clean up her mess to try to interpret it.

Then, Talon was gone. She walked off in the direction of her desk with her own coffee, and Emerson could only follow her with her eyes, turning her head a bit to stare at Talon's perfect ass.

"I'm a walking fucking lawsuit waiting to happen," she muttered to herself.

CHAPTER 6

It was day three of Emerson's brand-new, exciting, and well-paying job. She'd already managed to spill coffee over the counter and a little on herself, nearly choked to death on a chip, and got into a sexy staring contest with someone on her team, which would likely get her fired by day four if she didn't try to put some space between herself and Talon. That was already proving to be difficult. Talon's desk was just outside of Emerson's office. True, Talon was facing the other direction, but that didn't stop Emerson from wanting to look up at her constantly. Maybe she should move her own desk in the office. She could turn it around and face the wall, put herself in her own brand of time-out for as long as she and Talon both worked here. No, that would be weird. She just needed some self-control and to get laid. Yes, if she met someone she wanted to take home, she wasn't going to stop herself this time.

Miranda would have fit every definition of a clingy girlfriend. Emerson knew that now and wished their mutual friend would've given her the heads-up, but having sex with Miranda would've been a mistake. She likely would've just assumed they were a couple the following morning and started planning their move-in date shortly after. Emerson hadn't seen it at first because she hadn't really been paying attention, but now that Miranda was on Facebook bragging about her new girlfriend less than two weeks after the holiday, Emerson knew she should've seen the signs.

She left her boss's office after their first initial meeting, and her head was filled with action items. She'd taken notes, but the guy hadn't stopped talking the entire meeting, and the list in her notes app was likely short of a few dozen things he'd asked her to do. Dropping her laptop off in her office, she left again to go to the bathroom and returned to find Talon standing at that dry-erase wall again with someone else this time. No, it was two people. There was a third sitting at their desk, but they were turned to Talon as well. Emerson recognized one of them as a member of the sales operations team. He had his headphones around his neck and appeared to be paying close attention to Talon's explanation of something. Emerson stopped to listen herself but stood over to the side so as not to interrupt.

"Why can't we just bypass this?" Talon said, pointing to a step in her hand-drawn process. "We don't need it. There are three custom fields here that we're required to track, but we don't actually track them. One of them is the number of locations, but we have that earlier in the opportunity stage anyway. We have twenty custom fields included in our contract, and I know we have at least five new ones we want to add as well. If we delete these three and this stage entirely, the reps will save twenty minutes per deal in administration."

"But we still need the information," the sales ops guy said.

Emerson wished she could remember his name, but her brainpower was taken up by watching Talon, who today, had her hair pulled back, revealing a long neck and cute ears. Had Emerson ever in her life described a woman as having cute ears? She was leering. She was now a leering person. Emerson would be going straight to hell.

"So, we use the open field in the first stage," Talon replied, motioning to the first step in her process. "We're not tracking it, so we can just use it as an open text field instead. Reps can type the info for the two fields there, and when the account managers get the clients added to their portfolios later, they'll still have what they need. We'd cut three custom fields at once, so we could get at least three off of the backlog list."

Emerson smiled softly. Talon was commanding but not forceful. As a woman in sales, it was still difficult to be part of the boys' club. It was even more difficult to be a manager and be taken seriously and not be called a bitch or overly aggressive. Emerson was impressed. These three guys, currently captivated by Talon's plan, were taking her seriously. Hell, the sales ops guy was even taking notes. The other two were nodding along with her. Emerson knew how hard this was for a woman even today, which was annoying, but she and other women like her had to break that damn glass ceiling over and over again, and she was determined to let that glass fall.

"What about the other two?" one of the other guys asked. "Can we get all five of them in so we don't have to pay for adding more?"

That was the sales operations director. Emerson hadn't recognized him from behind because she hadn't yet spent much time with him. The director of the team who was supposed to do this stuff as their actual job, was asking Talon to help him figure out how to save the company a little money.

"The reality is, we need to go through the whole thing and delete, combine, and add new; not just custom fields," Talon continued. "There are fields we don't use that they include as standard. For example, franchise, union, privately owned, and publicly owned – we don't use that, but it's a dropdown. For some of the account managers, it would be good for them to know later."

"Why? We have customer size as a dropdown already," the sales ops director said. "That's what determines the customer's plan and all the manager needs."

"Franchises and unions have rules." Talon turned to him directly. "If the franchise headquarters, for example, decides they're going with our software, they're all required to use it. Knowing that from the SDRs, helps the rep not waste time in the demo. They have to use the system, and we're just signing the deal. When the account manager gets the account, if the customer threatens to churn, it's not a real threat unless we hear it from the headquarters – they can categorize and treat it differently."

Talon was right. The sales development representative teams were made up of entry-level and typically, post-college people who were looking for a way into an organization. Depending on their role, they could be tasked with either inbounding or outbounding. Outbound reps had the hardest job in the business, Emerson thought. They were responsible for making cold calls. All SDRs had the duty of booking as many sales demos onto an account representative's calendar as possible. They would then, hopefully, sell the product and hand it over to the account manager, who would manage its lifetime with the company. If account managers knew that the customer couldn't really churn, it would save them time to focus on the real threats, and the company could develop a strategy for handling those types of customers.

"We can test it in the sandbox," he said. "We need director approval for any changes."

"I know." Talon shrugged. "But you asked me why it was taking reps so much longer recently to move from stage one to stage four in this system, and that's why. Every field you make required, this damn system autosaves. I get why it does that, but every autosave takes at least two to three seconds. We usually have only five minutes, if we're lucky, between demos and calls. I've added it up: with all the required fields and autosave alone, it takes three minutes to get through one stage of this process. And that's just the required fields. We still have to take notes and then take the recording from the call and attach it – that takes another five to ten minutes."

"Are you ready for our meeting?" Nick asked.

"Oh." Emerson shook her head. "Yes, sorry. Come on in," she said, returning her attention to Talon for another moment before closing the door behind her. "Do you remember us talking about the system issues yesterday?"

"Yeah," he said as he sat in the chair in front of her desk.

"Sales ops is out there talking to Talon about it now," she said, sitting in her own chair.

"They do that. I told you, she's got a knack for this type of thing."

"How does it usually go?"

"Talon and sales ops?" Nick asked.

"Yes," she said.

"Honestly, this might be wrong to say, but I think Talon is smarter than the entire sales ops team combined at the stuff they were hired for, and it bugs the director, so they don't usually take her suggestions. If they do, it's because they have to, you know? Like, if they didn't, they'd be stupid. And I think they kind of take credit sometimes. I've been trying to work on that for Talon's sake, but she doesn't even want the credit herself." He chuckled. "She just doesn't like when her reps struggle to do their jobs because the system sucks."

Emerson smiled and said, "And they're too busy to redo the whole process right now, right?"

"I think so; I don't know. They always put it off."

She nodded and said, "Okay. Let's talk about you."

Thirty minutes later, with that meeting wrapped, Emerson headed to the director of sales operations' office.

"Hey, have a minute?" she asked him.

"Sure. What's up?" he replied, staring at the wall in front of him as if he were trying to solve some advanced math equation.

"I was wondering if I could take something off your team's to-do list. I'm new, so I've got some fresh eyes, and I've noticed the system could use an overhaul. I also noticed your team talking to Talon earlier."

"Yeah, we can't ever seem to get enough time to do it. We're always getting new crap put on our plates," he said, turning to her.

"I've got experience with this stuff," Emerson told him. "I could work with someone on your team but manage it myself with one of the other sales managers who could offer perspective, and we could get it done," she suggested, hoping he didn't think she was stepping on his toes.

"Talon?"

"Sorry?" she said.

"Did Talon put you up to this?"

"No, I haven't even talked to her about it."

"Nick?"

"No, I came up with this idea on my own. I'd like to borrow Talon for the project, though. She seems to have a good understanding of the needs of her team and has been here a long time, so she could offer context on why things were done the way they were done and what we've tried before."

"Yeah, Talon's cool," he said, nodding. "And she's got some good ideas."

"So, you'd be okay with this if I run with it? I don't want to cause any problems for your team."

"No, that would be great, actually. I've been swamped with this integration thing. The API is much more complex than we were sold on, and the vendor won't give us any more time with their team without making us pay for it."

"Okay. Great. I'll talk to Nick, and we'll get the project team started. Any ideas on who you'd want from your team? We'll need someone to test and implement later."

"Honestly, Talon has admin access to everything and knows how to test everything, too. She's been here so long compared to the rest of us, she was part of the original group who had to administrate everything prior to my team coming on board."

Emerson nodded and said, "Okay. I'll keep you posted."

She left quickly before he could change his mind. It was a big risk she was about to undertake. If the project didn't go well, it would make her look bad at her new job, but she'd somehow managed to put herself into a position where she'd be spending more time with Talon instead of getting that space from her that she was supposed to be getting.

***

"I know, Mom. It just happened," she said into her phone later that night.

"You just got this job," her mom replied. "And it's a good job, Emerson; you're making really good money. And with your student loans still not being paid off, you need this job."

"I know," she repeated. "And I'll have my loans paid off next year."

"If you keep this job. I know why you left *TechYes*. They didn't appreciate you or understand your talent, but it *was* a guaranteed salary. In this new role, you make peanuts unless your team sells."

That wasn't entirely true. Her mother was nervous because this role in leadership meant that Emerson made only about eighty percent of what she'd made before as a senior manager, and the rest was paid out based on the performance of her teams. If her reps sold well, Emerson could make forty percent more than she had at her previous job. On top of that, here, she actually had the opportunity to get a bonus every quarter, and those bonuses would be an additional ten to fifteen percent of her annual pay. She didn't ever count on bonuses, but she'd seen the numbers, and her team performed. She'd make at least the same amount as she made before, if not more.

"I'm okay, Mom."

"You can't flirt with this woman," her mom told her.

"I don't think spilling coffee all over us could be classified as flirting. So far, all I've really done is stare, but Mom, she's just…"

"Shut this down, Emerson," her mom said when she heard Emerson using her wistful voice.

"I know. I am."

"You're working on a new project with her. That doesn't sound like you're shutting anything down," her mom remarked.

"It has to get done, and she's smart, Mom. I watched her explain things to people today, and everything she said is what I've observed myself and can really make a difference. I'm not sure why they hired Nick, her boss, over her, but I can guess… She's a woman, and Nick has an advanced degree. Sound familiar?"

"Keep it focused on work," her mom said.

"I will."

"I've never heard you talk about a woman like this before," her mom added, sounding less authoritative now.

"I don't think I ever *have*," Emerson replied.

Her mother had only been sixteen when she'd had Emerson. As a result, it often felt like they'd grown up together. Emerson told her mother practically everything. Tonight, she'd explained seeing Talon at the party, feeling an instant desire to get to know her, and then finding out that they'd be working together and that Talon was on her team. She'd left out the part about how she regularly fantasized about having sex with Talon in her office. Emerson closed her eyes, thinking about Talon's head between her legs as Emerson sat at her desk and watched Talon work.

"Emerson?"

"Huh?" she said, snapping back to attention.

"You don't even know this woman. You can be attracted to someone, and that's it – it doesn't have to go anywhere. And if it did, it might not be good anyway. Sometimes, there's just chemistry between two people, but no compatibility."

"Yeah, I know."

"You want compatibility, too," her mom reminded.

"Yes, I do," Emerson replied, knowing her mom was right.

"So, keep it to just work, and find a woman that doesn't work there to date, okay?"

Emerson laughed and said, "As if it were that easy."

CHAPTER 7

It had been an interesting day at the office for Talon. She'd only stared at Emerson a dozen times as opposed to the five dozen from the previous day, and that, in Talon's mind, was growth. She kept running through the coffee incident in her head, except in Talon's fantasy, after their fingers touched, Emerson lifted Talon onto the counter, and as hot coffee continued to sputter without a receptacle, Emerson's lips attached themselves to Talon's before she began undoing Talon's jeans and sliding a hand inside. Okay… Talon had to stop doing this. Except that she couldn't. Emerson was in her head. She was also in her pants, but not in reality. It was just that every time Talon saw her, she thought about Emerson's eyes staring up at her from between her legs and how her fingers would feel buried inside Talon as Talon rocked against them.

"Everyone, this is Annie. Annie, you know Talon… This is Paisley." Weston pointed around the table. "This is Scarlet. Our friend Eleanor is on her way. Aria is the one missing tonight."

"She's having sex right now," Talon said, bringing her attention back to her friends and Weston's introduction of Annie to the group.

"Talon!" Paisley laughed. "Hi, Annie. It's nice to meet you. Sorry, our friend here couldn't keep it in her pants with your sister."

Annie laughed and said, "Yeah, if we could just avoid talking about that, I think that would be good for me."

"Thank God," Talon replied, blushing.

Sleeping with Aubrey had clearly been a mistake, and now the consequences of that mistake were becoming more and more obvious. When Weston had explained she'd be bringing Annie to their regular hangout, Talon had thought it a good idea for Weston but a bad idea for Talon.

"Here," Weston said, motioning for Annie to sit down.

Annie did, and Weston followed her, sitting on the outside of the booth as everyone scooted over to accommodate them. Weston smiled back at the woman and took a drink of her beer. Talon watched this dance between the two of them and looked over at Paisley, who rolled her eyes.

"So, how's the literary agent thing?" Scarlet asked.

"Sorry?" Annie asked.

"Literary agent? How is that going?" Scarlet repeated her question.

"Oh, fine. Thanks," Annie said, nodding. "What do *you* do?"

"I'm a boring data analyst."

"Why is that boring?" Annie asked seriously.

Scarlet looked at her like she hadn't expected Annie to respond that way, which was such a Scarlet thing to do.

"It's not. She's really good at her job," Weston said.

"Let's talk about Paisley's work; much more exciting," Scarlet deflected, taking a sip from whatever was in her glass.

"I'm an ERP consultant. How is that more exciting?" Paisley asked.

"ERP?" Annie asked.

"It's a fancy way of saying I help businesses integrate and improve their processes and systems."

"She owns her own company," Weston added.

"Of which, I'm the only employee, so not really all that exciting."

"You get to travel," Scarlet said.

"From business hotel to business hotel, yes," Paisley confirmed.

"Hey, sorry I'm late," Eleanor said, sliding into the booth next to Paisley.

"What are we talking about? What are we drinking?"

"Just going through what we all do," Talon said.

"Didn't you *do* her sister?" Eleanor joked.

Everyone laughed, but Talon wanted to lower herself until she was under the booth and no one could see her.

"Annie has requested we not talk about that, so you're making her feel uncomfortable now," Talon replied instead of doing that.

"I'm good. I think *you* might be the uncomfortable one," Annie replied, and everyone laughed again.

"Your next drink is on me," Paisley said. "Feel free to pick on Talon as much as you want."

"Hey!" Talon said.

"I'm going to grab a drink and be right back," Ellie said. "Anyone need a refill."

"I'll go with you," Talon said, sliding out of the booth with her.

"So, do we like her?" Ellie asked Talon when they arrived at the bar.

"Who?"

"Annie," Ellie replied.

"Oh, yeah. She's cool."

"Cooler than–"

"If you say, 'her sister,' I'm going to murder you."

Eleanor laughed and ordered a drink for herself.

"Still regret it?" she asked.

"Yes," Talon replied.

"Then, why did you do it? From what you've told us, you flirted right back. You might have even controlled the flirting."

"I didn't control it, but I did participate in it."

"Why?"

"Because it was just flirting at first. Aubrey is attractive and… I don't know. It felt like a good idea at the time."

"But you don't want to just hook up with women like Aria does," Ellie said more than asked.

"No, not really. It doesn't mean I don't want sex

sometimes, though, and she's the first person I've been with since Leigh. I think I needed to, like, cleanse myself of that relationship or something."

"So, have you been appropriately cleansed?" Ellie asked as her drink arrived in front of her.

"God, no. I had one baby orgasm. I'm still due for a *proper* cleansing," Talon replied.

Ellie laughed and said, "Baby orgasm?"

"El, I'm not even sure I came… The woman is determined; I'll give her that much. She wasn't going to stop, so at some point, when I felt like it was close enough and maybe it happened, I just got louder."

"Oh, that bad?" Ellie said as they walked back to the table.

"She can kiss… How can she not do anything else?"

"In the bedroom, apparently," Annie said as they approached the booth.

"What about the bedroom?" Ellie asked as she sat back down.

Talon sat down next to her.

"Nothing," Weston said.

"Wes was just filling me in on her relationship with Talon in college," Annie replied, glaring at Talon.

"Hey, don't look at me. Wes hit on me first," Talon remarked.

"I did not. You did that thing with your hair."

"Oh, that was after you did that thing with your mouth," Talon argued.

"What thing with your mouth?" Annie asked, turning back to Weston.

"Not *that* thing," Weston said quickly.

"I heard you two did *that* thing a lot back then," Ellie said, taking a drink of her red wine. "Like, a lot. Talon had marks on her knees from that rug you had next to your bed, Wes."

"Oh, my God," Talon said, laughing through her embarrassment.

"Knee marks?" Annie asked.

"We were nineteen," Weston said.

"And just figuring things out," Talon added.

"Yeah," Weston agreed.

"What? That you both really liked oral?" Ellie said.

"Eleanor!" Weston and Talon exclaimed at the same time.

A couple of hours later, Paisley had gone home to get some sleep after a long project at work. Eleanor and Scarlet had gone to the bar to chat with the bartender they both knew, and Talon was sitting across from Weston and Annie, just kind of moving her head to the music playing from the jukebox because it was awkward now.

"So," Talon said after a minute.

"So," Weston replied.

"This isn't weird," Talon said.

"Why would it be weird?" Annie asked her.

"No reason," she said. "I think I'm going to go, though – really tired and stuff."

"Sure you are," Weston said, laughing. "Do you want another drink?" she asked Annie.

"I'm okay."

"Let *me* buy you a drink." Talon stood.

"Because you slept with my sister?"

"And Wes technically, too," Talon replied. "Same thing?"

"Sure," Annie said.

Talon left the awkward third-wheel scenario that the night had rapidly turned into and had a feeling that even if it took them some time, Annie and Weston would be a couple eventually. They just had this vibe between them. That meant Weston would be happily coupled off soon, and Talon would still be alone. Sure, she had her other friends, and Weston had been in relationships before, but this time seemed different to Talon.

When she got home to her apartment, Talon tossed her keys on the table and headed straight to her bedroom.

She stripped quickly and hopped into the shower. When she wrapped the towel around herself after, for some reason, Emerson Bagley reentered her mind for the thousandth time that day. This time, it was about the project she'd been assigned. It had been Emerson's idea to include her, and now, Talon would be working with her directly, as Nick had explained before Talon had left for the day. She pictured long hours in Emerson's office, the conference rooms, the kitchen, and during those long hours, *some* work got done. Well, a little work got done. Talon dropped the towel to the floor and climbed into bed, but on top of the blanket, wanting to let the cool air dry her skin further. She reached into the drawer next to her and found what she needed. Then, she closed her eyes and pictured all that *working* she'd do with Emerson. With the vibrator pressed to her clit, it didn't take her long to come the first time as she pictured going down on Emerson, with Emerson pressed against a wall in her office. The second orgasm happened only moments later when Talon pictured Emerson standing in the freight elevator where, Talon happened to know, there were no cameras. Talon joined her, and within seconds, Emerson's lips were on her own in her imagination, but in reality, her clit was pulsing with need until she let the vision and her vibrator take her over once more.

CHAPTER 8

Yesterday had been a Talon-free day. It was surprising to Emerson how quickly she'd gotten accustomed to seeing the woman in the office. In the few days she'd worked here, she'd come to expect it and looked forward to watching Talon explain things to the boys or make coffee in the kitchen. Emerson knew that she couldn't just stare at her forever, but turning her head to look out her office just as Talon was walking back from a meeting, talking and laughing with someone, made Emerson smile and was something she hoped she got to see more of.

Yesterday, Talon had worked from home. Emerson had watched Talon's desk for a bit before a meeting where Nick had explained that Talon worked from home a few days a month to focus. Emerson could understand that, and as much as just looking at Talon did things to her, it also meant she wasn't focusing on doing *her* job. Emerson even had an office that she shared with someone who was hardly ever there, and she had a hard time focusing. Sometimes, it felt as if she were in a fishbowl. She was still the new kid on the block, and people often stared at her as they walked by the office. She could definitely use a work-from-home day, too.

Today, though, Talon would be in the office. Emerson knew that because they were slated to spend the entire day together on the project Emerson was running, and it would be just the two of them in a conference room. Emerson had done this to herself, but she also knew it was the right thing to do for the company. Talon was clearly talented in this arena, and the members of the sales operations team didn't seem to care if they ran with their ideas, so now, Emerson would be in a room all day with a woman she thought was remarkably sexy.

"She's an employee," Emerson muttered to herself just as she saw Talon approach her desk, opening her backpack and taking out a notebook and her computer. "She wore *that* today?"

Of all days, Talon had chosen today to wear a button-down shirt in charcoal-gray and a pair of dark jeans that looked a hell of a lot tighter than the ones Emerson had seen her in previously. Button-down shirts were Emerson's undoing, and she had to pick her jaw up off her desk when Talon turned to her and smiled at her. It was a soft smile that said, "Good morning" more than anything else, but that smile, in combination with the shirt, the tight jeans, and the boots with the short heel, had Emerson thinking about rescheduling their daylong meeting so she could get out of here and take care of herself back at home.

"Hey, can I come in?" Talon asked.

"Yeah, sure," Emerson replied, clearing her throat. "Morning," she added in a much higher pitch.

"Morning," Talon replied. "Are we still meeting? I just wanted to check."

"Unless you need to cancel," Emerson said for some reason.

"No, I'm good," Talon replied.

Emerson guessed Talon was *good* at a lot of things.

"Okay. Coffee?" Emerson asked, trying to take her mind off of those things.

"Sure," Talon said.

They made their way to the kitchen down the hall, and Emerson watched as Talon pulled a mug out of a hard-to-reach cabinet that appeared to be empty, save the mug.

"Is that your special spot or something?" Emerson asked.

"Yeah," Talon replied. "The kitchen was different when I first started working here: the fridge wasn't next to the cabinet, and the cups were stored there. I got used to getting my cup from there each morning, but then they remodeled, and it's harder to get to things up there, so I'm the only one that uses it, and I kind of like it that way. It means no one will steal my cup and leave it unwashed in the sink."

"Well, now, *I* might; now that I know your secret," Emerson teased.

"*You* can borrow my mug anytime," Talon said.

Was that flirting? Was Talon flirting with her?

"I mean, if you… If you need a cup. There are paper ones, but I prefer not to waste those, so I…" she continued.

"No, I have a water bottle. I try not to use paper cups, either," Emerson said.

Talon nodded. Emerson made herself a cappuccino and actually remembered to put a mug there this time. So, that was progress, at least.

"So, those are the company-provided ones for everyone, but if you're smart, you'll take one and write your name on it in permanent marker. Just rewrite over it from time to time if you put it in the dishwasher because it'll rub off. People tend to leave the claimed ones alone," Talon said.

Talon had just said the word *rub*, and now Emerson was thinking about things rubbing together and how nice that friction would feel right about now.

"I could just bring one from home that has my name on it already," Emerson said, swallowing.

"Do you have a cup that has Emerson on it?"

"I do. My little brother made it for me when he was in sixth grade."

"That's cute," Talon replied, placing her cup under the dispenser of the other coffee maker. "Are you older or younger?"

"Oldest of four," Emerson said.

"Really?"

"Yeah," Emerson said. "You?"

"I have a younger brother, too. He's, like, way younger,

though. My parents had me, took, like, sixteen years off from having sex, apparently – or, at least, that's what I choose to believe – and then had him. He's only thirteen."

Emerson tried to do the simple math, but her brain was stuck on the fact that Talon had just said the word *sex*, and now Emerson could *only* picture them having sex.

"He's annoying, but he's thirteen, and all thirteen-year-old boys are annoying," Talon added.

"Should we go?" Emerson asked once they both had their coffees, needing to leave the kitchen where they were talking about sex and rubbing things.

They made their way back to Emerson's office, where her officemate was taking a call. Emerson grabbed her computer and joined Talon by her desk, where Talon picked up her computer and notebook. Walking toward the reserved conference room, neither of them said anything, but Emerson didn't know *what* to say, because what she really wanted to do was ask Talon out on a date, and that wasn't possible.

"So, where do you want to start?" Talon asked, sitting down at the table.

"I thought we could start with you going over the whole process as it is right now. Then, we can talk about what works well and what doesn't and get some ideas on the board for how to change the parts we want," Emerson said, sitting down next to her so they could both face the dry-erase wall.

Ten minutes later, they were diving in headfirst. Talon was up at the board, outlining the first stage of the sales process. Emerson stood up, took a different color marker, and added a step she thought they needed. Talon stood back and looked at it as if seeing it written there would make it make more sense.

"Can't that happen later?" she asked.

"It could, but if we move it to stage two during the demo, that'll just make that longer, and the demo phase–"

"Is already long enough, yeah," Talon interrupted.

"What about the–"

"Third phase," Talon said. "But we lose the–"

"Dropdown where they indicate–"

"Yes," Talon said, smiling at her.

Emerson stared. She couldn't help it. She turned from the wall and stared at Talon, who was now leaning against the conference table behind them, looking ridiculously hot as she stared back at Emerson and then licked her lips. Emerson didn't mean to, but she licked *her* lips as well. Talon's eyes flitted down and watched the movement. Neither said anything.

"Hey, Talon, I need you to approve a discount for me," a guy said as he pushed open the door without knocking or asking if he could interrupt. "Sorry, it's over the thirty percent I can offer, and it's that deal I've been trying to close for months."

"What do you need?" Talon asked.

"Thirty-five, and they'll close," he said, holding open the door.

"How much?"

"Two hundred, all-in," he replied. "And up front, they're paying for the professional services package and activation fee."

"Okay. Put the opportunity in, and I'll approve it," she said.

"Awesome. Thanks," the guy said, letting the door close as he left.

"What can you approve?" Emerson asked.

"Up to fifty percent. Nick can basically give things away for free," Talon replied.

"Reps can do thirty?"

"Yeah," Talon said.

"What's the approval process?" Emerson asked.

Talon returned to the board and added a square in blue where she wrote down the process for discount approvals.

"Got it. Can we make that smoother?" she asked.

"Not really. If we let the reps go to fifty, maybe. We

don't do any more than that discount-wise unless they're massive enterprise deals, and those would all be negotiated and contracted more than just emailing an agreement for the customer to sign."

"But if we let them go to forty, is there a risk?"

"They only get commission on the paid amount, so I can't see them going to fifty often or ever, really – they'd make less money. Most don't even go to thirty. Very rarely do they ask to go to forty. Plus, we have reports on discounts, so we'd know who's discounting, by what, and for whom," Talon replied.

"If we changed it to forty, would that make it faster because you wouldn't have to approve anything?"

"Sure, but that's not something I can decide on," Talon said.

"*I* can," Emerson replied, smirking at her.

"Okay, girl power," Talon said, laughing.

"Hey, do you want to grab lunch to keep talking about this stuff?" Emerson asked without thinking.

"Sure," Talon agreed. "I like this stuff," she added. "And there's a good food truck outside if you like that sort of thing."

"What kind of food truck?"

"Amazing fish tacos."

"Insert lesbian joke here," Emerson said.

Talon's intense gaze returned to her.

"Talon, he's saying he'll only do forty now," the guy opened the door again and said it with an annoyed grunt.

"You're still on with him?" Talon asked, turning away from Emerson.

"Yeah, I'm on mute, though," he replied.

"Drop the activation fee; that usually does it. He's probably just playing hardball."

"Got it," he said, leaving them again.

"Activation fee is only fifteen hundred, but people love it when we waive it," Talon said.

"Right," Emerson replied.

Later, they took the elevator down to the lobby and joined the long line for the food truck.

"So, oldest of four?" Talon said after a long moment of silence.

"Yeah. I have two brothers and a sister," Emerson replied. "My sister is twenty-six, my brother is twenty-three, and my youngest brother is twenty-one."

"Pretty wide age gap. Like me," Talon said.

"I'm going to choose to think that you weren't just calling me old there." Emerson laughed a little. "My mom had me when she was young. My dad was young, too, so he didn't want anything to do with fatherhood. She got through high school, though, and with the help of my grandparents, raised me. Then, she met and married my stepdad. When I was six, they had my sister. Then, they got divorced – long story – but all of my siblings are technically my half-siblings. My two brothers have the same dad, but he didn't stick around long after they were born, so my mom raised us all on her own."

"She sounds like a badass," Talon replied.

"She is," Emerson said, laughing. "And I'm getting lunch today."

"You don't have to. I–"

"This is a working lunch; I'm expensing it," Emerson interrupted. "Now, tell me about this annoying little brother of yours."

"What does *he* have to do with our sales process?" Talon laughed.

"Any chance he's going to buy one of our products?" Emerson joked.

"With his measly allowance? I doubt it," Talon replied.

"Have you always lived here?" Emerson asked, changing the subject.

"Pretty much," Talon said. "On the bad side of town, though."

"Really? Me too," Emerson replied. "Fourteenth and Cherry."

"Sixteenth and Laurel," Talon said, smiling at her.

"You lived only a few blocks away from me," Emerson noted.

"Yeah, but you're what… like, three years older than me? I'm sure if I ran into you, you would've been too cool for me," Talon said.

"I *would* have run into you because I would've had my nose in a book and wouldn't have been paying attention," Emerson replied as they moved up in the line.

"I like to read. My friend Weston is a writer. She reads like crazy, too, and always recommends good books to me. Because she buys them herself, I just get to borrow them for free. She's like my own personal library."

"Has she written anything I'd know?" Emerson asked.

"She's about to publish her first novel. I'll get you a free copy when it comes out if you want," Talon said.

"What can I get you?" the guy in the truck asked.

"Two fish tacos for me," Talon said.

"Same," Emerson said and handed the guy her credit card.

CHAPTER 9

Emerson had sent her a request to connect on LinkedIn. It had only been a matter of time, really. Talon stared at the tiny image on her phone of Emerson with much longer hair. It was too small for Talon to really make out much because she had to accept the request first to see more details about Emerson, but Talon liked her with the much shorter hair better. It suited the woman somehow. There was a checkmark and an X, and Talon had no real option. Emerson would wonder why she hadn't accepted the connection, so she tapped the checkmark and bit her lower lip as she scrolled through the information now available to her, which wasn't much, to begin with, and was all professional. It wasn't enough; Talon knew that. She wanted to know everything there was to know about Emerson Bagley.

They'd eaten lunch the day before yesterday and hadn't talked at all about work, despite it supposedly being a working lunch. Emerson was interesting to her now; it wasn't just the lust anymore. Talon actually liked her, and that made it worse. If it were lust, she could deal with that. She could go on a date or two with a woman, have sex, and maybe get herself a girlfriend. That would curb the impulse she had to fuck her boss's boss in their office. Now that she actually liked her as a person, she couldn't get Emerson out of her head in a very different way.

"Sorry, I'm late," Aria said as she sat down in the chair across from Talon and hung her purse from it.

"No big deal. I was just thinking about how I'm going to get fired," Talon replied.

"What?" Aria said. "You're getting fired?"

"No. Well, not yet, but maybe."

"Talon, what the hell?" Aria asked. "You invited me to

lunch. Should this have been drinks instead?"

"We can have a beer at lunch. There's no rule against that," Talon said.

"I guess not," Aria said just as their waiter came over to their table.

Aria ordered them each a beer and selected an appetizer. Talon didn't know which one; she wasn't really paying attention. She was just staring out the window next to her, thinking about Emerson.

"Okay. What's going on? You're all, like, weird right now."

"I'm crushing so hard on my boss… My boss's boss, actually."

"You've got a crush? And that's going to get you fired?"

"I flirt with her constantly," Talon said. "And I think she's gay, too, but I don't know for sure yet."

"Signals?"

"Somewhat butch vibe, short nails."

"Anything else?" Aria said.

"She made a lesbian joke the other day."

"In a rude way?"

"No, like in a she's-part-of-the-fam way," Talon said, shrugging. "Fish tacos."

"I think there's more to the joke than that," Aria said.

"There was, and it was funny, but I didn't get to laugh at it or tell her I'm on the team or part of the fam myself because someone interrupted us."

"And you're mad you got interrupted?"

"Yes, and no," Talon replied as their drinks arrived at the table. "I can't date her, so it's a good thing someone interrupted us. God, Aria… Every time I look at her, I think about tearing her clothes off."

"Damn. Really?"

"I don't even really know why. Like, she's sexy, but it's more than that."

"Sounds like it's more than a crush, Tal," Aria said.

"I don't know enough about her for it to be more than a crush yet," Talon replied.

"But you want to," Aria said.

"Yes," Talon replied. "And that is why I will probably be fired."

Aria laughed and said, "Because you want to get to know someone at work?"

"Because of *how* I want to get to know her."

"Biblically?" Aria joked.

"Aria, I've…" Talon leaned forward and whispered. "Every night since I saw her."

"Gotten off?" Aria asked.

Talon nodded rapidly.

"Every night?"

"Yes." Talon's eyes widened.

"And you're thinking of her when you…"

"Every fucking time," Talon replied. "And sometimes, multiple times."

"Shit. You're getting off to this woman multiple times a night?"

"Here's your appetizer," their waiter said, setting the plate down between them.

Talon went red.

"Are you ready… to place your order?" he asked.

"I think we're going to need a minute," Aria said, holding back her laughter.

"I hate you," Talon said when the waiter walked away, and Aria finally let out the laughter she'd been holding in.

"Come on. That's funny."

"Now, he's probably picturing me with some woman."

"If he's a straight guy, yeah. But he was probably picturing you and me together before that anyway," Aria suggested.

Talon made a disgusted face.

"Hey, I don't think that's hot, either, but you don't have to look so grossed out by it," Aria said to her. "So, does she like you, too?"

"I don't know. Sometimes, it's like she does. Other times, it's like she can't get away from me fast enough."

"Example?" Aria said, taking a drink of her beer.

"We're working on this project together, and we spent the whole day in a conference room."

"Sounds good so far."

"It has a glass wall. Everyone can see us."

"Less interesting now that the story won't end with you taking her on the table, but go on."

Talon shook her head at that image and said, "We reached for the same dry-erase marker, and our fingers brushed. She pulled away really fast and then moved to the other side of the table."

"Okay. That's no big deal."

"The first time something like that happened, she kept her hand there," Talon remarked.

"And?" Aria asked, obviously interested.

"We stared at each other, and the world fell away."

"Tal, the world fell away?" Aria asked with her voice pitching higher.

"Yeah."

"Oh, you *like* her," Aria said, chuckling.

"I know. That's why I called you here. I need help."

"*My* help? I'm literally the last of our friends you should go to about relationships. Well, maybe Scarlet because she's pretty hopeless, but then it's me, and then Pais, and Ellie, and then–"

"Weston is all about Annie these days," Talon stated.

"And she's your normal go-to." Aria considered. "Well, you're not going to like my advice, but I say… Go for it."

"Go for it?" Talon couldn't have heard right.

"With the boss," Aria said.

"Go for it?" she checked again. "You're here to help talk me out of it."

"Why? It's tech, Talon. The rules are different, and if she's giving you vibes that she might be interested back, go for it. At least, let her know you're into it. If it's just sex, you'll get it out of your system. And if it's more, it's more."

"You're no help," Talon said.

Aria laughed and said, "You know I'm right, though."

"Just eat your appetizer. What did you order anyway?"

"Bruschetta."

"Is that cilantro?" Talon asked. "You know I hate cilantro."

"It's basil, Talon," Aria said.

"How do you know?"

"Because it's tomato and basil bruschetta with balsamic glaze. Do you really not know what basil looks like? I didn't order bruschetta with cilantro. I'm not a heathen," Aria said.

***

Later that night, Talon lay on her sofa watching something on TV that she wasn't actually paying attention to. Her brain couldn't focus on anything. In the group text with her friends, Eleanor sent a message asking if anyone wanted to grab drinks, but Talon had had two beers at her late lunch with Aria and wasn't feeling up for more. Paisley was out of town. Weston said she was busy. That left Aria and Scarlet. Talon watched as the typing bubbles appeared on the screen. Aria accepted. Scarlet said she could join them later but had some work to do first. They made their plans, and Talon tossed her phone aside. She wanted to ask Emerson for drinks. She pictured Emerson's smile that day at lunch and applied that image to a dimly lit bar, a small oak table between them, glasses with hands wrapped around them, and Talon's heart started to thud inside her chest. Then, she felt the pulse lower.

"Oh, come on," she said to her own body.

Then, she picked up her phone and dialed.

"Hey. What's up?" Paisley said.

"Which hotel?"

"Holiday Inn Express."

"Did you eat yet?"

"Ordered apps from the bar they have," Paisley said. "Not exactly the chef-made meals I grew up with, but not terrible."

"Are you working?" Talon asked.

"Yeah, but I can take a break," she said. "You okay?"

"No, I need you to stop me from masturbating."

"Excuse me?" Paisley said, laughing.

"Be my cooler, Paisley Hill," Talon replied.

"Um… Offense. I'm taking offense to that."

"I'm serious," Talon said, laughing.

"What the fuck, Tal?"

"I'm lusting after someone I can't have, and I can't stop touching myself thinking about her."

"I know we all share a lot, but that's *a lot*, Talon."

"Is it, really? You once told me you stuck a finger into– "

"I don't need to recall that," Paisley interrupted.

"I didn't need to *know* that," Talon argued.

"I was drunk when I told you that, and I thought you were just as drunk and, therefore, wouldn't remember. Anyway, who is this woman you're lusting after?"

Talon filled Paisley in on Emerson but gave her the short, less embarrassing version, leaving out all the times she'd stared at Emerson in the office.

"And Aria told you to go for it?"

"Yes, but I can't. I mean, even if there are no strict rules against it, she might not want it, and now it's–"

"Awkward," Paisley stated.

"Exactly."

"I get it. Thinking long-term," Paisley told her. "Aria tends to think short-term."

"Yes, and as much as I'd like to take Aria's advice and just ask Emerson out, if she said no, I'd have to look at her every day."

"So, ask someone else out."

"What?"

"Tal, just go out and meet someone else. If this Emerson woman is off-limits, go out there and meet someone that's not," Paisley said.

"I guess I could. I don't think it'll help the fact that I can't stop thinking about her right now, though."

"Hey, I don't want to know what you do when we hang up, but fantasies are a part of life. I say… Let yourself do what you need to do. It'll help you to not…"

"Burst right in front of her?" Talon asked.

"Not how I would have worded that, but you get the idea."

"Yeah, thanks, Pais," Talon replied.

"Sure. Happy to help. Have I sufficiently cooled you off?"

"No, I'm still going to–"

"Bye, Talon," Paisley said, hanging up the phone.

Talon laughed. She took a deep breath, felt the pulse between her legs, and slipped her hand into her underwear.

CHAPTER 10

A week had passed since they'd started having lunch together regularly. Emerson loved having lunch with Talon. Despite the cold, they'd bundle up and walk to a restaurant or a food truck nearby. On the days when there wasn't time to leave the office, they'd order in or grab snacks from the kitchen and make those their meal.

"I can't do the Hot Cheetos," Talon had said the first day when they'd been making their snack selections.

"Nick?" Emerson had asked.

"He eats, like, six bags a day," Talon had said, laughing.

"I know. The chopsticks he uses are stained red," Emerson had said, joining Talon in that laughter.

"Better than his fingertips, I guess. Imagine him typing on his laptop with red fingertips or touching the tables or something," Talon had replied.

"How about we grab the hummus and the baby carrots and avoid staining *our* fingertips?" Emerson had suggested.

"You read my mind," Talon had said, smiling at her as she'd opened the glass refrigerator door and pulled out two individual containers of hummus and two bags of baby carrots.

"Oh, grab the–"

"On it," Talon had said and reached for the sliced apples with the peanut butter dip.

Emerson had told her the day before that so far, that was her favorite kitchen snack, and Talon had grabbed two. They'd worked in Emerson's office since her officemate was working from home that day, and they'd somehow managed to be in sync on just about everything, with an ease Emerson hadn't ever found in someone she worked with. Hell, she'd never had that with someone she'd dated.

"How is it going?" her mother asked as Emerson walked from her car to the office.

"It's getting harder," Emerson replied.

"That's because you've done the opposite of what you were supposed to do, Emerson," her mom remarked.

"I know. I know. It's this project, though, Mom. It needs to happen, and we're doing such a good job with it."

"No one else could have helped you with it?"

"I don't think so, no," she said. "She just gets what I'm going for, and she's so smart, Mom. She just knows what needs to be done, and if we get this right, we'll end up saving the company–"

"Hey, good morning."

Emerson looked up, seeing Talon walk out of the building, wearing a navy-blue toggle-button coat that looked so good on her.

"Gotta go. Love you," she said quickly and hung up on her own mother.

"Sorry, I didn't mean for you to hang up," Talon said, approaching Emerson with her hands in her pockets. "I just saw you, so I thought I'd say hi."

"No, it's fine. My mom just called me. Checking in Mom stuff."

"Everything okay?" Talon asked as light snow began to fall.

"Yeah, everything's fine. We're just really close. I talk to her most days," Emerson said.

"That's cool. I talk to my folks about once a week, maybe. Depends on how busy *I* am and how busy they are with my brother. He wrestles, plays basketball and soccer, so they're always running around with him."

"Where are you headed?" Emerson asked.

"Oh, just to grab coffee," Talon said.

"You couldn't wait for me?" Emerson asked.

"*You* were supposed to be here fifteen minutes ago. I thought you might have decided to work from home today," Talon replied.

"Traffic," Emerson explained. "And we've been walking to coffee together, so I'm obviously deeply offended." She placed a hand over her heart in mock-outrage.

Talon laughed and said, "We've walked for coffee twice. Should I assume it's my responsibility to always check if you want to come with me whenever I'm leaving the office for coffee now?"

"Yes, obviously," Emerson said sarcastically.

"Well, do you want to drop your stuff upstairs, and I'll wait for you?"

"No, I can go with my bag," Emerson told her.

Talon nodded and said, "The coffee maker is broken again. Brittany called the guy to come and fix it, but I don't like the one you use."

"The one *you* taught me to use," Emerson replied, turning to walk next to Talon down the sidewalk.

"You *asked* me to teach you," Talon said.

"I like the strong stuff," Emerson replied. "And the one you use just makes regular coffee."

"It's a dark roast," Talon argued.

"That you add, like, a gallon of milk to," Emerson laughed.

"I do not," Talon said, laughing, too.

"I made you coffee the other day, brought it to you, and you said there wasn't enough cream in it. I'd filled half the mug with cream, Talon."

"First of all, I don't pick on *you* for your coffee."

"You just said you don't like the coffee I drink."

"Just that I didn't like it, but I didn't pick on you for it. I don't like those Veggie Sticks chips you eat, but I don't pick on you for eating them," Talon said.

"You've never even had them," Emerson replied.

"I snuck one from your bag. I'm not a fan."

Emerson liked this new development between them. This back-and-forth banter was nice. It probably shouldn't be *this* nice, and she knew it. She was allowed to get along with the people she worked with, though, so this was okay. She just needed to keep it at this. Emerson pulled open the door to the coffee place closest to their office, and Talon walked inside in front of her. Emerson had taken to opening doors for Talon recently, too, and while neither of them had spoken about it, Emerson liked doing it. It gave her a chance to sometimes hover her hand over the small of Talon's back as she ushered her inside, and while she'd yet to touch her there, the hovering was enough for now. No, it was enough *forever.* It had to be enough for forever.

"Can I get a large dark roast with room?" Talon asked the barista.

"Extra room," Emerson jokingly corrected.

"Shut up," Talon laughed. "And whatever caramel, hazelnut, vanilla thing with soy or almond milk that she wants, too." She hooked her thumb in Emerson's direction.

"Hey," Emerson said, laughing. "Just a large cappuccino."

Talon paid for both of them, which made Emerson smile. They waited for their drinks in silence since Talon had a few texts come in. Then, they left and began the short walk back.

"Sorry, my friends," Talon said, slipping her phone into her front pocket.

"It's okay." Emerson took a drink of the still very hot coffee.

"We have a group chat. It's usually pretty busy in there," Talon said.

"Yeah?"

"We've known each other forever and tend to overshare, so… Yeah."

"That sounds nice, actually," Emerson said.

"It *can* be," Talon replied. "They're my family, you know?"

"I don't, really. I mean, I have a few friends, but not many, and my family has been my family. I had a lot of responsibilities growing up. My mom needed my help."

"What was that like?" Talon asked. "I mean, I grew up poor, but I didn't have to help take care of anyone else."

"Oh, it was fine," she lied.

Talon didn't say anything for a moment. Then, she stopped walking, so Emerson stopped, too.

"It's okay if you don't want to tell me. It's really personal," Talon said. "I understand."

"What do you mean?" she asked, sipping her cappuccino as a distraction.

"I'm sure some of it was fine, but I'm also pretty sure that some of it really sucked. You were a kid, and you had to probably give some things up to take care of other kids. That couldn't have been easy; that's all I'm saying."

Emerson stared into those brown eyes that looked so open right now. How was it possible that eyes could look closed or open? Not in the way that they were physically closed or open, but in that way that either told someone not to broach a subject or that this person was ready and willing to listen to anything another person had to say. Talon's eyes looked as if Emerson could tell her anything in the world, and it would be okay, which only made Emerson *want* to tell her everything.

"It had its hard moments, yeah," Emerson admitted. "Want to get inside? It's cold."

"Sure," Talon said, nodding at her.

She looked, if Emerson could even describe it, disappointed a little, as if she'd been hoping Emerson would tell her more about her life growing up and all the difficult times. They hopped into the elevator and the subject changed from their personal struggles to the project they were working on, which made Emerson much more comfortable.

They spent the morning in their conference room, and it had become just that. There had been a sign placed on the door by someone saying it was reserved for the next couple of weeks for the project. Emerson wondered who had put it there. They'd already reserved the room in the online system, so there was no need for the sign, but if it kept random reps from trying to jump into the room to make a quick call, she figured she'd keep it up.

She watched as Nick walked past the room with likely his second bag of Hot Cheetos in hand and wondered if it had been him with the sign. She had hardly spent any time with him since she'd started working with Talon, and she needed to invest more time in her direct report. It likely bothered him that Emerson had clearly connected with Talon more than him so far, and she'd have to put in the work with him and his ego to make sure things were okay between them. She'd only just started, after all. She couldn't go around pissing everyone off already.

"I played around with it in the sandbox last night," Talon said, bringing Emerson's attention back to her.

"And?" she asked, leaning over Talon's shoulder to look down at her laptop screen.

Her hair smelled of snow. Was that even possible? Did snow smell? Emerson's eyes couldn't stay on the screen and moved to Talon's neck, which looked so soft. She wanted to touch it. Emerson wanted to press her lips to it and slide her hand down into Talon's shirt, massaging her breast until Talon begged her to fuck her against the table.

"Emerson?" Talon said.

Her head turned a little until their eyes met. Talon licked her lips. Emerson did the same. Then, she looked up and moved away.

"Can you put it on the big TV?" Emerson asked, clearing her throat.

"Yeah, sure," Talon replied.

***

After work, Emerson drove home, trying to figure out a way to have it all. She couldn't afford to lose her new job. She had her student loans to pay off and still sometimes helped her siblings make rent or pay utility bills when they needed a little cash. She couldn't ask Talon out then, because even if Talon said yes, it wouldn't look right. Emerson had selected her for this project and had spent all this time working with her and taking coffee breaks and lunches with her. People would talk. Hell, HR would probably pull her into an office and give her a warning or just go straight to firing her to protect themselves. It would be worse if what she thought she was feeling from Talon was wrong, and Talon wasn't into women or, at least, wasn't into her. So, Emerson walked into her apartment knowing she'd never be able to have it all. It was time for her to stop thinking about Talon Mitchell as anything other than a colleague and try to meet someone else.

Tomorrow. She'd do that tomorrow. Tonight, she wanted to take a long, hot bubble bath and think about Talon being in there with her as she touched herself to relieve the sexual tension. Then, she'd pull out her laptop and test some of the changes they'd made that day to the process.

After her bath and the orgasm that was enough for now but not nearly good enough, in her opinion, she opened her email and noticed one from Talon. She smiled as she opened the message.

Emerson,

I will be walking to get coffee tomorrow morning at nine since Brittany said the coffee guy needs a part to fix the one in the office. This is me letting you know that if you also need coffee around nine in the morning, you can join me at my desk. If I don't see you there by five after, I'll leave without you.

Talon

P.S. But seriously, if you can't go but want me to grab you a cappuccino, just let me know.

Emerson laughed as she replied.

CHAPTER 11

"You two are getting along," Nick said.

"Huh?" Talon asked.

"You and Emerson," he said.

"Oh. I guess, yeah." Talon sat at her desk.

Nick sat down next to her in Dimitri's chair and moved in a little too close for Talon's liking.

"How's the project going?"

"Fine," she said.

"Can you walk me through the changes you're suggesting so I can approve them?"

Talon turned to him and said, "I can, but Emerson is already approving them."

That was probably the wrong thing to say, but she didn't care. Nick had been giving her a hard time since she and Emerson began working together. Talon was used to the guys pushing her buttons; it came with the territory. But Nick's attitude toward her had shifted as of late, and it was starting to piss her off.

"I'd still like to know what's going on, Talon. I'll probably be put in charge of rolling the changes out to the greater team," Nick replied.

"I thought Emerson put Talon on that," Dimitri said, walking toward his desk. "That's what she said in the team meeting this morning."

"I'm Talon's boss, so it'll really fall to me," Nick said.

"Nick, can I borrow you?"

Talon looked up to see Emerson standing just outside her office now.

"Sure," he said, smiling a fake smile.

He stood, giving Dimitri his chair back, and headed into Emerson's office. Emerson closed the door behind them. That was when Talon noticed Chet from HR sitting in the office as well. One of the downsides to having glass walls everywhere was that when someone needed to have a private conversation, it wasn't all that private. Talon turned back to her computer.

"Hey, don't worry about him. He's just jealous you're better at this stuff than he is," Dimitri said.

"What?" Talon asked.

"Nick. You're better than him at just about everything, from what I can see. Now that you're finally getting some major projects, he's upset about it, but that's on him." He shrugged. "You keep kicking ass."

"Thanks," Talon said, laughing a little.

A few minutes later, Nick emerged from Emerson's office and headed toward the elevators. Talon pretended not to notice and just kept her eyes on her computer screen.

"Talon, can I talk to you?" Emerson asked.

Shit. Now, it was her turn. Talon reviewed everything she'd done in the past few weeks. Was there something she should be getting in trouble for? She'd been staring at Emerson, but that was it. She couldn't get fired just for staring, could she? She stood and turned, noticing Chet left Emerson's office, which meant the meeting wouldn't involve HR; it was probably just about the project. She sighed, feeling relieved, and walked into the office. Emerson closed the door behind them, and Talon sat down.

"Hey, I'm sorry," Emerson said, sitting down in her chair.

"For?" Talon asked.

"For Nick," she replied. "I had a chat with him with Chet."

"Chat with Chet?" Talon teased. "Sounds like a terrible talk show or web series."

"I know." Emerson laughed lightly. "Nick is the one that put that sign on the conference room door."

"The one where it says it's reserved for us?"

"The one that now has a pen drawing of stick figures of you and me holding little stick figure hands," Emerson said. "Incredibly immature. I also heard he's been making some comments about how I've made you my favorite, even though he's your boss. I wanted to put a stop to it, so I've involved HR."

"I can handle Nick," Talon said.

"You shouldn't have to, and neither should I. Others reported him, including *my* boss, so I wanted to let you know that because you've been mentioned, HR might want to talk to you."

"Mentioned?"

"Your name came up in the complaints. Plus, I just heard what he said to you out there, and so did Chet. He's probably going to ask to talk to you after he finds Nick."

"Finds him?"

"He said he needed some air. I can't tell you about the crux of the conversation, but he needed a few minutes, so we thought it best to let him go outside. Chet is checking on him now, though."

"Okay," Talon said. "What does this mean, though? Does Nick still work here?"

"For now," Emerson said. "Look, I'm probably breaking *all* the rules telling you this stuff, Talon, but he's bordering on the line between immediate termination and a final written warning."

"So, I still have to work for him?" Talon asked.

"Do you have concerns for how he's been treating you?"

"No, I mean, it's–"

"Because I do," Emerson said.

Talon stared into her green eyes, which showed that concern. It was nice. She wasn't sure she'd ever seen concern in Nick's eyes directed toward her. Now, if they were out of Hot Cheetos, his concern was legendary around the office.

"I'd like to move you over to another manager, but I wanted to talk to you about it first."

"You want to move me?"

"You haven't done anything wrong, so I won't if you tell me not to. I just hate the idea of you working under someone who clearly doesn't appreciate your talents and makes rude comments about you because you and I are working on a project together."

"But if I move, everyone will know what happened," Talon said.

"I think they already do," Emerson replied. "Brock tore down the sign on the door and was the one that brought it to me. He's a good manager, from what I can see. His teams perform almost as well as your team does."

Talon laughed and said, "Yeah, they usually come in second, third, and fourth every month."

"While we figure out what to do with Nick, HR and I think it's good to put you on Brock's team. He spoke very highly of you."

"So, I'm on Brock's team now, and Nick just has Dimitri and Ruben?"

"While the investigation is conducted."

"Investigation?" Talon asked. "He hasn't been *that* bad. He's immature, yeah, but he's just giving me a hard time. It's–"

"Talon, he's said other things. I can't share the details with you, but it's not just what he's said to your face." Emerson paused. "On a more personal note, we're women in a male-dominated profession – we already have to put up with a lot. The high-fives are the least of our concerns. There are comments made daily that they probably don't mean or think we're okay with but we don't deserve and shouldn't have to put up with. I remember last week, when you told me about the off-site meeting last year where you all went to the park…"

"And played touch football?" Talon recalled telling her.

"Yeah. You told me that they passed to you, and you scored a touchdown, making you one of the guys, but Chantal missed a pass, and they never threw to her again. They made some comments about her in the huddle."

Talon nodded and said, "I should've said something, but I let it happen."

"They shouldn't have said it at all," Emerson replied. "If it were up to me, Nick wouldn't work here anymore, but there are policies, paperwork, and concerns about wrongful termination lawsuits. I, personally, don't care. I dare Nick to file a lawsuit saying we had no right to fire his ass – I'll get up on that stand and tell whoever needs to hear it that he deserved it and then some."

"Slow down, Rosie the Riveter," Talon said, laughing because she needed to make light of the situation right now.

Nick had been an immature asshole, but it was something she'd gotten used to. She hadn't realized it went beyond that, though, and knowing that now… well, it hurt.

"Do you want to work from home for the rest of the day?" Emerson asked.

"What? No way. We have a meeting," Talon replied.

Emerson smiled and said, "We do. I have notes from the testing I did."

"I don't want to lose traction because of Nick," Talon stated.

"What if we go down to the operations' floor? They have those rooms in the corner–"

"With the beanbag chairs? Yeah, that sounds good."

It sounded even better to not be on this floor after Nick stormed off and Chet from HR ran after him. They rode the elevator down a floor, and Emerson negotiated with some operations people to use the room they were in. Once they were gone, she and Emerson each took a beanbag chair, laughed because of how ridiculous it looked, and then got to work.

***

"That asshole," Scarlet said, and *that* meant something because Scarlet rarely swore.

"Can I stop by your office and kick him in the nuts? They can't fire me," Ellie added.

"But he could file assault charges," Paisley said.

"It's fine. I mean, it's not – it sucks – but I guess I'm on Brock's team now. He's good. He's at least been here for four years and really earned the job he has. Plus, he defended my honor, which is kind of cool," Talon replied.

Paisley was in town for just the day and had asked Talon and the rest of the group to join her for lunch before her next contract forced her on the road again that night. Aria and Weston had been busy, but Talon and the rest of them had joined her. The restaurant they chose was only a few blocks from the office, which meant Talon could eat and then get back without a problem. She had another afternoon with Emerson ahead of her, and they were getting started at two.

"I'm glad about that, and I'm glad Emerson stood up for you, too," Scarlet said, taking a bite of her salad.

"Yeah, he said some stuff about her, too, so it stands to reason."

"Plus, she probably has a thing for you," Ellie said.

"She does *not*," Talon played it cool, laughing.

"The way you've described your interactions with her, yeah, she's got a thing for you," Ellie added.

"Whether she does or doesn't, Talon can't go there," Paisley said.

"Right," Talon replied.

"Haven't you been hanging out with her outside of the office?" Scarlet asked.

"So?"

"Like, coffees and lunches?" Scarlet said.

"Yes, Scar. We're working together, so we go to lunch and–"

"And why didn't you invite her to join us?"

"Paisley's invite, not mine," Talon said.

"Yeah, right. That's never stopped you before," Ellie said.

"You didn't invite her because you really like her. And you know if she were here, we'd be able to tell if she really likes you, and then you'd have to decide what to do about it," Scarlet said, being the shy, perceptive one she always was in the group.

"She was busy," Talon replied.

"Which is it? She was busy, or this was Paisley's invite?" Eleanor asked.

"Okay. You guys are ganging up on me like we're in an episode of *Law & Order* and I'm the bad guy. I don't like it," Talon told them. "And I have to get back anyway."

"To Emerson," Ellie said, smirking at her.

"To work," Talon corrected.

"And the girl you like."

"Yes, Ellie. I like her. That's obvious."

"If you're not going to do anything about it, Tal, you should go out, try to meet someone else," Ellie said.

"Or, I could just wallow," Talon replied. "I'm good at wallowing. I've been doing it since my ex dumped me in front of family and out of the blue."

"Fine, keep wallowing. But if you have to see her every day, I don't see that ending anytime soon," Paisley replied.

"Don't I know it," Talon said.

CHAPTER 12

Emerson had hated having to talk to Talon about Nick. She hated moving Talon to another manager when she'd done nothing wrong. Women always seemed to have to change something about their lives because of things men did or didn't do, and it annoyed Emerson that this was still true in this day and age. Brock was a good manager. Emerson could tell that from his numbers alone, but also the way he supported and bragged about his team, not himself. On top of that, when he'd heard about the thing Nick had been doing, he hadn't been afraid to turn him in. At another company, in another situation, Brock would be worried about snitching on a peer and facing a bunch of crap from everyone, but he hadn't cared about that. On top of it, Emerson hadn't seen or heard much crap come his way, so maybe Nick was the bad apple and everyone else was okay here.

Either way, when Nick had cursed Chet out after Chet had followed him outside, saying that Talon was only a manager and he was a *senior* manager and should, therefore, be working on this project instead, or should at least be approving Talon's work, Chet had made the right decision and fired Nick on the spot. The rest of the sales team was pulled into a few conference rooms for some important meetings where they were all told that Nick no longer worked for the company and that they'd be posting his position shortly. That had been the thing to push Emerson over the edge with her plans tonight.

Talon would get that position. She'd apply, and she'd get it. She should have gotten it the last time, but the company had made a mistake. Emerson had only spent a couple of weeks working closely with Talon, but she knew that no outside hire would be able to compete with her skill or knowledge about the company. Others might apply internally, but Emerson couldn't see any of them comparing, either. So, Talon would get the job and report directly to Emerson, making things even worse for Emerson's feelings now, which had gone from pure lust to more actual feelings. The lust was still there. It was very much still there. Talon had worn a few button-downs recently, and Emerson had daydreamed about taking them off by tearing at the buttons until they were bouncing off the floor. Her new daydream, though, was more about slowly unbuttoning them as she kissed Talon just as slowly. She guessed that showed the evolution of her feelings.

"Actually, I'm leaving, too. This place is dead tonight," a woman said as Emerson opened the door to the bar. "Can you take me home, Wes, so I don't have to get a car?"

"Sure," another woman said.

Then, Emerson saw her.

"Oh, hi," Talon said, noticing Emerson at the same time.

"Oh, hi," Emerson repeated, wide-eyed.

"I didn't know you–"

"Yeah, me neither," Emerson said, interrupting Talon.

This was a gay bar. Emerson was walking into a gay bar to meet a friend, and here was Talon. Neither of them had confirmed their sexuality to the other. Emerson had made a joke, and there had been a couple of pronouns tossed around, but she'd been careful because if she told Talon she was gay, and Talon was, too – or, at least, had the same feelings for Emerson that Emerson had for her – that would somehow make it more possible for them to pursue this, whatever *this* was. And it was something they couldn't pursue.

"My friends and I were just leaving," Talon said.

"Okay," Emerson replied to Talon's abrupt comment.

"Talon, do you want to maybe introduce us to your friend?" the first woman asked.

"Oh, we're not–" Emerson started and stopped. "I'll just let you go."

She moved out of the open doorway, allowing them to pass.

"Sure. Thanks. Bye," Talon said.

Why had Emerson tried to correct the woman? They *were* friends, weren't they? Sure, they were colleagues, but it wasn't like they were *just* colleagues anymore. They'd talked about personal things; they'd hung out at lunch and had gotten coffee together. Hell, they'd even left the office together the other day and proceeded to stand by Emerson's car talking for over an hour, braving the cold and claiming they wanted to try to miss the worst of the traffic, but that hadn't been the reason, and Emerson had known it.

"Hey, I wasn't sure what you wanted, so I didn't order you anything," Shea said.

"That's okay. I just had the weirdest thing happen," Emerson replied, sitting down next to her friend.

"Really? What?" they asked.

"I ran into someone from work."

"Here? Are you outed now?" Shea asked.

"I don't know. I mean, I'm out everywhere. It didn't exactly come up in the interview process that I'm a lesbian, but it's obvious, right?" Emerson motioned to herself.

"Oh, yeah," Shea stated, taking a drink of their beer. "Then, why is it weird?"

"Because it's Talon."

"Talon? The woman you called me about, begging me to drop what I was doing and come for a drink so I can play winghuman and help you find someone to maybe take home because you can't stop thinking about Talon between your legs doing–"

"Okay. I get it," Emerson said, laughing. "And yes, *that* Talon. She was here with a couple of her friends, I guess."

"Maybe I noticed her. What does she look like?" Shea asked.

"Straight long brown hair, brown eyes, and an adorable button nose that I also find incredibly sexy."

"And you want to see what it feels like when it's…" Shea pointed down between their legs.

"Shea!"

"You're blushing," Shea said, laughing.

"Because I came here tonight to *not* think about that," Emerson replied.

"And you're thinking about it now?"

"Yes. And she looks so good in that navy coat…" Emerson said dreamily.

"Oh, now I know who you're talking about. She had a couple of friends in here."

"Yes," Emerson said.

"She's cute," Shea noted.

"She's more than cute," Emerson said as the bartender finally arrived to take her order.

"What'll it be?" the woman asked.

"Whiskey sour," Emerson said.

The bartender nodded and turned to make Emerson's drink.

"Clearly, you've got it bad for this girl," Shea said. "I think tonight, we need to focus on finding you someone to *definitely* take home, not *maybe* take home. Let's find you a woman so you can buy her a drink. You never slept with Miranda, right?"

"No. And while I'm grateful for that fact because I think she would've proposed by now, given the pictures I've seen on social – I'm also wondering if I'm just really…"

"Horny?" Shea asked.

"Hey."

The voice came from behind Emerson's stool but was unmistakable. Emerson swallowed, praying Talon hadn't heard everything they'd just said, and turned.

"Talon? Hey, I thought you left."

"I was just seeing my friends off." The woman hooked a thumb in the direction of the door. "Well, that's not true. I *was* leaving, but then I saw you, and I think it was weird back there, so I wanted to come back in and apologize if I was rude."

Shea cleared their throat.

"Oh, sorry. This is my friend Shea."

Talon turned to Shea as if finally realizing Emerson wasn't alone at the bar.

"Hi," Talon said, holding out her hand to shake. "Sorry for interrupting. Nice to meet you."

"You weren't interrupting anything," Emerson said a little too quickly, earning a lifted eyebrow from Shea.

"Nice to meet you, too," Shea said. "I was just about to order a girl a drink. I'll leave you two to catch up."

Emerson's eyes went wide as she watched Shea stand and take their beer with them. Shea walked over to a group of women and just kind of joined in how they always did.

"Shea's always been able to just walk up to people like that," Emerson commented.

"Yeah? Not you?" Talon asked.

Emerson's drink was placed in front of her, and she picked it up just to have something to hold on to.

"Only after about three of these."

"You seem so confident, though," Talon said.

"At work, maybe," Emerson stated, taking a drink. "Here. Have Shea's seat. They'll be gone for a while."

The bar wasn't packed, but Shea's stool was the only empty one. Talon sat down, and Emerson hadn't even realized how close she and Shea had been sitting until Talon occupied the stool and was practically on top of Emerson now.

"Oh, sorry," Talon said, scooting the stool over a bit.

"It's okay," Emerson replied, laughing a little. "So, can I get you a drink?"

"I'm okay," Talon replied, staring ahead at the bar and not looking anywhere near Emerson.

Emerson wasn't sure what she should do now, so she picked up her own drink and took a sip.

"What are you having?" Talon asked her.

"Whiskey sour."

"Ah, the hard stuff," Talon commented, laughing softly.

"I guess." Emerson laughed a little, too.

"You know what, maybe I *will* have another drink." She waved over the bartender.

"I thought you left," the woman said to Talon.

"I did. I came back. Can I get a mojito?"

"I'm out of fresh mint," the bartender replied. "That group over there is a bachelorette party and has an obsession with mojitos."

Talon laughed a little louder and said, "Okay. Martini?"

"Extra olives?" the bartender asked.

"Yeah," Talon said.

The woman nodded and went to make the drink.

"You must come here a lot," Emerson said.

"It's one of a few hangout places my friends and I have. We have a regular old pub, too, but this is the only lesbian bar in a few towns. There are a few gay clubs, but I prefer the quiet like this most nights," Talon explained.

"So, you're…" Emerson wasn't sure how to say it.

If Talon weren't an employee, it would be easier, but Emerson wasn't sure if there was some HR violation just for asking when they were out in public like this.

"Yeah. You?"

Emerson nodded and said, "You couldn't tell?" She smiled.

Talon laughed and said, "I could, but I never assume."

"Me neither."

"But could you tell with me?" Talon wondered.

"Not exactly," Emerson replied honestly. "There were moments."

"Moments?" Talon lifted an eyebrow.

"Yeah. Like, when you talked about that ex that broke

up with you, you failed to say *she* and said *they* instead. I guess *they* could have been non-binary, like Shea over there. Another reason I never assume," Emerson said.

"She was a she," Talon confirmed for her. "And yeah, I was cautious."

"I get it." Emerson took another drink.

"So, you're here with Shea?"

"They're an old friend; grew up in the neighborhood with me. We hadn't talked in a long time. Then, I ran into them at a neighborhood block party thing a couple of years ago, and we hang out from time to time now."

"Cool. That's cool," Talon said as her martini was placed in front of her.

"So, extra olives?" Emerson said because she had no idea what else to say.

"Yeah, extra olives," Talon replied, shaking her head and laughing a little.

CHAPTER 13

Talon hadn't planned on seeing Emerson that night. She hadn't planned on having a drink with her in a dimly lit bar. Well, she'd had that one fantasy, but this was reality, and now she was sitting next to the object of her affections and sipping a martini while Emerson worked on her second whiskey sour. Talon had already had a drink with her friends, so she wanted to take this drink slow. She didn't have to drive; Weston was going to take her home. But, technically, Talon could walk from here. She wouldn't walk alone at night, but she could get a car for herself. She just hated getting into the back of a stranger's car too intoxicated to take care of herself, so she'd pace herself with this drink. Also, there was the fact that Emerson's green eyes looked amazing in the bar light, and Talon needed to keep herself in check, so getting drunk wasn't an option.

"Hey, I'm thinking about heading out. You cool?" Shea asked after approaching them.

Emerson looked from Talon to Shea and back to Talon. Talon looked down at her martini, giving Emerson an out if she wanted to take it.

"I'm good, yeah," Emerson said to Talon's surprise.

"Awesome. There's a girl over there that asked me to have drinks back at her place," Shea said. "So, wish me luck."

"Good luck," Emerson said, laughing.

"Good luck?" Talon asked more than said.

"Hey, thanks. Nice meeting you again," Shea told her.

And then, they were alone at the bar again.

"Do they normally pick up women and leave you alone?" Talon asked of Shea.

"No, but we don't hang out all that often these days. They must really like the girl," Emerson said. "You came with your friends tonight, right?"

"Yeah. And I should have introduced you. It was just weird running into you outside of work. Kind of like running into a teacher outside of school or your therapist outside of their office. Not that I go to therapy… I mean, not that there's anything wrong with going to therapy. I think it's great," Talon blurted out.

Emerson laughed and said, "It's okay. I get it. I don't feel like I give off teacher or therapist vibes, but I get it."

"It's just that I expect to see you at work."

"Not out at a gay bar?" Emerson smiled.

"Yeah," Talon said, finishing her martini.

"Do you want another?" Emerson asked.

"I shouldn't. I've had a drink with my friends, and they make strong drinks here."

"Really? Mine is pretty weak, actually," Emerson noted. "Actually, my first one was fine. My second one was weaker."

"Yeah?" Talon asked, pushing her martini glass away.

"Another one, Tal?" the bartender asked almost immediately.

"No, I'm good. Just the check, please," Talon said.

"On the house," the bartender replied. "Another one for you?" she asked Emerson.

"I'm good."

"I'll grab your check, then," she said and walked over to the computer.

"I get it now," Emerson said, laughing.

"What?" Talon asked, wondering what she was talking about.

"She likes you," Emerson stated, pointing to the bartender.

"Who?"

"Talon, the bartender," she explained.

"She does not," Talon argued.

"Yes, she does. You just got a free drink. And while my first drink was fine – you sit down next to me and we start talking, and my second drink isn't as good. And *I'm* about to get a check."

"Here you go," the bartender said to Emerson, placing the check on the bar.

Talon got to it before Emerson could and slid cash out of a wallet she kept in her back pocket. She paid for the two drinks and left a generous tip.

"Thanks," she said to the bartender.

"See you next time?" the woman asked.

"Sure," Talon said, unaffected. Then, she turned to Emerson and added, "You ready to go?"

Talon knew she couldn't be on a real date with Emerson, but she also wasn't interested in the bartender at her regular lesbian bar. That just opened up a whole lot of possible complications she didn't want to deal with, and she was still getting picked on for sleeping with Aubrey by her friends, so she didn't need to have to pick a new hangout because the bartender started making them all bad drinks when Talon screwed her over or something.

"Oh, sure," Emerson replied, looking a little surprised.

Talon stood, and Emerson did the same. Talon had no idea where they were going. She hadn't yet ordered a car and hadn't planned on just announcing that they were leaving like that, so she'd have to improvise. Emerson opened the door for her, as usual, and followed Talon outside, where it was cool but not cold for once.

"I don't know why I did that," she admitted.

"Me neither," Emerson replied, laughing.

"Um… I need to order a car." Talon pulled out her phone. "I can walk, but I don't walk at night."

"You live that close?"

"Yeah, just over there a few blocks and then two blocks down." Talon pointed.

"I can walk with you," Emerson said. "I can order myself a car from there. I took one here. This was Shea's recommendation, and I thought they'd take me home, but…"

"They went home with someone else," Talon finished.

"And they're probably feeling that someone up in a car right about now, which I think is what that bartender wanted to do to you," Emerson said.

"I hardly know her; she just takes our drink orders. I think that's the first free drink she's ever given me," Talon replied, tucking her phone back into her coat pocket. "Are you sure about the walk? I can just get a car."

"No, it's fine. It's a nice night. I miss nights like this in the winter."

"Yeah, it's February 1st – it's supposed to be way colder than this," Talon said.

"You know how every year we get, like, one or two days like this?" Emerson asked as they started to walk. "They kind of come out of nowhere. Like, it'll be twenty degrees one day and sixty the next."

"Yeah, I wonder why that is," Talon commented.

"No clue, but it's nice. I remember one year; I was about eleven or twelve, so my sister would've been about six or seven, and my brother was really little. I don't remember if my youngest brother was born yet or not. Anyway, it was St. Patrick's Day, and there's this annual block party thing that the neighborhood did back then. They still do, and my family still goes, but back then, it was just the block, not the people that left and come back from time to time. It was the weirdest thing because the day before, it had been about forty degrees or something. We woke up on St. Patrick's Day, and it was eighty-five," Emerson recalled.

"Really? I don't remember that." Talon said, and she really didn't.

"My mom's boyfriend at the time was crazy Irish. His whole family loved the holiday, I guess, so we celebrated it, and it became a thing. The older boys on the block set up the sprinklers, and we all stripped down to our underwear and bathing suits if we had them and ran through the water. It was such a great day. My mom had it off work, and we all ate burgers, hot dogs, and other things we couldn't afford to have regularly because the whole block chipped in."

Talon smiled as Emerson shared this part of her childhood with her. It was nice to see this part of the woman, and Talon could picture younger Emerson running with the other kids through the sprinklers, laughing and having a blast.

"That sounds like a pretty perfect day."

"At the end of that party, I remember my Mom came into my room before bed and gave me an extra piece of chocolate cake with bright-green icing she'd saved for me. I had to eat it after my sister fell asleep because she'd tried to steal it from me. My mom tried to do those little things for me when she could. It wasn't always easy, and there wasn't always extra, but when she had something, she gave it to me. I think, looking back on it, that was her way of thanking me for helping out so much with the other kids."

"I'm sure you're right. She sounds like a great mom, Emerson," Talon said.

"She is," Emerson said. "What about yours?"

"My mom?" Talon laughed. "She's a good mom, too. I was basically an only child since my brother wasn't born until I was sixteen. We didn't have much. My parents both worked blue-collar jobs. My dad was in a factory for twelve hours a day, five to six days a week, always trying to get overtime, until he got injured on the job about ten years ago. Now, he's on disability, but he's able to move around and stuff; he just can't do much beyond that. My mom worked at a donut shop for a while."

"Donuts?"

"That was pretty cool, but some nights, there would only be donuts for dinner, so Talon ended up gaining the freshman fifteen as a ten-year-old," she said of herself.

"Oh, no," Emerson said, chuckling. "I bet you were adorable, though."

"I was *not*," Talon replied, shaking her head. "She left the donut shop, which was great for my figure as a teenager, and ended up working at a regular restaurant and some other odd jobs here and there once my dad got injured. She worked so much, I didn't see her all that often, and by the time my dad got injured and was at home all the time, I–"

"You were a teenager and wanted nothing to do with your parents anymore because you were so cool?" Emerson concluded.

"Exactly," Talon stated, laughing again. "My brother was born, and I got a scholarship to college, so that helped them out with having to feed him, too. My mom worked her way up at work, and they were able to afford a different apartment on the decent side of town. That's where they are now. I still help out when they need it and I can."

They walked for a bit in silence, which Talon found to be comfortable until they hit a stoplight and had to wait for it to change to cross the street.

"You can probably order your car now," Talon said. "My place is just over there." She pointed. "Actually, you walked me home. Let *me* order a car for *you*."

"You paid for both of my drinks, Talon. I think the least I could do is walk you all the way to your front door," Emerson told her in response.

The light changed, and they walked across the street. Talon saw a man and a woman holding hands as they walked past them, and it took everything in her somewhat tipsy state to not reach over and take Emerson's hand. She wanted to hold it so badly. There was this pull that went straight from Talon to Emerson. So much so that Talon couldn't care less about that bartender or any other woman in the place that would've looked her way.

"This is my place," she said, stopping at her front stoop.

Emerson looked up and said, "Which floor?"

"Third. It's a six-story building, and I'm on three. It has an elevator, though. Other places I've lived have been walk-ups, and I hate walk-ups."

"Oh, me too," Emerson said, pulling out her phone to order her car. "My first apartment was a five-story walk-up. I had amazing legs but hated every minute of it. One time, I was having…" She looked up at Talon. "I was having a woman over. We'd been dating for a while, and she said she was ready for… Is this weird? We're hanging out tonight, but we work together…"

"It's fine," Talon said, lying because the last thing she wanted to hear about was Emerson having sex with another woman.

"Well, I'd bought the expensive wine, and two bottles at that."

"I think I know where this is going," Talon said as Emerson slipped her phone back into her pocket.

"I was cooking dinner, too, and had everything I needed to make a gourmet meal. Well, a meal cooked by me, so it probably would've been fine, but not gourmet. I was on the steps to the fourth floor, and I tripped. The bags slipped out of my arms, and the wine bottles broke, seeping wine all over my French bread, the shrimp I'd bought, and just about everything else. On top of all that, I had also picked up a few things for breakfast. My bacon was fine. The eggs – not so much. The pickles I'd bought just because I liked pickles busted, too. The entire stairwell smelled like pickles until after I moved out." Emerson laughed.

Talon had to laugh, too, even though she was still thinking about the fact that Emerson had bought dinner and wine for a woman she was going to sleep with, and then breakfast because she would have stayed the night after.

"What did you do for dinner?"

"We ordered in, and I told her the whole story. She had to walk up those stairs to get to my place, and the first thing she said when I opened the door was, 'Why does your stairwell smell like pickles?' I probably still smelled like them, too, even though I showered before she got there."

Talon wanted to ask if the woman stayed over, but that would be inappropriate, so instead, she just turned her head and noticed the car slowing to a stop behind Emerson.

"I think your car is here," she said.

"Oh, right," Emerson said as if she'd forgotten she'd even ordered one. "Well, I should go, then." She turned and waved at the driver.

"Yeah, thanks for walking me. I'll see you at work."

"No problem. And yeah, at work," Emerson said, nodding.

Talon thought Emerson wanted to say more, but instead, she just kept nodding. Then, she turned around, opened the car door, looked back at Talon for a second, gave her a quick wave, and climbed inside.

CHAPTER 14

The night hadn't gone as Emerson had expected. She'd invited Shea there to help her meet women in hopes of meeting one she could ask out for coffee or drinks another time. While sex that night would've been a bonus, it wasn't what Emerson really needed, and she knew that now. At first, she'd been all about wanting to get Talon naked, so finding another woman who she *could* actually sleep with to take her mind off of Talon had been something of interest. Now, Emerson knew it wasn't just sex that she wanted. Yes, she definitely still wanted sex, but she also wanted to keep getting to know Talon Mitchell.

The walk home the other night had been amazing. There had been other people around, but to Emerson, it had felt as if they were completely alone. The only exception had been when a couple had walked past them holding hands. Emerson had noticed them and had wanted to do the same with Talon. Her hand had actually twitched in anticipation, and if her brain hadn't talked her out of it, Emerson would have reached over and taken Talon's.

Emerson had spent her Sunday alone in her apartment, working and catching up on some TV show she'd recorded and hadn't yet watched. It played in the background as she checked her email, scrolled through social media on her phone, and was just really, really bored the entire day. She called her sister, who, at twenty-six, already had a husband and two kids and was, therefore, too busy to talk long. After about ten minutes, Emerson heard her yelling at one of the boys, and then there was a click. She'd laughed at that but remembered the times when her sister had been childless and more available for Emerson. Emerson loved her nephews more than life, but she still missed how much closer she'd been with her sister prior to their arrival.

Now, it was Monday, and she'd be seeing Talon today. Lunches and coffee trips were one thing. This was entirely different. They'd run into one another at a gay bar. They'd shared a drink; an intimate drink in a room with low lights that allowed Emerson to stare just a little longer at Talon – whenever Talon looked away – without appearing to be creepy. Talon had even bought Emerson's drinks, and instead of Emerson meeting a stranger and asking them out or taking them home, she'd walked Talon home instead. Every time she made a plan to avoid the complication that was Talon Mitchell in her life, somehow, they ended up being pulled back together; or, if she were being honest, *she* pulled them back together.

She woke early on Monday, unable to make it to her alarm clock as she'd hoped, and decided to take an extra-long shower to help her prepare for the long week ahead. She turned the water on and got inside, closing the frosted door behind her. One thing she wanted to be able to do the moment her loans were paid off, was to get an apartment with a bigger shower. She made good enough money to afford a better place under normal conditions, but she was still helping her youngest brother with some of his college tuition, rent for the other, and still had her student loans and some credit card debt she accrued before she got her last job. It was all worth it since it meant her family was okay and she was stable enough, but she still wanted a bigger shower.

This place was unique in that it had an old clawfoot tub and a shower next to it, but the shower itself was much smaller than she'd seen elsewhere. Emerson hadn't noticed it when she'd toured the place, and when she went to take her first shower there after renting, she must have smacked her elbow at least ten times. She'd perfected the art of the shower in the space now, and it *was* an art. She had to turn slightly when she bent over to wash her legs and feet, for example, or she'd hit the faucet. So, she did that this morning, washing quickly so she could then just stand under the hot spray and think about her workday. If she thought about her to-do list prior to getting into the office, she felt more productive.

Emerson had another full day with Talon in the conference room. Before that, she had a quick check-in with Brock on the changes and then Dimitri and Ruben, who they were moving to the other senior manager until they hired Nick's replacement, which would likely be Talon…

Shit. Talon. Now, she was thinking about Talon. Would the woman be wearing another button-down today? Emerson's mind wandered now. She thought about the beanbag conference room on the operations floor and how it didn't have glass walls. She thought about how the last time they'd been there, Talon had leaned over to see Emerson's screen, and Emerson had licked her lips with Talon's neck being so close. Emerson's right hand moved to her right breast on its own, and she began to massage it.

This was the point of no return. Her nipples were incredibly sensitive, even more so in the shower under hot running water, for some reason, so if she began to play with one, she'd have to touch herself. If she stopped now, she could get by without; for the day, at least. She'd been perpetually turned on for weeks now, and she knew why. She knew it was because of the way Talon stared back at her. Emerson knew it was *there* between them. Now that she knew for sure that Talon was gay, the meaning behind that intensity between them was perfectly clear.

"God, I want her," she said to herself and twisted her nipple.

That did it. The pulse between her legs took off. She turned around and faced the back wall of the shower, knowing just the right angle she had to take to do this. The water hit her back like firm raindrops in a downpour as she used both hands on her nipples now, twisting and tweaking until she could feel how hard her clit had gotten without even touching it yet. As she played with her breasts, she thought of Talon spreading her legs in this very shower, despite the fact that they could never do that in this tiny shower. She looked down in her imagination and found Talon's brown eyes, dark and filled with the lust Emerson always felt for her. Then, she felt Talon's mouth on her as she began stroking her clit.

"Fuck," she said as she realized how turned on and sensitive she was already. "Talon, suck me."

Talon wasn't there. Emerson was going crazy; she knew that. She also knew that just saying those words out loud was enough to make her clit come. She lowered her left hand to her clit and slipped two fingers from her right inside herself. She couldn't always come like this, but if she found just the right angle and was turned on enough, she knew it was more than possible, so she curled inside herself and rubbed her clit hard and fast. She lifted her right leg up onto the soap ledge, watching as the soap slipped to the floor. Now she had to worry about falling in this shower as she fucked herself. Just great.

Emerson closed her eyes again, picturing Talon on her knees, moaning as she sucked on Emerson's clit. Talon's fingers were inside her, and they were deeper than her own. God, they were touching her just right. Emerson knew all too well that they weren't really, but just thinking about Talon inside her pushed Emerson over the edge until she had to put her forehead against the wall to keep herself steady as she brought herself down slowly, fingers lingering on her clit, which clearly still needed more from her, but Emerson would leave it for the day. She'd given herself this moment to fantasize about Talon making her come. That was all she was allowed.

***

Talon hadn't worn a button-down today after all,

which would've been a disappointment except for the fact that she *had* worn a skirt. Talon had worn an actual pleated skirt in gray and black plaid with a black sweater that made her look like she could have been an extra in a movie about a boarding school. No, Talon would've been the star; she was no one's extra. Emerson got her first real peek at Talon's legs. The woman was wearing one-inch heels that only served to lengthen them, and Emerson stared as Talon made herself a cup of coffee from the now-fixed coffee maker. Emerson had decided to sit at the giant communal table in the kitchen for a few minutes to start her day, gather her thoughts, and get prepared for her meetings. She was regretting not letting her clit come again now. Hell, Emerson even spread her legs under the table on impulse and actually wished she could touch herself while Talon made herself coffee. She needed to see a therapist. There was definitely something wrong with her.

Talon turned around, and Emerson closed her legs, even though Talon couldn't see them spread wide for her. Talon smiled. Emerson smiled back. Talon walked over to the table, and Emerson thought she'd just say good morning, but Talon sat down across from her, pulling out the bench seat first to slide along it and right in front of her.

"I didn't check to see if you needed coffee. Am I in trouble now?" Talon asked with a wink.

"Definitely," Emerson teased, lifting a flirtatious eyebrow back.

"I can make you something," Talon offered, smiling at her still.

"No, I'm good. I do *not* need caffeine right now," she said.

Why had she just said that?

"No?"

"Nope," Emerson said, shaking her head.

"Did you sleep extra well or something? I always need caffeine in the morning."

"No, normal sleep," Emerson said quickly.

And she should've just said yes. She should've just said she'd had the best sleep of her life, because Talon was staring at her inquisitively, which might be one of Emerson's favorite expressions of hers.

"Okay. Cryptic," Talon replied after a moment.

"I just had a good morning," Emerson said.

Shut up. Emerson, shut the hell up, she thought to herself.

"How good?" Talon asked.

"Very good," Emerson said.

And Talon's eyes darkened. They fucking darkened right there in front of Emerson; *directed* at Emerson. Did she know what Emerson was saying without really saying it?

"Me too," Talon said. "Last night was really good, too, though."

"Last night?" Emerson asked, clearing her throat.

Then, she felt Talon's knee hit hers under the table. That was probably an accident, but the knee didn't move, and Emerson didn't move her leg, either. They just sat there, staring at each other, with their knees obviously touching despite there being plenty of space for their knees to go and not touch.

"Yeah, last night was really good. This morning was even better, though," Talon said, eyes darkening further.

Emerson swallowed. Her legs parted slowly. She could feel Talon's other knee now, and that meant that Talon's legs were spread wider than hers under this damn table. Talon's legs were spread, and Emerson wasn't able to see what she had on underneath that skirt. There was something so very disappointing about that and also so very necessary.

"Anyway, I should go," Talon added. "I have my morning stand-up and then our meeting."

Talon's legs were no longer touching Emerson's. She slipped out of the bench seat and looked down at Emerson, who, if she'd been anywhere else, her jaw would've been on the floor.

"Hey, this is new. What do you think?" Talon touched

the side of her skirt just below her hip, drawing Emerson's eyes there.

Emerson cleared her throat again and said, "Yeah. Yeah. It's good. I mean, it looks good on you."

"Yeah?" Talon checked. "I wasn't sure."

"Be sure," Emerson said. "Definitely be sure… about that."

Talon nodded with that intense gaze still locked on Emerson's. When the woman smiled at her, walking away, it was wicked. Emerson closed her damn legs under the table and checked the time on her computer. She had just enough. Emerson dropped her bag off in her office and hurried to the elevator. She took it down to the parking garage. Directors got their own assigned spots, and right now, she was very grateful for her own, which was against one concrete wall and had three handicapped spots next to it that were rarely occupied. She thanked God she'd gone for the tinted windows in her car and climbed into the back seat. This was bad. This was very, very bad. But if she didn't do this now, she'd spend all day with Talon wearing that sexy skirt, and she'd regret it.

Emerson unbuttoned and unzipped her jeans, feeling her clit relax a bit once the pressure from the jeans being so tight was released. Then, she slid her hand inside her underwear and felt how wet she was. She really needed to change her underwear now, but she didn't have any extra clothes with her – she'd have to walk around the office like this all day now. Emerson stroked quickly, not wanting to be out here any longer than she needed to be, but her clit wouldn't come.

She took a deep breath and thought of Talon in that skirt, spreading her legs for her under the table. Emerson pictured herself slipping beneath that table with all of their coworkers around them not knowing what she was doing. In her mind, Emerson didn't remove the thong Talon was wearing. She licked over it until Talon's hand covered the back of her head. Then, Emerson moved it aside and sucked on her until Talon came quietly so no one would know what had just happened. Emerson came in her own hand at the sight of Talon's swollen clit with the thong pushed aside. In her fantasy, she licked it as a promise for more later and put the thong back in place before moving back to her own side of the table and using a napkin to wipe her face. After that, Emerson looked across the table and saw Talon's flushed skin and unfocused eyes, and she came a second time accidentally and unexpectedly. Then, she pulled her hand out, because she couldn't keep getting herself off like this in the parking garage at work.

She needed to cool down, though, so she buttoned and zipped her jeans back up, feeling her now-cold wetness soak through her panties. *This* would be uncomfortable. She took several deep breaths and tried to picture her calendar and to-do list instead of Talon's sex inches from her face. That didn't work as effectively as she'd hoped, but she had no choice. She climbed ungracefully into the front seat so that it wouldn't look like she was climbing out of the back, got out of the car, and took the elevator straight up to the floor where she ducked into a bathroom, cleaned herself up as best she could, and then went to her office. Picking up her things, she went to her first meeting of the morning. This was going to be a long day.

CHAPTER 15

"Hey, I'm here," Talon said from the living room of Weston's place.

"Did I know you were coming by?" Weston asked, likely from her office.

"No, but I need to talk. Can you take a break?" Talon said, sitting on the sofa.

Weston walked into the room and sat down next to her.

"Sure. Is everything okay?"

"No," Talon said, sighing. "I've got a problem."

"What problem?"

"I'm crushing on my boss. Well, she's my boss's boss, technically."

"Oh, shit," Weston replied.

"Yeah, *oh, shit*," Talon said. "Wes, I'm, like, getting myself off just thinking about her."

And wearing skirts for her. And buying her drinks. And obviously flirting with her. Talon didn't say all that to Weston, though.

"Okay. I don't know that I need to know that to help you," Weston said.

"It's just the two of us here. No one's going to make fun of us, so we can be real. You and I used to date, and it was good; we just weren't meant to be. You've seen me naked, and I've seen you naked. You've touched me everywhere in just about every way, and I did that to you. What I'm getting at here is that you've watched me touch myself, Weston. I think we can both just acknowledge that and talk about sex like two adults."

Weston laughed and said, "Okay. I get it."

"She's the new sales director, and I am legit walking around with a hard-on, like, constantly these days. I think she's so sexy, and we're working on this project together, and it's so nice. She's gorgeous and funny, and I like her."

"So, it's not just a sex thing?"

"No, I have an actual crush. It's not just lust."

"Why are you calling it a crush?" Weston asked.

Talon looked at her, confused.

"Because it *is* a crush," she said.

"Or, you just like her. I don't know all that many crushes that have to do with lust. Isn't the definition of a crush that it's relatively innocent?"

"You're asking me to define words right now? I used a vibrator to give myself three orgasms this morning. All I can think about is Emerson."

"Her name is Emerson?"

"Isn't it pretty?" Talon asked almost wistfully.

"Yeah, it is," Weston laughed lightly. "What do you like about her?"

"Everything," Talon replied. "I don't know all that much yet, but what I *do* know, I like."

"And she's off-limits because of work?" Weston asked.

"Yup," Talon said. "If you want to date someone at work, it's frowned upon, but whatever. When it's your boss, or your boss's boss in my case, though, it's–"

"Complicated," Weston said.

"*Sexual harassment* is the term they use most," Talon replied. "But if I like her, too, where's the problem?"

"She likes you?"

"Huh?"

"You said if you like her *too*," Weston said.

"Oh, I don't know." Talon shrugged a shoulder. "It seems like she might, but I could just be imagining that like I imagined her head between my legs this morning."

Weston laughed and said, "You've got it bad, my friend."

"Duh. That's why I'm here. Help!"

"What can *I* do?"

"Well, you and Annie aren't exclusive yet. Can you and I have, like, one no-strings sexual encounter so I can at least have someone else's hands on me and maybe get Emerson out of my head?"

"What? No way," Weston said, laughing.

"I know." Talon sighed again. "Dumb idea."

"Very dumb."

"Wes, I like her."

"I know," Weston said. "Maybe you should just tell her. Put it out there and see if she's interested. If not, you let it go. If she is, you two can talk about it and see what makes sense, given the working relationship."

"That's logical, so I doubt it will work," Talon replied. "I know that's basically what you did with Annie, but Annie is your agent; she isn't your boss."

"She might not be my agent any longer," Weston said.

"What? Did her dad find out about you two or something?"

"Or something," Weston replied. "She forgot about a date, and I ended up having to go over to her place to check on her. She was writing and just–"

"Forgot the world existed, like you do sometimes?" Talon asked.

"Yeah. And that wasn't a big deal. I brought dinner to her, and we were going to watch a movie together when she checked her email, and the publisher that I was kind of interested in messaged that they're moving on without me because she failed to get back to them with a decision. They have another series they're interested in. They were giving me the slot, but they moved on to the other author when Annie didn't get back to them by the deadline they'd given her."

"She cost you a deal?"

"I know she didn't do it on purpose, and I know this deal wasn't exactly the best in the world, but she was supposed to clarify things with lawyers. I'd even gotten my attorney to give her some info that she could use, and she forgot."

"Shit, Wes. I'm sorry. What happens now?" she asked her friend.

"She seems convinced that I'll get offers from other publishers, but I've turned down two so far because she said the deals weren't good. Well, one was the woman who harassed Annie, but still – I had a chance there, and I said no. Now, this third one is a no-go, even though Annie left me a voicemail saying she explained things to them, but they'd already made the offer to the other writer who snatched it up right away."

"Do you think your relationship is getting in the way of her doing her job with you?"

"I don't know. I think her finally getting into writing and loving it isn't something she's accustomed to, and it's hard when you first really get into it. I would know – I've been there. You can't focus on anything else. I know I turned down nights hanging out with you guys and told my parents and brothers I couldn't do dinners or family events because I had a chapter to finish. Your mind is so focused on the story and getting the words down on the paper, and it's always urgent because you're worried you'll lose the train of thought. No matter how much you outline or take notes, you're still always worried," Weston explained.

"It sounds like you understand what she's dealing with," Talon said.

"I do," Weston agreed. "But I've never missed a date, Talon. I've had girlfriends, and while none of them really understood what it meant for me to be a writer, when something was planned or scheduled, I didn't forget it."

"So, you're hurt she forgot about you?"

"I guess. I mean, maybe I'm more in this thing than she is."

"You don't know that. Like you said, she's new to this thing. She might need to adjust."

"What if I don't get any other offers, and the one I could have had is gone?" Weston asked.

"I am confident that Annie is right, and you'll hear from other publishers. And remember, you can always publish yourself. You're all hell-bent on going this route, but you can always put it out there on your own," Talon tried to reassure her.

"Yeah, I guess," Weston said, sounding unconvinced. "You didn't come over here to talk about *me*, though. What are you going to do about this Emerson?"

"Nothing." Talon sighed. "Well, drink a lot, probably, maybe pick up some woman at a bar to try to take my mind off of her, and end up thinking about Emerson during."

Weston laughed and said, "Just don't call Aubrey, please."

Talon laughed too then and said, "She did literally nothing for me, so no chance of that."

"Annie said she's asked about you at least four times, so you *definitely* did something for her," Weston replied.

"I did something for you about a decade ago, too," Talon joked.

"Many, many somethings. Emerson is missing out," Weston replied.

"Damn right, she is," Talon said. "Oh, you saw her, by the way."

"Saw who?"

"Emerson. You saw her at the bar. That's who I ran into when we were leaving."

"*That's* Emerson?"

"Yeah. Before that, I didn't even know if she'd be into women, but it was a gay bar, and… Anyway, we talked for a while," Talon explained.

"She's cute," Weston said, remembering the woman she only saw briefly.

"She is not cute. She's…"

"Okay. I don't want to know what you're thinking right now."

"Just about her fingers as she held her drink. They're long, Wes."

"Yup, I was right: I didn't want to know."

Weston's phone buzzed on the table, and Talon picked it up.

"Oh, it's her," she said, meaning Annie.

"Give me that," Weston said, taking the phone. "She wants to meet."

"To apologize, probably."

"She's already done that," Weston said.

"What are you going to tell her?"

"I want to be mature about this."

"You're better than me. I'm passive-aggressive all the way. Leave her on *read* and wait an hour. Then, respond by saying you're busy tonight, but maybe tomorrow. You'll get back to her."

"Yeah, I'm not doing that." Weston typed a response. "And if you like this Emerson, don't act like that with her."

"I can't act like anything other than disinterested – she's my boss's–"

"Boss. Yeah, I know." Weston's phone buzzed again.

"You're meeting with her?"

"Yeah," Weston said. "I still have to finish the chapter I was working on."

"I'll take the hint. I think I can use a walk to clear my head anyway," Talon said, standing up. "Call me later?"

"Sure. Hey, it'll be okay. Either you'll get over these feelings and find another woman soon, or you won't, and Emerson is the one for you." She smiled at Talon.

"How unlikely is that last part…" Talon said. "She's way out of my league."

"No one is out of your league, Talon."

Talon gave her a shy smile before she left. She loved her friend. Maybe it was because she and Weston had dated all those years ago, but Weston had this way of making Talon feel like she could do anything, have anything, even though Talon never really felt that way about herself. She hadn't wanted to reveal everything to Weston, though. She'd already crossed so many lines with Emerson. Now that Nick was gone, there was a chance Talon would get his job. She hadn't applied yet, though, despite the fact that the role had been posted, because, for the first time in her career, Talon didn't want that job. Well, she did, but not if it meant reporting directly to Emerson. Working on this project with the woman and not being able to tell her how she really felt was already hard enough. Weston was right: this wasn't a crush; this was real. Talon liked Emerson.

She drove from Weston's to her own apartment and got out of the car, locking it and then deciding to walk off the frustration she was feeling, which was now much more than just sexual. After the first block, her phone buzzed in her pocket. Talon pulled it out, expecting it to be Weston telling her about something having to do with Annie, but she was surprised to see Emerson's name on her screen instead. Talon stopped abruptly, forcing the person walking behind her to bump into her.

"Hey, watch it," the guy said rudely.

"Sorry," Talon replied as he walked past her.

She moved off to the side and unlocked her phone.

Emerson Bagley: Hey, I don't know what you're up to, but I couldn't focus, so I came into the office to get some work done. No one else is here. It's kind of eerie, actually. I thought I'd see if you wanted to join me. I wanted to test a few of the changes before Monday, and you have the admin access. If you can't, that's okay. I just thought I'd check.

Emerson was at the office by herself. She should say no. The whole company had been given the day off. It was a quarterly thing that was supposed to support work-life balance and mental health. Talon usually just stayed home and read or something, pretending like her life wasn't mostly about work. She looked around her as if the city would reveal correct answers to her, knowing she should just go home and tell Emerson she was too busy. She thought for another few seconds. Then, she typed her response.

CHAPTER 16

Emerson had woken early that day and thought about lying in bed, reading a book, or catching up on some laundry, but lying around and doing menial tasks would still make her think of Talon, that skirt, and that flirting. It was flirting, wasn't it? Talon had flirted with her, and it had been awesome. That was the only word Emerson could think of to describe it. It had been torture, but such *awesome* torture. She swore she used to have a much larger vocabulary than that, but awesome was the only word that came to mind.

Instead of lying around, she opted to head to the office, taking advantage of the security badge she had that would let her in twenty-four-seven instead of the more standard ones that only worked from seven in the morning until seven at night. Arriving at just before seven in the morning, Emerson enjoyed the quiet space of her office with no sound coming from the sales pit, grabbed a snack from the kitchen, uninterrupted, and then went into the big conference room with three full dry-erase walls and a large TV and got to work reviewing stages three and four of their new proposed process. When a sales rep was first booked for a demo, that created a prospect, or what the system called, an opportunity. This opportunity process was six stages, which for the timeline of their sales seemed far too long for Emerson, so they were working on getting down to at least four stages. If she could swing three without making the third step extra complicated, she'd go for that.

Unfortunately for her, Emerson didn't have full admin rights to the system, and she needed to run a quick test for validation errors in their sandbox environment, which was just a play area that enabled them to test and have quality checks prior to launching the new process. *Talon* had administrative access to the sandbox. Talon also had killer legs, full lips Emerson wanted to kiss, and eyes that made Emerson go weak in the knees every time they connected with her own. She knew it was the quarterly day off the company offered along with other paid holidays and unlimited paid time off, but she wondered if Talon would be able to come in just for an hour or so to test this. It was wrong to ask. She didn't want Talon to think she didn't support her team getting a well-deserved day off, but if she messaged and Talon said yes, they could get ahead and maybe go for a late lunch afterward. Okay. Emerson really wanted the late lunch.

When she texted, she didn't think she'd get a response right away, so she set her phone down and went back to the kitchen for another coffee. She got back to the room and saw her phone light up and ping with a notification. Emerson smiled when she saw that Talon had accepted and would be in soon. Several minutes later, her phone rang. Emerson saw Talon's name and assumed she was calling to say she couldn't make it, after all.

"Hey," Emerson said.

"Hi. My badge isn't working. Can you let me up?"

"Oh, shit. Sorry, I forgot."

For the day off, the company deactivated the badges of almost everyone to encourage them to stay home. Emerson not only forgot that part but was also actively encouraging Talon to come to work.

"I'm on my way," Emerson added.

"Cool. Thanks," Talon said.

Emerson headed to the elevator and took it down to the lobby, where she saw Talon waiting.

"Hey," Talon said with a smile.

"Hey. Sorry, I forgot they deactivated the badges for today. I feel awful texting you and asking you to come in," Emerson told her.

"It's fine. I wasn't doing anything anyway. I just had to go home and grab my computer."

Talon followed Emerson into the elevator, where Emerson swiped her badge, enabling her to press the button for their floor.

"Home? You weren't at home, and I made you go there and then come here? I'm sorry, Talon."

"I decided to take a walk," Talon replied. "No big deal. I can do that later."

"If you're interested, lunch is on me. Have you eaten?"

"Not yet, no," Talon replied as the elevator arrived at the floor and they both attempted to get off at the same time. "Sorry. You first."

"No, you first," Emerson said.

"It's fine. You–"

The doors started to close.

"Shit," Emerson said, putting her arm out to stop it.

Talon laughed.

"I'll just go," she said, leaving the elevator.

Emerson followed her, watching Talon's ass in those jeans. She wasn't wearing her usual, longer navy coat today. Instead, she was in a short leather jacket that had Emerson's mouth watering. Talon in a leather jacket and tennis shoes might be the hottest Talon of all, and Emerson had ranked skirt-wearing Talon as the hottest Talon of all just the other day.

"Coffee?" Emerson asked, clearing her throat as they walked past the kitchen.

"No, but I'll grab a water. I didn't bring my water bottle." Talon grabbed a plastic cup and filled it at the water cooler. "Okay. Ready."

Was *Emerson* ready for the sight of Talon drinking that water, tipping her neck back and revealing the V-neck t-shirt under that leather jacket, which gave Emerson just the slightest view of the dip between Talon's breasts? They walked to the conference room, where Talon got her laptop out of her bag and took a look at the screen where Emerson had placed a zoomed-in view of a change she wanted to test. Emerson sat on the other side of the table, a safe distance away, and tried to focus her gaze on the image and not on Talon, who looked focused as she stared at her own computer screen now.

"I can turn that on. Do you want to run it on the test account we made the other day and see if there are any validation errors?" Talon asked.

"Yes, that'd be great."

Validation errors would appear if anything in any of the fields screwed up anything else in the process or came back as incorrect information. For example, if in one field, the rep put their location as CA and in another California, the way the system was now, they'd get an error and would have to fix it. Emerson and Talon wanted to change some of those unnecessary things so that they could only use CA, for example, which would be easier to type, would save time, and would prevent them from receiving an error.

"Okay. Let's run it," Talon said, pressing a button.

"Anything?" Emerson asked.

"A couple, but nothing we can't fix. Can I put my stuff on the screen now?"

"Sure." Emerson disconnected her computer from the remote screen.

"So, what made you want to come in on the day off?" Talon asked as she connected her screen.

"Just bored at home," Emerson said. "And my family was all busy."

"What about Shea?" Talon asked.

"They're out of town. Something for work, I think," Emerson replied. "And I have other friends, by the way."

Talon laughed and said, "I assumed you do. I just don't know any of their names."

"You have, like, five really close friends, and I don't know all their names."

"Weston, Aria, Paisley, Scarlet, and Eleanor, but we call her Ellie unless she's in trouble."

"How often is she in trouble?" Emerson smiled.

"Depends on the day," Talon said, laughing.

"Weston is the one you're closest with, right?"

"Yeah. How'd you know?" Talon asked.

"You've talked about her before, and you said her name first."

"I guess I did," Talon said, realizing it at the same time. "She's my best friend, yeah. We're all really close, though."

"I'm envious. I really only have one more friend, and I hardly see her because she lives in Portland," Emerson replied.

"What's *her* name?"

"Jenny. She moved to town when we were in high school. We sort of dated first. Then, we broke up and became friends. She's married now and has three kids, with a fourth on the way, which is crazy to me because I can't even keep a plant alive." Emerson laughed a little.

"You dated first?" Talon asked.

"Yeah. And we managed to salvage a friendship out of it. Doesn't happen often."

"I know. I got lucky with Wes," Talon said.

"Wes… Weston?" Emerson asked.

"Yeah. We technically were friends for a bit first, but we dated back then," Talon said.

"You dated Weston? The woman at the bar that one night?"

"For, like, two months when we were still teenagers."

"Which one was she?" Emerson asked.

"Um… short brown hair. Aria was the blonde," Talon replied.

Emerson tried to recall the brunette, and she did with ease.

"She's pretty," Emerson said.

"Wes? Yeah, she's hot. She was at nineteen, too," Talon said, laughing.

Emerson watched as Talon looked up from her laptop and met Emerson's gaze.

"You two didn't work out?"

"God, no. We're much better as friends. What about you and Jenny?"

"First love; not forever love. So, what did it for you and Weston?" Emerson asked, leaning over the table.

"It wasn't one thing. I think we just both realized we shouldn't date. I mean, the sex was amazing, but she was also my first, so I wanted it, like, all the time after we finally did it the first time, and… you know, she wanted a real girlfriend, not someone who wanted to jump her bones every time I saw her, which I did." Talon laughed.

"Are you still…" Emerson swallowed as Talon lowered her laptop screen.

"Into Weston? No, that ship sailed a decade ago," Talon said. "No more Jenny for you?"

"No," Emerson said, laughing a little. "I think her wife might have a problem with her visiting me once a year if I was still lusting after Jenny." She licked her lips. "So, no more Weston for you. What about your… other friends?"

Talon shook her head and said, "Just friends."

"And bartenders from lesbian bars?"

Talon laughed and said, "The one lesbian bar in town?"

"Yes."

"Not into it," Talon said. "Shea?"

"Who went home with someone else the night at the bar?" Emerson said, rolling her eyes. "No, Shea's a friend only."

Talon nodded again and said, "Anyone else you're lusting after?"

Emerson's eyes went wide. She thought about what to say. She wasn't a liar, but this wasn't exactly the situation to be one hundred percent truthful in, either. So, she shook her head. Talon nodded slowly, seemingly disappointed.

"Me neither," she said, opening her laptop back up. "I've got it on the screen. We can run it again."

"Talon?"

"Yeah?" She wouldn't meet Emerson's eyes.

"If things were…"

"I can knock this validation error by just switching the field from open text to a dropdown if you want," Talon said.

"Are you going to apply for Nick's job?" Emerson asked, changing the subject.

"What?" Talon did meet her eyes then.

"Nick's job; you haven't applied. I thought you would."

"Why?"

"Because you're ten times the manager Nick ever will be, and you're ridiculously smart and so talented. You should have the job, Talon."

"Is that you talking as my manager's manager, or you talking as something else?"

"What else would I–"

"Jesus Christ," Talon interrupted her.

Then, Emerson watched as Talon opened a Word document that Emerson could see on the big screen.

"What do I need to write for this to happen?" Talon asked.

"Huh?" Emerson asked back, turning to Talon.

"Do you want this?" Talon asked. "What's been brewing between us since the moment we first laid eyes on each other; do you want it?"

Emerson realized what Talon was saying, swallowed, and thought about how to respond.

CHAPTER 17

"It's called a consensual relationship agreement," Talon said. "Look." She pointed to the screen. "If I type this and sign it, and you sign it, can we just…"

"You typed *how to tell HR you're in a relationship at work* into Google?"

"Yes," Talon replied. "And we type the thing and sign it, and we can just…" Talon faded out as she took in Emerson's confused expression. "Shit. Am I wrong?"

"No," Emerson said. "No, you're not. You're not wrong."

Talon's breathing intensified as she watched Emerson's chest rise and fall. She was wearing a relaxed flannel shirt today that was green, white, and brown, and it made her eyes pop in a way Talon hadn't ever seen before.

"I want it, and I'm tired of pretending like I don't," Talon told the woman.

"You wore that skirt for me?" Emerson asked, swallowing.

"Yes," Talon stated.

"Fuck, Talon. We can't."

"Yes, we can. I want you," she replied, copying and pasting a templated letter from the Internet into the document she'd just opened.

Before she could stop herself, she hit print and left the room. She rushed to the printer next to the room, grabbed the paper that had just printed, and rushed back to the room. Emerson was standing now. No, she was pacing. Talon searched for the pen in her backpack, found it, and quickly scrawled her signature at the bottom.

"There," she said. "Emerson, there."

Emerson turned around to face her. She looked down at the piece of paper next to Talon's computer, and for a second, Talon worried she'd taken this too far. Emerson wanted this; Talon had known it all along. She'd just been doubting herself, but Emerson wanted her, and Talon was over pretending like they weren't into each other.

"We can't do this here," Emerson said softly as she took two steps toward Talon, took the pen from her, and signed the paper.

"But we *can* do this?" Talon asked.

"Fuck, Talon," Emerson repeated her words from earlier.

Before Talon knew it, Emerson was pressing Talon against the table. Her lips were on Talon's, and Talon was kissing her back. She guessed they *could* do this here. Emerson's lips tasted like strawberry ChapStick. Her tongue was pure velvet, and her hands were soft as they moved up under Talon's jacket and t-shirt with ease until Talon was sitting on the table and spreading her legs for Emerson to stand between.

"God, I want you," Talon said as Emerson's lips moved to her neck.

"Jacket," Emerson said, sucking on Talon's neck.

Talon unzipped the jacket and tore it off her own shoulders, letting it fall behind her on the table. Emerson lifted Talon's shirt up and off, dropping it off to the side. Then, her hands were on Talon's belt. She pulled until the buckle was undone, and Talon couldn't wait for what would come next. She undid her own bra as Emerson paused to stare at her now exposed breasts. Emerson moved to suck a nipple into her mouth, and Talon leaned back to let her have whatever she wanted.

"Yes, that's…" Talon couldn't finish.

Then, Emerson unbuttoned and unzipped Talon's jeans. Talon wanted her to slip inside and touch her until she came, but Emerson stepped back. Talon worried it was all over then. They'd gone too far. While she knew there were no cameras on this part of the floor because she'd seen the server room where the screens were, Emerson didn't know that and was likely freaking out. But Emerson didn't freak out. She pulled until Talon's jeans were hanging around her ankles along with her panties. Talon kicked them until they were on the floor as Emerson looked her up and down, licking her lips. Then, she leaned forward again, spreading Talon's legs once more. Without warning, Emerson swept Talon's arms that had been behind her, holding her up, until Talon was flat on her back.

"Inside, Emerson," Talon said as she watched Emerson climb on top of her.

Emerson hovered and kissed Talon again, a little softer this time, but not so much softer that Talon expected them to slow down. Then, Emerson filled her.

"Oh, Talon," Emerson said softly against Talon's ear. "I've wanted this."

She thrust hard as her thumb met Talon's clit, and Talon had nothing but Emerson to hang on to as Emerson fucked her hard. Talon closed her eyes and let the sensations of finally being with this woman take her over completely. It didn't take long. Emerson's strong strokes had her coming before she could stop herself to delay the orgasm she'd wanted for weeks now.

"Emerson, I'm…"

Emerson grunted against her neck and kept her thrusts steady until Talon tapped her shoulder blades, letting her know she couldn't take any more.

"Do you know what I wanted to do to you when you were in that skirt?" Emerson whispered into Talon's ear as she slipped out of her.

"What?"

Emerson kissed her again, letting their tongues play as Talon ran her hands under the shirt Emerson still, unfortunately, wore. Then, Emerson climbed off the table and knelt in front of her.

"Oh, fuck," Talon said.

Emerson didn't wait for permission. She pulled on Talon's legs until her sex was at the edge of the table. Then,

Emerson's mouth was on her. Talon didn't wait, either. Her hand was on the back of Emerson's head.

"I've wanted your mouth on me since the first time I saw you," Talon confessed. "God, that's good."

"Yes, it is," Emerson said, licking Talon before she returned to sucking on Talon's clit.

Talon opened her eyes and stared down, feeling like this was even better than every single fantasy she'd ever had about Emerson. Hell, this was better than every sexual encounter she'd ever had. Emerson's lips engulfed her clit as if they'd done it a hundred times before, and her tongue flitted out at just the right moments until Talon screamed her name and came harder than before. Emerson slowed but didn't stop. Talon watched as Emerson looked up at her and made eye contact with her.

"Okay. That's the sexiest thing I've ever seen," Talon said in a husky, post-scream voice.

"You're naked on a table – I challenge your opinion," Emerson replied, kissing her clit and licking it again.

"Fuck."

"I want you again," Emerson said.

"I've let you have your way with me," Talon replied, smirking.

"I want you again," Emerson said more firmly this time. "On the floor."

Talon watched Emerson's eyes darken even further. She'd never been taken like this, been the one to let the other person take total control. She swallowed as she nodded because she wanted Emerson to do anything and everything she wanted to right now.

Emerson helped Talon up. Then, she kissed her and moved them until Talon was pressed to the wall. Emerson's hand roamed until it was lifting Talon's leg.

"This isn't the floor."

"In a minute," Emerson said, slipping her other hand inside. "Why do you feel so good to me?"

"I don't know. You feel… Oh, God, Emerson," Talon

said, lowering her hand to Emerson's shoulder and just letting the woman fuck her because it felt so damn good.

"I saw you on New Year's Eve, Talon. I wanted you then, too," Emerson said into her ear.

"What?" Talon asked, lifting her head and moving until she could meet Emerson's eyes.

"I was at the same party." She thrust harder.

Talon moaned.

"I had a date."

She curled her fingers.

"Her name was something… I can't… remember… right…" She pushed in deeper again. "Now."

"I'm going to come," Talon said, lowering her head again and biting Emerson's shoulder through her shirt.

"I took her home, and she wanted to do this," Emerson said, flicking Talon's clit with her thumb. "But I couldn't. I thought of you."

"Me?" Talon asked as her head smacked back into the wall.

"Yes, you," Emerson said. "Then, I saw you here, and I wanted you again."

"I'm coming!" Talon practically yelled as Emerson thrust inside.

"I've never wanted anyone how I've wanted you," Emerson said.

"God, me neither," Talon said, lowering her leg to the floor as Emerson slipped out of her, and putting her hands on Emerson's flannel. She pulled hard, yanking until a few of the buttons popped. "Now, take this off. I need to see you."

Emerson started with the bottom button, but she was taking too long, so Talon yanked harder until the shirt was open, and Talon could see the black bra beneath.

"Jesus, a black bra? Are you trying to kill me?"

Emerson laughed, but Talon cut her off with a heated kiss, and the shirt fell to the floor. Emerson had her own bra off a second later, and finally, Talon's hands were on the breasts she'd been dying to touch. Emerson's hands were on her own jeans, unbuttoning them until they were at her ankles. Talon felt more than she saw Emerson kicking at them until they were off her ankles and somewhere else entirely. Talon looked down then, noticing Emerson had removed her underwear, too.

"You're so sexy," Talons said, lowering her mouth to Emerson's breast and sucking on a nipple.

"God, I've dreamed about this," Emerson said.

"This?"

"Your mouth on my nipple? Yes, Talon, I got off to this."

"Fuck," Talon replied, sucking right after and pushing at Emerson's hips until Emerson finally got the idea.

Talon pulled back as Emerson lowered herself to a kneeling position. She kissed Talon's stomach and the inside of her thighs. She pulled Talon's sex to her, kissed the hairs she found, and licked Talon once more. Talon pushed at Emerson's shoulders until Emerson was lying on the floor and Talon was on top of her, staring down at her.

"You said you wanted me on the floor," Talon said, smirking and then kissing Emerson as her hand wandered to between Emerson's legs. "God, you're wet."

Emerson moaned into Talon's mouth. When Talon slipped between Emerson's folds, she knew this wouldn't be the last time she did this. It couldn't be. It felt too good. When she slipped inside her, she pulled back to take in Emerson's face and tried to save the image forever in her mind. Then, she thrust. Emerson moaned again. Talon moved her own sex until it was over Emerson's thigh. She rocked, and Emerson grabbed her ass, encouraging her to continue. Talon didn't stop. She couldn't. She needed to come again.

"Tal, that's…" Emerson faded.

Talon noticed that was the first time Emerson had used her nickname, and it sounded so good coming from her. Talon moved her mouth back to Emerson's neck.

"I like you calling me that. Say it again."

"Tal, fuck! That's so… Touch my clit," Emerson said.

"No, that's for my mouth to do in a minute," Talon replied.

"Jesus."

Talon felt a fresh coat of wetness come over her fingers.

"You like that?"

"Yes."

"Me talking about what my mouth is going to do to you?" Talon said and sucked on Emerson's earlobe.

"Yes," Emerson gasped out.

"The first time," Talon began as she rubbed herself over Emerson's thigh, pressing down harder. "I'm going to let you come fast. I'll suck you until you tell me to stop."

"Yes. Yes," Emerson said fast, and Talon felt her clenching around her fingers.

Emerson was coming. Talon watched.

"The next time, I'll lick you and let you come slowly. When you do, I'll put my tongue inside you."

"Tal!" Emerson's face scrunched and turned red.

Talon rode her thigh as Emerson came, waiting for her own orgasm to take her over the edge, too. When it did, she had her mouth around Emerson's nipple and her fingers still inside her. Emerson somehow came again as Talon sucked and Emerson's hips took what they wanted from the still fingers inside her body. Talon growled against Emerson's body. She'd never growled during sex before, but she'd also never wanted sex this much before, either.

"Come again for me," Talon said.

"Put your mouth on me, and I will," Emerson replied.

Talon let go of Emerson's nipple with a pop and stared down at her.

"Wait. You were at the New Year's Eve party?" she asked, realizing what Emerson had said earlier.

"Talon, focus," Emerson said.

CHAPTER 18

Now, *this* was *the* fantasy come to life. Since the kitchen was covered in cameras, for whatever reason, Emerson couldn't have exactly what she wanted, which was what she'd imagined the other day: Talon in that skirt and thong, Emerson under the picnic table, sucking on her until she came. That no longer mattered, though, because after they'd finished in the conference room and lay on the floor spent, Emerson had dressed and had gone to the kitchen to get them food and something to drink. When she returned, Talon and her belongings were no longer in the conference room. Emerson's computer was gone, too, and the TV had been turned off. She had a moment of panic. Talon must have regretted what just happened and rushed out of there, but she wouldn't take Emerson's computer if that were the case.

"Hey, in here," Talon said.

Emerson stuck her head out the glass door, despite being able to see through it anyway, and saw a dressed Talon in her own office door. Well, she was dressed but still disheveled-looking, and Emerson loved that she'd done that to Talon's hair.

"You're in my office," Emerson said, walking in that direction.

"And your office has the windows that frost when you press a button," Talon replied, reaching to the light switch and raising the switch next to it, frosting the windows and the door entirely.

"What the fuck? I thought that was a dimmer switch," Emerson said in amazement.

Talon laughed and said, "Why would they put a dimmer switch in here?"

"I don't know. Why did you use it?"

"Because I want to have sex in here, and there are

cameras in the sales pit. None of them directly aim right here, but they'd get a show." Talon closed the door once Emerson was inside. "Now, they can't see what I want to do to you."

"No?"

"Nope," Talon said, reaching for that flannel shirt that now had no buttons holding it together. Thankfully, Talon had had a t-shirt in her backpack for the times she went to the company gym. "Now, everything comes back off."

"I left all the snacks and stuff in the conference room," Emerson said as Talon pulled off the flannel, followed by the t-shirt.

"It can wait. I put your bra and panties in my backpack when I came in here; I'm thinking about keeping them."

"Oh, yeah?" Emerson asked as Talon sucked on her pulse point. "Do I get to keep yours?"

"They're in my backpack, too. You can take them out later, but right now, I want you to sit in your chair," Talon said.

"Oh," Emerson said, realizing what Talon wanted. "Yeah? I've wanted that, too."

"Good. Pants off," Talon instructed.

Emerson kicked her shoes, socks, and jeans off for the second time that day. Now, she was bare again to Talon, whose eyes raked over her skin with something Emerson hadn't ever seen in a lover. And now, Talon wasn't just a colleague; she was also Emerson's lover. At least, for today. They hadn't even talked about this. They'd signed that document that *might* offer Emerson some protection, but also might not because it's just a piece of paper that she had no copy of for her own files.

"Hey, are you okay?" Talon asked softly, cupping Emerson's cheek.

"Huh?" Emerson asked, being taken aback by the soft gesture.

They hadn't exactly been this gentle with one another today.

"Are you okay? Should we stop?"

"No," Emerson replied, pulling off Talon's t-shirt. "But I do want to know how you seem to be aware of every camera in this place."

Talon removed her own jeans and said, "I've worked here forever, remember? I helped the one IT guy we used to have set some of them up, and I have the key to the server room where the screens are because that's where we store some of the sales team swag for the new hires and award winners."

"*I* don't have the key to the server room," Emerson replied.

"It's a physical key," Talon said. "And if you want one, I'm sure you can ask, and they'll give it to you. Sit."

Talon placed both hands on Emerson's shoulders once they were around her desk, and Emerson sat. Talon walked back around her desk, and Emerson followed the naked Talon as she walked confidently and somehow seductively. Then, she knelt. Talon knelt and crawled under Emerson's desk. She reached for and spread Emerson's legs, staring at Emerson's still ready sex. When Talon licked her lips, Emerson gasped, and Talon looked up at her.

"Slow this time," Talon said.

Emerson shifted until she was uncomfortably closer to the edge of the chair. Talon smirked. Then, she took her. And yeah, *this* was *the* fantasy. Talon was under her desk with her hands on the top of Emerson's thighs, licking her clit. Emerson couldn't look away. This was the most erotic moment of her entire life, and she'd never be able to look at this office or that conference room the same way again.

***

The angle was off for Emerson, but Talon wasn't complaining. After their time in Emerson's office where Talon made her come with her mouth twice, they'd decided to grab their snacks and drinks and take them down to the operations floor and go into the beanbag room, which had actual solid walls, and according to Talon, no cameras.

Talon was lying on one of those beanbag chairs, and Emerson was thrusting into her from above. Emerson had sweat pooling at the base of her spine and some on her forehead as well. Her upper arm was exhausted. Her wrist was killing her, but Talon was about to come again, so that pain would all be worth it.

"Fuck, yes!" Talon came.

Emerson felt her clench around her fingers, so she slowed but didn't stop her movements inside the woman.

"God, you're good at that," Talon said, covering her face with her arm, elbow out to the side a bit. "I've never come so much in my life."

"Not even when you and Weston went at it like rabbits?" Emerson teased, kissing Talon's chest.

Talon laughed a husky laugh. Emerson had done that to her. She'd brought Talon so much pleasure that she could no longer laugh her usual laugh.

"Not even then," Talon said. "Are you in some kind of competition with Weston I don't know about?"

"Maybe."

"Roll over," Talon said. "I'm in a competition with Jenny, then."

Emerson laughed and said, "Jenny and I were kids. You've already defeated Jenny."

"Who was your best sex, then?" Talon asked as Emerson moved to the other beanbag chair.

"Um…" Emerson pointed at Talon, who was moving to climb on top of her.

"It's me?" Talon asked, sounding surprised.

"It is *now*, yeah," Emerson said.

"Oh, I like that," Talon said, lowering herself and placing her hands on either side of Emerson's head. "I like this, too." She kissed Emerson softer than she'd done before.

Maybe they were losing energy; they'd been having sex

for hours now. Emerson didn't know that for a fact because there was no clock in here, and she had no idea where her phone was right now, but it felt like hours. Her body was screaming at her to stop, but then Talon kissed her softly, and Emerson never wanted it to end. She cupped Talon's cheek, letting her know that this was good. This gentle and slow kiss was just as good as the hard and fast stuff they'd both needed after weeks of wanting one another. Talon explored her mouth as she settled between Emerson's hips. She didn't rock into her; she just settled there, pressing their centers together in a way they hadn't done yet, and while Emerson was still turned on and wanted more, she wanted this right now. Just this.

Talon moved to Emerson's neck and continued her slow kisses, adding in some licks and a few light nibbles that Emerson hoped wouldn't leave marks. At that, Emerson laughed.

"What?" Talon asked, stopping to look down at her. "Did I tickle you or something?"

"No, I just realized we have to work tomorrow," Emerson said, laughing. "Here. They needed the big room for something else tomorrow, so I reserved this room for us."

"Really?" Talon asked, chuckling a little, too. "I don't suppose we can do this…"

"No way," Emerson said.

"But, Emerson, there are walls."

"There's no lock on the door," Emerson reminded, holding on to Talon's ass and pressing her into her. "Better make the most of it now."

Talon rolled into her and said, "Like this?"

"Yes, just like this. Maybe add in some of that kissing, though."

Talon smiled, leaned down, and they kissed for a long time before Talon sped up her hips and slipped a hand between them, stroking Emerson gently and slowly until Emerson came in her hand. When Talon moved inside,

Emerson spread herself wider for her. Talon didn't so much thrust this time; she rocked her hips as her hand moved in time, and she let Emerson rise this time instead of focusing just on taking her over. When Emerson *did* come again, it was after several minutes of Talon kissing her neck, then her breasts, and that amazing rocking.

"We should talk, right?" Talon asked minutes later after they'd both dressed again and returned to the big conference room.

Emerson hadn't bothered with her flannel shirt because the buttons were currently all over the floor of this room, and she and Talon needed to find all of them to get rid of the evidence of what they'd done.

"We should wipe this table," Emerson said, staring at the large conference room table.

"We probably should clean the beanbag chairs, too, but I don't know how to do that without ruining them. Want me to wipe down your desk chair, though? I think you got it a little wet." Talon wrapped her arms around Emerson's neck from behind and kissed her neck. "Not that *I* mind, but you'll have to sit on that thing tomorrow."

Emerson laughed and said, "I'll take care of that tomorrow morning. And don't talk about how wet I was; I'll want it again."

"Really? You're not sore as hell?"

"No, I am, but I can't stop the wanting," Emerson said, wrapping her arm around the back of Talon's neck and turning her head to kiss her.

"Want to grab dinner?" Talon asked.

"It's dinnertime?" Emerson asked back, checking her phone now that she had it in her pocket. "Shit. I had no idea."

Talon laughed and sucked on Emerson's earlobe.

"We could go to your place and order in," Talon suggested.

"My place?" Emerson asked.

Talon pulled back and said, "Or not. Sorry, I'm getting

ahead of myself."

Emerson turned around and said, "No, it's not that. I just... Talon, I didn't expect this to happen. I've been trying to ignore the feelings I have for you this whole time, and then today, we've had sex all over the office."

"Not *all* over. There's still a lot of uncovered rooms we could have sex in. For example, the gym showers have no cameras, obviously."

"Not here again, Talon," Emerson said.

Talon looked hurt for a second but then nodded in understanding.

"Today has been so good – you have no idea how good, but we can't do this again here," Emerson said. "I can't look at my chair the same way anymore, and if we do this in the gym showers, I won't be able to see them the same way, either."

"How do you see the gym showers now?" Talon asked, looking confused and utterly adorable.

"Put on that sexy leather jacket of yours, and let's go to my place. We'll order dinner as we walk to the parking garage."

"It's pleather, by the way; not real leather," Talon said.

"Still badass and sexy," Emerson replied.

"Good to know. I'll have to keep that in mind and wear it to work more often."

"Tease?"

"What? Problem?" Talon asked, lifting a sexy eyebrow.

"No. I got myself off to you in that skirt in the parking garage the other day. The back seat of my car, hand inside my jeans, panties ruined, and I had to walk around in them *all day*. Oh, and I came twice." Emerson held up two fingers.

Talon's jaw dropped.

"Problem?" Emerson teased.

CHAPTER 19

Talon woke up sorer than she'd ever been in her entire life. She'd lost track of the number of orgasms she'd had the previous day, and well, in the middle of the night, too. Her head was foggy, as if she were hungover, but she hadn't had any alcohol. After their final round at the office, Emerson had made Talon take her to the server room to verify that none of the cameras had any angles of what they'd just done to one another. They'd watched on tape as Talon walked from the conference room and into Emerson's office. Then, Emerson joined her, and the frosted glass was put into action. Emerson had been worried that there would be shadows, making it perfectly clear what they'd gotten up to, but thankfully, the location of the window and the sun made that impossible.

They looked like they were two people working on a project together in an empty office, but nothing more than that, and Talon was sure no one would be reviewing security footage unless there was a break-in or robbery that required it. Brittany had also explained once that the footage overwrote after seventy-two hours anyway, so Talon made sure to share that with Emerson, too. That seemed to make her feel better, and they headed out of the office and down the elevator to the parking garage, where Talon made fun of Emerson getting herself off twice in the back seat of her car there. Emerson told Talon to follow her home and shut up about it, or she wouldn't ever see Emerson's hands slip into her own panties. Talon shut up.

They got to Emerson's apartment shortly after, and even though Emerson had ordered food that would be there any minute, Talon had still pressed her up against the wall and got what she wanted when Emerson's hand moved into her unbuttoned and unzipped jeans. Talon had watched Emerson touch herself without being able to really see anything at all.

"God, you're so sexy," Talon had said.

Emerson came after a few minutes, and Talon had bitten her lip to keep herself from touching her. When Emerson's hand emerged, Talon took a step to close the distance between them. She took that hand and slipped the fingers into her mouth, sucking on them, wanting to taste Emerson again. Then, the doorbell rang.

Dinner was shared, but there was no movie after and no hand-holding or snuggling on the sofa. Instead, there had been a round on the sofa, a break as they ate the ice cream Emerson had in the freezer for dessert, another round in the kitchen after, and then a final round in the bedroom. Well, it was *supposed* to be the final round. Then, Emerson had suggested they take a bath since they couldn't both easily fit in her shower. Emerson had lay behind her at first, slowing stroking Talon's thighs and stomach. Then, she moved to Talon's clit, and as much as it felt to Talon like she was so sore, she'd never come again, Emerson got her there. Talon had turned them around and sucked on Emerson's nipples, knowing they'd be sore too by now, and hearing the water slosh around them.

It hadn't taken long for her hand to be placed by Emerson between Emerson's legs, and Talon had rubbed slow circles until Emerson came yet again. It felt like the past few weeks of wanting each other meant that they needed to get all of this out at once, when all Talon wanted now was a thorough night's sleep and to talk to Emerson the following morning about what this meant for them now.

Now, it was morning, and Emerson was on her side, facing away from Talon. They hadn't talked about whether or not Talon would stay over. Talon had just stayed, and Emerson had let her. Talon stared at Emerson's bare, somewhat muscled back and wondered if she worked out.

The woman didn't have abs, exactly, but she had more definition than Talon did, and it worked for her. She'd ask her later if she worked out regularly, but right now, she just wanted to trace Emerson's spine with her fingertip, which she did and then did again.

"Can I help you?" Emerson asked in a groggy voice.

"No, I'm fine," Talon replied, sliding over to Emerson and kissing her shoulder. "Now, I'm better."

"Oh, yeah?" Emerson said.

"Yeah," Talon replied, smiling as she kissed Emerson's back. "I'd be even better if you rolled over onto your back."

"Tal, I cannot again," Emerson said, laughing a little. "I think you broke me."

Talon laughed and slid a hand down Emerson's thigh.

"I gave you a break," she replied.

"To sleep for, like, four hours," Emerson remarked.

"Hey, *you* woke me up in the middle of the night and touched me," Talon replied.

"I did," Emerson said, and Talon could feel the smirk without seeing it.

"So, can I…" Talon's hand moved to Emerson's ass and slid down. "Just once before I go. We have to get up for work anyway. I could just make sure you're one hundred percent satisfied before I go."

"Trust me; I am definitely satisfied."

"Yeah?" Talon asked, moving into Emerson's folds from behind. "You feel… hard and wet to me."

"Fuck. How am I still turned on?" Emerson asked, her body tensing as Talon began to rub slowly.

"I don't know, but I'm happy to take care of this for you whenever you need me to," she replied.

Talon kissed Emerson's neck. Then, she saw Emerson's hand go to her own breast and begin to massage it.

"I didn't think it was possible to come this much," Emerson said between breaths.

"Neither did I, but it's a very good discovery," Talon said, slipping inside Emerson with two fingers. "You can touch your clit while I do this now."

"Yes," Emerson breathed out and reached down to stroke herself while Talon moved deep inside her. "God, that's…"

"Yeah? Already?" Talon asked, sucking on Emerson's earlobe.

Emerson came as a response, which surprised Talon because that was the fastest she'd come so far.

"My face," Emerson said, rolling onto her back. "Sit on…"

"Oh," Talon said, understanding what she meant.

"Now, Tal. I want you," she ordered, and Talon had no trouble obeying.

***

"So, I should shower at my place and then head in. I might be a little late," Talon said, standing up minutes later.

"Shower here. I'll go in after you. It's annoying it's so small, I know," Emerson replied, covering herself with the sheet.

That made Talon laugh. The room reeked of sex. She'd seen every single inch of Emerson's body, and Emerson was covering herself up.

"It's fine. I need new clothes anyway. We're pretty close to the same size in shirts, but–"

"Not in pants," Emerson said.

"Yeah," Talon put on her jacket and zipped up her jeans.

"You are sexy as fuck in that jacket." Emerson stared.

"I've heard that before," Talon said, smiling.

"Yeah? From whom?"

"You," Talon said, walking over to the bed and leaning down over Emerson. "Wait. I don't…"

"What?" Emerson asked, looking concerned.

"Do I kiss you goodbye? Was last night a date? Dinner on the sofa, lots of hot sex… but we haven't talked about what this is. And I know we need to go, but we should talk about this, right?"

"We should," Emerson said, tucking the sheet in closer to her chest.

Talon sat down on the edge of the bed and said, "Oh, I know *that* look."

"What look?"

"The bad-news look. You're about to tell me this can't happen again."

"Tal, I'm not… It's…"

"Over?" Talon asked.

"I just don't know. I love what we did. I've wanted it, and–"

"You've had it, so you're good now?" Talon asked.

"What? No," Emerson said, leaning forward and taking Talon's hand. "Talon, I need this job. And as much as I've loved every minute of this, it shouldn't have happened. Before you ask, I don't regret a single minute of it. I just don't know what I can offer you."

"We signed the paper," Talon said. "I have it in my backpack. We can give it to HR."

"Talon, if we do that, people are going to think you get what comes next for you because you're sleeping with the boss."

"What comes next?"

"You know you're going to get Nick's job, right? All you have to do is apply."

"But I haven't applied," Talon said.

"Why not?" Emerson asked, still holding on to Talon's hand.

"I don't know. I thought I wanted it before Nick got here."

"And now?"

"And now, I'm not sure I do."

"What do you want, then? Career-wise, I mean."

Talon looked down at their linked hands and said, "You saw me at that party. What was it about me that made you think about this?"

"That's not at all a segue," Emerson said, laughing.

"So?"

"Okay. If we're doing this, we're doing this, I guess." Emerson took a deep breath. "My date was annoying me that night. I wasn't sure it would go anywhere, but I hadn't decided yet. Then, I see you at the food table talking to someone, and you just had something about you. Maybe it was those eyes or your soft hair that I've wanted to touch since that night." Emerson held out her free hand and ran it through Talon's hair, smiling. "I just wanted to know you, Talon. I had no idea I'd be working with you. I thought I'd never see you again, actually. I only went to that party because of my date. I knew no one there, so I didn't think there was a chance I'd ever…" She ran her hand through Talon's hair again.

"And you couldn't… with her that night?"

"No. We kissed, and there was a moment when I had my hand… somewhere."

Talon laughed and said, "You've had that hand all over my *somewhere*, and you can't even say it?"

"Her pussy, Talon; I had my hand on her pussy."

Talon stopped laughing.

"Over her thong, and I was about to–"

"Okay. Never mind. I don't want to know." Talon shook her head.

"But I didn't because I saw this stranger's face. And then I saw that same stranger at work a couple of weeks later, and I haven't been able to get my mind off of her since."

"Then, let's just try this," Talon replied, squeezing Emerson's hand.

"A piece of paper won't help you when it comes time for a promotion or for credit on your work."

"I don't care. I'm used to being looked over for stuff."

"And I hate that, Talon. You're so good at what you do."

"So, if I sucked at my job, you'd date me?"

"No," Emerson said. "You being good at your job is one of the things I like about you. It's sexy how smart you are and how you explain things to the guys who should know already what you're telling them because it's their actual job."

"Then, what are you saying, Emerson?" Talon asked.

"Can we just get a little space from last night and this morning? The room does smell like sex. And I promise, when I asked you to come to the office yesterday, I did *not* expect this to happen."

"So, space?"

"I swear, it's not a line or a dismissal."

Talon nodded reluctantly and said, "So, it's over, then."

"No, that's not–"

"That's pretty much what space means, Emerson," Talon said, standing and letting go of Emerson's hand. "Look, I do understand what you're saying; I'm not naïve. It just hurts."

"Will you please sit back down? We can be late for work."

Talon reached down and picked her backpack up off the floor, unzipping it and pulling out the piece of paper that was now slightly crumpled.

"Just in case." She placed it on the bed. "I don't want you to worry or think that I'm going to say or do anything about this."

"Talon, I don't need that," Emerson told her. "I know you wouldn't–"

"Keep it anyway." Talon shrugged a shoulder. "And I'm not mad. I'm confused, and yeah, it hurts, but I'm not mad. I just want to go home and be alone for a bit."

"Will you please stay?" Emerson said, standing up and losing the sheet.

Talon looked her up and down, taking in Emerson's perfect form because it might be the last time she'd see it.

"You wanted space, Emerson. I want to give that to you. If you haven't noticed yet, I kind of really enjoy giving you what you want."

Then, she left the bedroom.

CHAPTER 20

"You look exhausted," Talon said to Aria.

"Well, I was up all night," Aria replied, sipping her martini.

"Regular hookup?" Weston asked.

"Yeah… And she told me she was interested in someone from her office."

"Oh, like *interested* interested?" Talon asked.

"Like she's asked the woman out, and the woman said yes. They've actually been out a few times since then, and while they're not even close to exclusive, she's not sure she can keep doing what we're doing."

"Sorry, Aria," Weston replied.

"It sucks, but she said she's going to let me know either way. Last night, we kind of had a send-off just in case it's the last time. She did things to me that she's never done before."

"Is that why you kind of waddled into the bar?" Talon teased.

"Shut up," Aria said, laughing. "Someone else has some sexy times news for us, I hear."

"I did, but now I don't," Talon said, bringing her beer bottle to her lips.

"What do you mean?" Weston asked.

Weston had been a bit out of the loop with Talon since she'd shown up that day and told her about the woman from work. Ever since, Weston had been writing and waiting to hear back from Annie either about a possible deal or their fledgling relationship. Talon hadn't really done her part to help keep Weston involved in her life recently, but Weston was focused on other things right now, which made sense, and Talon didn't want to have to keep going back to her to talk to her about the ups and downs of being crazy into Emerson Bagley.

"You haven't filled Wes in?" Aria asked.

"Not yet. She's been busy, and I have been, too, technically."

"Emerson?" Weston asked.

"Yeah, we've… Well, you know."

"Really? Why wasn't this in the group text? Why didn't you call me?"

"Like I said, you've been busy. But it's over anyway," Talon said.

"What? Why?" Weston looked concerned.

"The day I went to see you, she asked me to come into the office to work on the project I told you about. I went in, and we… Well, we didn't do all that much working."

"I heard from Ellie that you told her it was the hottest sex of your life," Aria said.

"Oh, definitely," Talon replied, looking skyward. "It was amazing, and there was more after that, but then she told me she needed to get some space from what happened because of work or something. So, it's over already."

"Does it really have to be, though?" Weston asked her.

"She says it does, so that's that," Talon replied, sounding defeated. "I don't want just sex with her. What we had was fucking amazing, but I want more. I'm ready for something real. If she's unable to give that to me because we work together, I don't know what I'm supposed to do."

"Me too. I'm ready for something real, too," Aria said, surprising them both.

"What?" Weston asked her.

"I don't know. Maybe I'm not. I just don't know that I want the regular hookup anymore. She's got someone she likes now; that changes things. I don't want her thinking of someone else when she's with me, and I don't know that I really want even the hottest sex with someone who wants someone else like that, too."

"Have they had sex yet?" Weston asked.

"I don't know. I didn't ask."

"Aria, even if it's not an exclusive thing – it's a safe sex thing. You should know if she's hooking up with someone else, have her get tested before she–"

"I know. I know. I made a bad call." Aria sipped her martini again. "I'm in a weird funk, and I don't know how to get myself out of it."

"Maybe try not meeting woman after woman and taking them to bed," Weston suggested.

"Maybe. I don't know," Aria said.

"What if, tonight, we both try to meet women, but not for sex," Talon offered. "We could just enjoy conversations and maybe buy them drinks or get a dance or something, but we end it there."

"I thought you were still pining for Emerson," Aria said.

"I am, but if it's not going anywhere, I can be your wingwoman and maybe just, I don't know, meet a nice girl and strike up a conversation. I have no energy for anything else."

"Weston, you in?" Aria asked.

"Weston is taken," Talon replied. "Right?"

"Not technically, no," Weston said. "Annie and I aren't together."

"But that's just the technicality, though. It's not like you want to date other people," Talon remarked.

"No, I don't," Weston said. "But she's got some things to sort out now, so we're not even just dating."

"You're not dating anymore?" Aria asked.

"Not right now. She asked for a few days to get things together. It's been a few days, and I still haven't heard from her. I don't know what I'm waiting for. Maybe it's just not meant to be. She's got so much going on, and I want to be supportive, but I also want to be with her, and that means actually being *with* her."

"She wants to be with you, too," Talon said. "That was

obvious the night we were all here. Seemed to me like she didn't care for the fact that I'd seen you naked years ago, and that was before you two were even dating."

"I don't doubt that she likes me," Weston commented. "But if she's right, and we met at the wrong time, it might not work, and I can't just wait around forever. I mean, it's not like we've been together for years or something. We haven't even known each other that long."

"So?" Talon said. "I haven't known Emerson that long, and I know what I feel for her. It won't go anywhere because of our circumstances, but time doesn't make a difference – you feel what you feel." She shrugged a shoulder.

"You really like her, huh?" Aria asked Talon.

"Doesn't matter," Talon said. "So, are we going to put ourselves out there and meet women we *won't* try to sleep with?"

"I'm in," Aria said, finishing her martini.

"I'm out," Weston added. "I think I'm going to go home and pack for the cabin. The renters are gone, so I have the place to myself now that it's off the market."

"How long will you be gone?" Talon asked.

"I don't know. I'll text you guys when I've figured it out, though."

"What if Annie comes around while you're gone or something?" Aria asked.

"She'll have to wait for me this time, I guess," Weston said.

***

Neither Talon nor Aria really found anyone they were interested in that night. Talon bought one woman a drink, and they talked for a while, but when Talon thought about continuing the relationship with coffee or dinner on another night, there wasn't anything there for her. They had a few things in common, she supposed, but there was no spark, nothing that would make Talon believe this would go anywhere. So, she politely excused herself and went home.

She stared at her ceiling and tried to think about getting herself out of this funk. Maybe she could go digital and try a dating app. Sure, she'd made fun of Ellie for suggesting it, but that was mainly because she always picked on Ellie. Hell, they all picked on each other.

Just as Talon stood to take a hot shower before bed, her phone pinged. She'd walked out with Aria, but maybe Aria had gone somewhere else and had picked up someone and wanted to brag. Talon swallowed when she saw it was Emerson.

Emerson Bagley: Can we talk?

Talon didn't know what to say. It had been a few days since they'd had their day and night together. Being at the office and working on the same project hadn't been easy, but Talon figured that the more time they put between what had happened between them and the present, the easier it would be for her to be able to work on projects with Emerson again. It would just take a while. She messaged back and waited for the next text to come in, but instead, it was a call.

"Hello?" Talon said.

"Hey," Emerson said, sounding exhausted.

"You okay?" Talon asked.

"You're a good person for even asking me that after I told you I needed space to figure things out. I should be asking *you* that."

"Well, ask me," Talon said, lying back down.

"*Are* you okay?"

"No," Talon said.

"Me neither."

"Why not?"

"You know why not."

"And I need to hear you say it," Talon replied.

"I miss you," Emerson said softly.

"In bed?" Talon needed to know.

"No, Talon. I miss *you.* I wanted to have sex with you, but I don't *only* want to have sex with you. I love our lunches and our coffee walks. I love getting to know you and working beside you on this project."

"Then, why did you tell me it wasn't going to happen?"

"I didn't. I just said I needed some space to think. We're women in a male-dominated field, and we're lesbians at that. I wish those weren't things we needed to think about here, but they are, and I need this job. It's not just for me; It's for my family, Tal. I help all of them out financially in one way or another."

"I know," Talon said. "And I'd never do anything to jeopardize that for you."

"I know, but I don't want to jeopardize anything for you, either. I mean, look at stupid Nick: he noticed us just working together and getting along and started rumors. What happens if you and I actually date, and we go public?"

"We have more amazing sex?" Talon joked.

"Babe, I'm serious," Emerson replied but laughed all the same.

Talon smiled because Emerson just called her *babe.*

"I know," Talon said. "And I know you want me to take Nick's job, but I don't know that that's what *I* want. If you and I do this, I won't apply for it, Emerson. But I don't want you to decide on our personal relationship because of that. It's *my* decision."

"Can you honestly tell me that if you and I weren't incredibly attracted to each other, you'd still not apply?"

Talon thought about that for a minute and said, "I might have, but I don't know. When they hired Nick and passed me over, I kind of gave up on it. I like my job enough. My team performs well, and I make good money; it works for me. Emerson, if we decide to go on a date, we don't have to tell anyone until if or when we're ready to tell them. It's our personal business. It won't belong to them."

"What if it gets out anyway?"

"Then, we deal with it. I didn't care about Nick's

rumors or comments anyway. When I go home, I'm home. I don't bring shit from work home with me. Well, maybe actual work, but not the juvenile bullshit."

"God, say that again. It's sexy."

Talon laughed and said, "I don't bring the juvenile bullshit home with me. I *do* bring *you* with me, though."

"You do?" Emerson asked.

"Yes," Talon said.

"I'm sorry," Emerson said.

"Yeah? Are you done with this space thing?"

"It's still complicated, Tal."

"Call me *babe* instead. I like that better than *Tal* now."

Emerson laughed and said, "Will you go out with me? For real?"

"Come over here and ask me in person," Talon smirked even though no one could see it.

"No way. We'd end up naked against your front door."

"So?"

Emerson laughed again and said, "I want a real date, babe."

"Fine. But only because you called me *babe* again." Talon sighed dramatically. "When?"

"After Valentine's Day," Emerson said.

"*After*? That's, like, days away."

"I know. But I don't want our first date to be on Valentine's Day – it's too much pressure."

"Pressure? Why? We've already slept together," Talon said.

"The 16th," Emerson stated.

"Huh?"

"The 16th. Can we go out then? I have a family thing with my mom and sister and her kids tomorrow night, and a work drinks thing the night after that."

"Okay. That takes us to the 13th," Talon remarked.

"*You* have something on the 13th."

"Shit." Talon smacked her forehead. "The stupid team awards dinner."

"Yes," Emerson said, laughing. "And the 15th, I have that full day of team-building for the executive team. I don't want to go out with you right after that. I'll be wiped."

"So, the 16th?"

"Yes," Emerson said. "Until then, I'll just stare longingly at you from across the rooms we're in together."

"Longingly, huh?" Talon joked.

"Yes, Tal."

"No, go back to babe – that one's better."

Emerson laughed again and said, "I should let you go."

"Okay, babe. I'll see you at work?"

Emerson's laugh made Talon smile as they hung up the phone.

CHAPTER 21

"Emerson?"

"Huh?" Emerson asked.

"Where are you right now?" her sister asked, glaring at her.

"What?"

"Hi, I'm your sister." She waved. "And I'm at dinner right now. Where are you?"

"I'm here," Emerson said, looking from her sister to her nephew, who was sitting next to her, coloring on the kid's menu and not paying any attention to them.

"Are you?"

Their mother had gone to the bathroom a minute ago, taking Emerson's other nephew with her. That left just the three of them sitting in the booth of the Italian restaurant chain.

"Yeah, I'm right here. I just zoned out a little."

Emerson's phone buzzed on the table. She glanced at the screen and saw Talon's name there. She smiled without meaning to.

"Who is that?"

"No one," she lied.

"You are a terrible liar. Always have been," her sister said.

"You lie?" her three-year-old nephew asked. "Aunt Emson lied."

He had a hard time saying her actual name, so he'd been calling her Aunt Emson for a while now. Emerson thought it was adorable and hoped he always called her that.

"No, buddy," she said. "Aunt Emson didn't lie."

He returned to coloring, seemingly no longer caring about what the adults were talking about.

"Out with it," her sister said.

"There's nothing to come out with," Emerson replied, picking up her phone and reading the message.

Talon Mitchell: This waiting thing is torture.

Emerson smiled again and typed a message back. She saw the three bubbles almost immediately and waited for Talon's response.

Talon Mitchell: Yes, we waited before. But now that I know what it's like to touch you, it's harder.

Emerson knew she was blushing and didn't even bother to hide it.

"Okay. You have a new girlfriend, don't you?"

"What?" Emerson said, looking up at her sister, who had their mother's eyes but her father's blonde hair.

"You seem happy and distracted. That can only mean one thing," her sister replied.

"I don't have a girlfriend." Emerson's phone buzzed again, and she looked down.

Talon Mitchell: Come over after your dinner.

Her thighs clenched just thinking about it, but she wanted more than just sex with Talon; and if she went over to Talon's place late, that would be all they'd do. Emerson messaged her back, and then came the reply.

Talon Mitchell: I'm touching myself right now.

"Oh, my God," Emerson said, biting her bottom lip.

"Are you being gross right now?" her sister asked.

"Gross," Emerson's nephew said and then promptly laughed.

Their mother returned to the booth meant for six, and Emerson's four-year-old nephew sat next to her, which meant the phone had to go away given Talon's most recent message.

"Mom, Emerson has a girlfriend," her sister said.

"How old are you?" Emerson asked her.

"You're seeing someone?" her mom asked.

"What? No," Emerson lied.

Her mother's eyes seared into her soul, and Emerson knew she was caught.

"Want to try that again?" the older woman asked with a lifted eyebrow in that way only mothers could do.

"We haven't started the seeing-each-other part yet," Emerson said. "It's complicated."

"That's a Facebook relationship status, not what you tell your family," her sister argued.

"You're a real pain in my…" Emerson stopped when she looked down at her nephew, who was staring up at her in confusion. "You know what."

Her sister laughed.

"Who is it?" her mother asked.

"You know who," Emerson replied, looking down at her phone in her hand, which buzzed again right after she tucked it into her pocket.

"No, I–" Her mom stopped. "Wait. Talon?"

"Who's Talon?" her sister asked.

"Oh, Emerson… No, honey."

"Mom, it's complicated, like I said. We really like each other."

"You know she likes you now?" her mom asked.

Emerson swallowed and thought of Talon's head between her legs.

"Yeah, I know she likes me," Emerson said.

"Who is Talon?"

"Talon!" her youngest nephew shouted.

His mother passed him another crayon, which he took and continued coloring. Emerson kind of wished she could just be coloring right now, too.

"She's someone I work with."

"You're dating someone you work with?"

"We're not–" Emerson took a deep breath. "We haven't gone on a date yet."

"The last I heard, you were interested, unsure if she

was too, and you weren't going to do anything about it because she's a subordinate," her mother said.

"You're dating someone who works *for* you?" her sister asked this time.

"Again, we haven't gone on a date yet," Emerson reminded her. "We're going to go on our first one after Valentine's Day."

"Why not *on* Valentine's Day?" her sister asked.

"Because that's a lot of pressure for a first date, and I want it to go well."

"Emerson, this is dangerous," her mom said.

"I know, Mom, but she's already signed a form thing that says it's a consensual relationship. I have it. If it turns into something, I'll give it to HR."

"And that's enough to keep you from getting into trouble?" her mom asked.

"I've worried about nothing else ever since I saw Talon the first day at work. Mom, I am crazy attracted to her, but it's more than just that. We talk. We've spent hours and hours together at work by now, and we get coffee together, eat lunch together, we ran into each other at a bar, shared a drink, and I walked her home. I just wanted to kiss her. I wanted to hold her hand while we walked."

"So, it's not just the–" Her sister stopped herself and looked down at the table. "The *crayon* that you want?"

Emerson stared at her in confusion.

"The *crayon*, Emerson." She nodded to her son. "You know? The thing some people do on the third date as if that's some rule."

"Are you talking about–"

"Yes, a *crayon*," she said, eyes wide.

Emerson laughed. Neither of her nephews appeared to be paying attention, but they were inquisitive. If Emerson said *sex*, they'd ask what that was, and her sister obviously wasn't ready to deal with that conversation yet.

"Yes, I also want a *crayon*," she said, feeling really weird. "But I want the other stuff, too. And so does Talon."

"You've talked about it?" her mom asked.

"We're going on a date, Mom. Plus, I know her well enough by now to know that it's not just *crayons* that she wants."

"How can you know for sure if she hasn't had the crayon yet?" her sister asked. "She might just want that, and when she gets it, she–"

"Because we've already done that. We've… *colored* together," Emerson said.

"You did what?" her mom asked.

"Mom, I'm thirty-two years old. You know I have…" She looked at her nephew. "This is ridiculous."

"Ridlis!" he said and laughed.

"Ridiculous, baby," her sister said to her son softly, sounding out the word for him.

"Riclis?"

"Close," she replied, laughing softly at him.

"You've…" her mom said, giving Emerson a look.

"Yes. It wasn't planned, but it happened. Then, the morning after, I told Talon I needed some space because I wasn't expecting it, and the look of disappointment on her face about killed me, Mom."

"She was disappointed after *crayons*?" her sister teased. "Did you do it right?" She smirked at her own joke.

"Oh, she was anything but disappointed," Emerson said. "Trust me. We were both very satisfied by the… *color selection* of our crayons."

"Selection, huh?" she asked, leaning over the table. "Do tell. Some of us have just the one or two color options. Let me live vicariously."

"Please don't," their mother said, taking a drink of her nearly finished ice water. "Emerson, is this a good idea?"

"I don't know, but I trust Talon. And like I said, we can give HR the form when we're ready. That will offer me protection from a lawsuit, but I'm still worried about the rumor mill and Talon's career being harmed because of me."

"What does she say about that?"

Emerson's phone buzzed again.

"She says this is what she wants," Emerson replied.

"Be careful, honey," her mom said.

"I will," Emerson replied.

***

"I cannot believe you did that to me," Emerson said into the phone the moment she got inside her apartment and closed the door behind her.

"What?" Talon played coy.

"You texted me that you were getting yourself off with my four-year-old nephew sitting right next to me."

"Shit. Can he read?"

"Sort of, but I hid it from him," she said.

"Okay. So, the problem is really that I messaged *you* that, and it got you all hot and bothered then," Talon teased.

Emerson flopped onto her sofa and said, "Did you really do that?"

"Yes," Talon said.

"How?"

"You want to know?"

"Yes."

"I can just show you. Come over, Emerson," Talon told her.

"If I do–"

"We'll have sex, yes," Talon stated.

"Do you just want that?" Emerson asked, letting her mother and sister get into her head.

"What?"

"We're going on a date, Tal, but do you just want–"

"Am I doing it again?" Talon interrupted.

"Doing what?"

"I lost a girlfriend because once we started having sex, all I wanted to do was have sex," Talon replied.

"Babe, I would have sex with you all the time if I could.

I just want to know that you want the other stuff, too."

"I do. I do want the other stuff. I just… You turn me on, Emerson."

"You turn me on, too," Emerson said.

"And now that I've touched you, and you've touched me, it's just hard to think of anything else. Not that I *was* thinking of much else before that happened."

"So, you'll let me take you out on a real date?"

"Yes," Talon said, laughing. "Sorry if I'm coming on really strong. I just see you at work, and I think about what we did there…"

"What do you think about?" Emerson asked.

"If I tell you that, I'll have to get off again," Talon said.

"So?"

"So? Do you want to listen?" Talon asked.

"Maybe I want to do it with you," Emerson offered back.

"You just said–"

"That I would have sex with you all the time if I could," Emerson completed. "And I wish that I could, because you are so…" Emerson lay down on the sofa and held the phone down to her jeans, where she popped the button and unzipped them. Then, she brought it back to her ear. "Hot."

"Did you just…"

"Yes."

"Get over here. *I'll* come there. Let me touch you for real," Talon said.

"No, I kind of like this part," Emerson replied. "You got me wet tonight just messaging me. You can deal with hearing how wet I am for you now."

Emerson lowered her jeans and panties to her knees and put the phone on speaker.

"Are you in bed?" Talon asked.

"Couch," Emerson said, placing the phone on her thigh. "Now, tell me what you were picturing earlier. Which part?"

"Fuck, Emerson," Talon said.

"Are you touching yourself now?"

"Yes," Talon said.

Emerson smirked and slid her hand between her legs, hearing for herself just how wet she was for Talon.

"Fuck. Is that–"

"Yes," Emerson said, closing her eyes. "Tell me, Talon."

CHAPTER 22

Talon had managed to make it through the few days she and Emerson had to wait for their first official date, but it hadn't been easy. They'd talked on the phone every night and seen each other at work, but they'd kept it professional there and personal when they'd talked at night. They'd only done the whole phone sex thing that night. After that, Talon thought she should cool it a bit. She wanted Emerson, and she made no apologies for it, but she wouldn't make the same mistake she'd made in college. She wanted all of Emerson; and that meant going on a real date together, not just getting off on the phone while the other person listened in or late-night booty calls.

Being in the same space at work had been the hardest part. They were finalizing the project they'd been working on and still had to spend time alone together to make that happen. While the glass walls and people outside them certainly helped them keep it professional, the comments they shared when no one else was listening were clear innuendos. Okay… They didn't keep it completely professional, after all.

"You went away for like a week or so and came back with a girlfriend?" Scarlet asked. "How do *I* do that? Is that cabin magical or something? Are there fairies in the woods sprinkling you with their dust, making women fall in love with you?"

"Yes, Scar. That's obviously what happened," Weston teased. "It had nothing to do with the fact that Annie and I were dating *before* I went to the cabin."

"I really like her for you," Paisley said, drinking her bottled beer. "And this place is all right, too. I'm not normally a big beer drinker, but I didn't trust the whole four wines they have in their selection, so I went with this thing, and it's not awful." She held up the bottle to review the label.

"That's high praise coming from you." Aria smirked. "And Annie *is* good for you," she told Weston. "You two look, like, crazy happy right now."

"It's the sex," Talon suggested. "They finally started having sex."

"And the fact that they really like each other," Ellie said.

"Yeah, that too," Talon replied, sipping her own beer.

Talon didn't want to miss Weston's return to the city from the cabin. That was especially true because Weston had come back with a full-on girlfriend in Annie. They'd worked things out while they were away, which was great, but now Talon was regretting going out because she was nervous. She hadn't been at all up until now, but her first date with Emerson was tonight. Maybe she should still be at home getting ready, and not out for a quick drink with her friends.

"I'm falling in love with her," Weston said. "I think I'm there already. I almost let the words slip out when we were…"

"Having sex," Aria said. "Yeah, we get it."

Weston laughed and said, "Yes. It came out of nowhere. We're not ready for that yet."

"Who's in charge of determining that?" Ellie asked.

"Yeah, there's no rule, right? Not that I'd really know, but I don't think there's a rule," Scarlet added, picking at the panini she'd ordered and got made wrong, but in true Scarlet fashion, she said she'd eat it anyway instead of sending it back to the kitchen.

"I don't think you should profess your undying love to the woman in the middle of sex," Paisley said. "I mean, they say the hormones alone are enough to make you say things that you might not mean. It's like alcohol, lowering your inhibitions. You're supposed to wait at least fifteen minutes after an orgasm to say anything big like that."

"Where did you learn that?" Talon asked her.

"The Internet."

"Which is *always* right," Talon teased.

"It was an academic article," Paisley remarked. "Not Wikipedia."

"Dr. Sophia Clark and Dr. Takura Miroco?" Aria asked.

"What?" Paisley asked. "Maybe. Why?"

"I edited that one, I think," Aria replied. "She's right. The science was pretty sound in that one."

"You edited that article?" Talon asked.

"I even did my own personal study," Aria said. "With my regular, when I was working on that one, I timed myself from orgasm to the moment I felt like I had full brain function and control over the shit I wanted to say – it was about fifteen minutes."

"What shit did you want to say to her?" Weston asked. "You're not telling someone you're dating that you love them."

"No, I told her it was over, though. I wanted to be sure that was what I wanted, and it was. She's ready to be official with that woman she's dating, and we had a real farewell this time. It wasn't as hot as it usually was, but it was good. And now it's over, and I know for sure – because I waited – that that was what I wanted."

"Well, all right," Talon said. "Guys, can we talk about me for a minute?"

"She has a date tonight," Ellie said.

"With whom?" Weston asked. "And it's six. Why are you *here* if you have a date?"

"Because you came back from the cabin today, and Paisley was in town, and this is what we do when we're all here. Plus, Annie is here, and you're together now, so I wanted to show my support," Talon replied.

"Who's it with?" Weston asked again.

"What do you mean, who's it with? Emerson," Talon stated.

"Emerson? I thought you said that was done."

"Well, we talked, and we're going to go out," Talon replied matter-of-factly.

"What did I miss?" Annie asked, returning to the empty chair next to Weston after having gone to the bathroom.

"Just me telling everyone I'm about to go on my first real date with a woman I work with, who is my boss's boss, who drives me crazy in all the best ways, and who I've already slept with, so I know it's amazing," Talon rambled.

"Oh. So, a lot," Annie replied, turning to Weston and giving her a smile.

Weston wrapped her arm around Annie's chair in response.

"Cute," Scarlet said.

"Act like I've never had a girlfriend in front of you guys before," Weston said sarcastically.

"I'd prefer that, actually," Annie joked.

"Her other girlfriends weren't anything for you to worry about," Paisley said.

"Hey," Talon said in mock-offense.

"We've been over this," Paisley added.

Paisley was right. Talon couldn't both tell them not to bring up the fact that she and Weston had dated, and then get mad when they did that.

"Back to me, please," she changed the topic. "How the hell do I do this?"

"Go on a date?" Weston asked.

"Yes. We've had the whole hot, sexy thing, and I think it will translate into a real relationship, but sometimes, it's just the hot and heavy sex, and it turns out, there's nothing else there."

"Take it from the person that just has the hot and heavy sex," Aria said. "You can just have that, and it's fine."

"*Amen* to that," Paisley said.

"But if you want more than that, that's fine, too," Annie added, placing a hand on Weston's thigh, or that was what Talon thought she saw.

"Okay. You guys can't be unbiased now," Paisley said. "You're all loved up."

"Oh, stop. We are not," Weston said, laughing.

Annie turned and whispered something into Weston's ear that had Weston smiling. Then, Annie lowered her head back to Weston's shoulder.

"For real… How do I do this? I've always dated and *then* had the sex. Now, I've had the sex first, and I'm going on a date with her, and I want the sex again, but it's a first date."

"Talon, slow down," Ellie said, placing her hand on Talon's shoulder. "And no more of this." She pulled Talon's mostly finished beer away. "Ladies don't like beer breath."

"Ellie, I'm serious," Talon replied.

"So is she. This stuff isn't going to get you kissed," Paisley said, sliding Talon's beer over to her side of the table. "And what's the big deal, Tal? You're acting like you've never been on a first date before."

"Not like this," Talon said.

"You really like her," Annie said, smiling at Talon sweetly.

"Yes, I do. And look, this is probably not the best group to bring this up in with Annie here now, but when Wes and I broke up, part of the reason was that I went all-in with…" She cleared her throat. "*Something*, and Wes thought we lost the other part of our relationship."

"Sex. It's okay. I know," Annie said.

"Sorry," Talon replied.

"Talon, that was college, and I was your first. You've dated women since then and haven't had that problem," Weston said.

"Not exactly true," Talon replied, squinting her eyes.

"With whom?" Scarlet asked.

"Not Leigh," Aria said.

"No, but we never really had the hot-and-heavy phase. Our sex was always just okay," Talon replied. "Chloe."

"I remember Chloe," Ellie said. "Like, three years ago, right?"

"Four," Talon said. "And we dated for a few weeks. Then, we started sleeping together, and… I don't know. I kind of lost sight of the other stuff. She'd come over, we'd have sex, and I'd just order in something for us to eat after. I'd go to her place, and it would be the same thing. Then, we're, like, three months in, and she's complaining that we never go out anymore."

"So, did you?" Annie asked.

"We tried, but we had, like, three dates, and each time I was just thinking about what would happen at the end of the night."

"Tal, you had chemistry," Aria spoke. "That's okay. It just doesn't mean you had relationship compatibility."

"*We* had chemistry," Weston added, too. "But no compatibility in an actual relationship, so we're friends."

"You don't *still* have that chemistry, do you?" Annie asked.

Weston kissed her forehead and said, "No, babe."

"It's gross now," Talon explained to Annie. "Thinking about that time."

"Hey!" Weston laughed.

"I want there to be compatibility with Emerson."

"Isn't there already?" Paisley said. "You've been to lunches and hang out."

"I hang out with Wes now, too," Talon replied.

"Okay. We're just going to go," Weston said, laughing. "New girlfriend constantly hearing about how I used to sleep with someone at this table is a little much for me."

Annie laughed and shook her head. Talon knew she was being a good sport about all of this, but also that it probably bugged the woman to think about Weston with anyone else; especially, one of her best friends that she still spent a lot of time with. Talon would be frustrated, too, if

Emerson was hanging out all the time with someone she used to sleep with – and they weren't even a couple. She was thinking about Jenny now and how Emerson had described the woman as her *first* but not *forever* love. Emerson only saw Jenny a couple of times a year now, if that, and Jenny was married with kids, so at least, Talon wouldn't have to spend a lot of time with the two of them thinking about them together.

"It's okay. I'm going anyway. I have to get home and brush my teeth for like a half-hour so she'll actually want to kiss me, and get dressed," Talon announced to the group.

"What are you going to wear?" Paisley asked.

"I was thinking this skirt and my jacket. She loved them both individually; said they were hot on me. So, I'm going to wear them together."

"Oh, no," Paisley said, shaking her head. "If you're trying to show the woman you just want a date tonight, you can't wear the sexy outfit."

"She can't?" Scarlet asked.

"No. And don't shave your legs when you shower," Ellie suggested. "You won't want her to see your grizzly hair, so you'll be less–"

"That's outdated," Aria said. "Some women don't shave at all. Does Emerson shave?" she asked Talon.

"Yes," Talon said, and now she was thinking about Emerson's soft legs. "And this isn't helping. I'm going to wear something else, but I'm shaving my legs."

"Talon, it's going to be fine," Weston said, smiling softly at her. "You are amazing; and from the little you've told me, it feels like Emerson sees that about you. Just be yourself. She obviously likes you, or she wouldn't be going out with you."

"You *have* to say that; you're my friend."

"No, I *get* to say that because I'm your friend. We all are, and we all love you. Emerson will, too. Just be the funny, smart, and caring Talon that you are, and you'll get a goodnight kiss and maybe a second date out of it."

Talon was glad Weston was back because she'd been missing her friend who was now happily in love with Annie and about to have her first book published. It was great for Weston and Annie but meant that Talon wouldn't get to see her best friend as much. Annie would start staying over all the time since Weston owned her place and Annie rented. Eventually, they'd move in together, and likely later, they'd move to that cabin Weston loved in the middle of nowhere.

Talon knew that she and all of her friends were on borrowed time as it were. They'd all somehow find someone to love or something to take them away from this place; maybe both. She sighed, wishing that she could stop time and keep them all in this place, but also that she could speed up what she had with Emerson to look ahead and see if it would all work out. She decided she'd just be herself tonight, after all, and hope for the best. If it was going to work out in the end, she had to be who she was; and that had to be whatever Emerson was looking for, or else it wouldn't last anyway.

She said goodbye to her friends, went home, showered and brushed her teeth for a solid five minutes, and popped a mint after. She only hoped Emerson liked wintergreen. Talon searched her closet for something that was casual with a hint of sexy. She settled on her navy coat with a cream-colored sweater and a pair of her nicer jeans. She added her boots with the small heel and put on just a little bit of makeup. She didn't wear much, to begin with, and Emerson hadn't ever seen her in a full face of makeup, so she went with her normal look and kept her hair down with a slight curl at the end. She checked herself in the mirror at the same time the doorbell rang. Talon nodded at herself and walked to the door, which she opened.

Emerson looked at her, sighed, and said, "You're gorgeous."

CHAPTER 23

Talon smiled and took Emerson in. She was wearing a pair of dark jeans and her usual tan coat that looked like cashmere but probably wasn't *actually* cashmere. Talon couldn't tell what was underneath it, but her mind was definitely filling in that knowledge gap with images. Emerson was topless under that coat. In fact, her jeans were undone and ready for Talon to slip into them. Of course, Emerson wasn't really topless, and her jeans were likely buttoned and zipped.

"Talon?" Emerson said.

"Yeah? Talon asked.

Emerson laughed and said, "You okay there?"

"Yes. I was just picturing you naked. Well, topless," Talon rambled.

Emerson lifted an eyebrow and said, "You were?"

"Yeah," Talon replied, shrugging a shoulder. "But you look great in that, too."

"You wish I were topless, though?"

"I *always* wish you were topless," Talon stated.

"God, why? My boobs are tiny," Emerson said.

"Your boobs are perfect. They fit in my palms, and I can–" Talon cleared her throat. "But we're on a first date."

Emerson laughed again and said, "Yes, we are. And I thought we could drive out of town for dinner if that's okay."

"Out of town?"

"Honestly, I was thinking it would be better for us not to be seen. It's a big city, but you never know."

Talon nodded and said, "I get it. That's fine. Just let me grab my phone and my keys. Oh, and come in."

"I better not," Emerson replied.

Talon walked over to her table and grabbed her phone and keys.

"Why not? I can show you around. It's not much, but it works for me."

"If I cross this threshold, I'm likely to take that coat off you, and we'll never get out of here."

Talon lifted an eyebrow at her and said, "Really? *You* wanted a real first date."

"Doesn't mean I'm not picturing you topless right now, too. I've seen you topless now, and it's not hard to…," Emerson faded out, staring at Talon's chest.

Talon laughed a little and walked out of the apartment, locking the door behind her, feeling pretty good right about now. Emerson was struggling not to tear her clothes off, too. That was a good thing.

"Okay. So, we keep it PG," Talon said. "I can do that. I've had to the past few days anyway."

"You call wearing that skirt to the office again PG?"

They walked down the hall as Talon laughed.

"I almost wore it tonight, too," she admitted.

"What? Really? We can go back real quick and you can change," Emerson said, hooking her thumb back in the direction of the apartment.

"That skirt is not PG."

"Not with *you* wearing it, at least."

When they got to the elevator, Talon pressed the button and turned to Emerson.

"I could wear it for you another night."

"And then *not* wear it for me later?"

Talon nodded slowly.

"We're off to a great start with this whole PG thing," Emerson said sarcastically as the elevator arrived.

***

"Why sales?" Emerson asked her as they sat across from one another at the table.

"I was good at it. I got the job because I needed a job, but it turned out, I was pretty good at convincing people of stuff."

"You convinced me to take you on a conference room table," Emerson said, taking a bite of her scallop.

"I don't recall you requiring all that much convincing."

"That's true," Emerson said. "Did you like it?"

"You taking me on the conference room–"

"Sales," Emerson said, laughing.

"Enough, I guess. I was happy when they promoted me, though. I like being a manager more than making the calls myself, and the money is a little better. At first, I worried I'd make less because the reps kill it and make great commissions, and I *was* making good commissions then. When they promoted me, though, they made sure to bump me up enough, and I can maybe think about buying a house one day. I put some money away already for my brother's college. I know my parents won't be able to afford to pay for everything, and I don't know if he's going to get any scholarships, so I put a little in each check away for that. I got a scholarship to school, which helped, of course, but it didn't cover everything. There was work-study to help out, but I ended up having to take out a loan, too, and I'm almost done paying that off."

"You want a house one day?" Emerson asked her.

"I hate living in an apartment. A few of my friends have houses, and I'm seriously jealous. Do you not want one?"

"Of course, I want a house," Emerson said. "You've seen my shower, Talon. If I gain twenty pounds anytime soon, I won't be able to fit inside it."

Talon laughed and said, "It is really small, but the claw tub is nice."

"But I can get one of those in a house with a bigger shower," Emerson said.

"That's true, I guess." Talon thought about the whole chemistry and compatibility thing and asked, "So, what kind of house do you want?"

"One big enough for me, my wife, and our kids," Emerson said, taking a sip of her red wine.

"How many of those?"

"One or two," Emerson replied. "Not four. I don't know how my mom handled four."

"Yeah, four's a lot," Talon said.

"What about you?"

"Yeah, I guess."

"You guess?"

"I've kind of been focusing on finding a girlfriend first," Talon said. "I had one up until late November. We were together for a year. I thought…"

"Leigh, right?"

"Yeah," Talon said.

"You thought she was the one?" Emerson asked, looking down at her plate.

"No. I don't know. I think I'm confusing to most people."

"Confusing?"

"Like, I'm not really femme, but I'm not totally butch, either. I have a decent job but don't necessarily have any big aspirations like everyone else seems to have. I mean, Paisley has her own company, Weston is publishing a book. Aria is kind of adrift sometimes, but people still *get* her. She works *when* she wants and has a ton of money, so she doesn't have to have aspirations for anything."

"You do that a lot, you know?" Emerson said, looking up at her with a serious expression.

"What?"

"You compare yourself to your friends a lot," Emerson said.

"They're my friends – or, my family, really," Talon replied.

"Talon, I don't know your friends. Maybe I'll get to meet them one day soon, but I have all the confidence in the world that you don't need to be comparing yourself to *any* of them. Babe, you fixed a broken process that had been sitting there for years with no one else thinking it could be done in just a few weeks. I actually think *I* slowed you down. You were teaching me things, and without me there, you would've implemented the whole thing in a couple of days. Do you have any idea how much time you'll save the reps and managers?"

"A few minutes per call maybe," Talon said. "I haven't really tracked that yet."

"I have," Emerson said. "It's three minutes per call, and they have six to eight calls a day. In a year, that's over six thousand minutes per rep. And for the managers who have to approve sales – you made it faster for them, too. I talked to one of the managers on the account management side, and he said the changes make it easier for his team to know what they're getting into with customers. You even thought to make them a view that's just for them so they don't have to scroll through the details they don't need." Emerson smiled softly and then sighed. "Babe, you've saved the company millions of dollars, and it was nothing to you. You're remarkable at your job, and you have no idea. I watch you with Brittany, who works the front desk, and you don't treat her like some receptionist who just greets people and stocks the printers with paper how everyone else does. You ask her how her day is going, help her restock those printers, and I've seen you restock the sugar caddies and the coffee when she's busy and you want to help. You're saving money for your kid brother's college education because you know he'll need it, Talon. You probably could've bought that house already, but you didn't. You're taking care of your family."

"It's not a big deal. You're doing the same thing."

"I am, but you discount what you're doing, and you shouldn't. I like you, Talon. I don't just like having sex with you. I like that you're a good person. I just wish you'd stop comparing yourself to your friends because I don't know them, but I *do* know you, and I think you are remarkable."

Talon stared at Emerson then and couldn't do anything but nod once because that was the nicest thing anyone had ever said to her.

"Now, in this house you're thinking about, claw tub or no claw tub?" Emerson said, likely sensing Talon's need for a break from the compliments.

"Can it be both? One claw tub in the main bath and a regular tub in another," Talon suggested.

Emerson smiled and returned to her scallops.

***

"Okay. So, I was thinking we could walk down to the fountains in front of city hall. They have them set up with lights and stuff, and there are food trucks. I looked it up; they have two dessert trucks. One has churros," Emerson said as they walked out of the restaurant. "It's only about half a mile from here."

"You looked it up?" Talon asked.

"Yeah. I've never really spent any time over here, so I wanted to make sure I picked a good place."

"You're cute," Talon said, stepping into Emerson's space.

"I am?"

Talon nodded and moved a step closer.

"So, yes, on the churros?"

"One condition."

"Condition?"

"Yes. The last time we walked somewhere, I really wanted to hold your hand."

Emerson smiled and took Talon's hand in her own, slipping her fingers between Talon's.

"Better?"

"Better," Talon said.

They walked slowly, taking their time to get to the fountain and the food trucks. When they finally got there, Talon couldn't care less about churros. She just wanted to stand there next to Emerson, who had moved behind her and wrapped her arms around Talon's waist as they watched the fountain do some kind of choreographed dance.

"I'm having a great time," Emerson whispered in her ear.

"So am I," Talon replied, covering Emerson's arms with her own.

"But…"

"Churros, yeah." Talon laughed. "I get it."

"It's fried dough in cinnamon sugar, Tal. Can you blame me?"

Talon turned in Emerson's arms and kissed her quickly on the lips.

"You're amazing. Can you blame me?"

"Not if you do that again, but slower," Emerson said, pressing her forehead to Talon's.

"Slower, huh? I can do that."

Emerson cupped Talon's cheek. Talon wrapped her arms around Emerson's neck and pulled her in close. She reconnected their lips in their slowest kiss to date. The crashing water behind them disappeared for Talon as Emerson's tongue moved into her mouth and stroked her own. Emerson's hand lowered from Talon's cheek and joined the other one on her back instead, pulling her fully against Emerson's body.

"I hope that's not a goodnight kiss," Talon said when they finally pulled apart.

"It can't be yet. We still have churros," Emerson replied, kissing Talon quickly again.

CHAPTER 24

Emerson sat in the conference room listening only about halfway, which was wrong, but she couldn't exactly help it. Talon was sitting next to Emerson while the VP of Sales presented something to the entire management team. It had been a few days since their first date. Their second one was later that evening, and it was all Emerson could think about. That fountain kiss, sharing churros, and walking back to Emerson's car holding hands had pretty much sealed it for her. She turned to Talon and offered her a shy smile. Talon gave her one back and then returned her attention to the presentation.

After Emerson drove them back to Talon's place, she'd thought Talon would invite her inside. After all, Emerson had gotten her real first date and wanted to stay over, but Talon had insisted on just a goodnight kiss at her front door, and Emerson had left after that. It was a great goodnight kiss, though. The kiss was different than all of their previous ones. The first several were shared the day they hooked up and didn't know what it was they had between them. Those kisses said that they wanted to connect and reconnect as many times as possible, in case this was the only day they got. The one at the fountain said tentative first real kiss. The one at Talon's door meant promise. They'd arranged their second date the following day over text, and Emerson had been waiting for tonight ever since. She just had to get through the entire working day first.

"Emerson, can you hang back?" her boss said.

Talon heard and stopped walking out the door, turning to Emerson with a look of concern on her face. Emerson waved her off, and Talon walked slowly out of the room with all of the other managers. The VP sat down in the chair he'd occupied for the meeting and turned to her once the door was closed.

"I can talk to Brock if I need to, but I wanted to ask about Talon."

Emerson swallowed and said, "Talon?"

"Yeah, Talon. She still hasn't applied for Nick's job. I thought you said she was interested and a shoo-in. I've looked at her most recent numbers, and even with taking on that project with you, they're outstanding."

"Oh, right," Emerson said, laughing for some reason. "The job."

"Is she going to apply? If not, we have to start interviewing the other internal candidates and maybe go external if we don't find anyone here."

"I'll talk to her about it again," Emerson said.

"Okay. Tell her that we can't keep spreading the other seniors too thin, so we want to make a decision quickly."

"I will," Emerson said.

"Talon's great," the VP continued. "I think she'll do a good job in the role."

"Can I ask why she didn't get it the last time then?" Emerson asked.

"Nick's position?" he asked. "You know, it was strange. We interviewed her, and she said she wanted the job, but it just didn't feel like she actually did. Nick came in all guns blazing; he was qualified and seemed like he genuinely wanted the job. We weren't sure with Talon, and your predecessor was the one that made the final call. I only talked to the candidates for about fifteen minutes apiece, but I backed him up. Talon's heart didn't appear to be in it, and that's important in sales, as you know. The only reason I'm asking you about her now is that you said she was really interested when we lost Nick. Maybe she just needed time to get there or see what happens when we bring someone in from the outside, and she has to essentially carry them."

"Yeah. Maybe," Emerson said, feeling like she might

have misspoken about Talon's interest in the role, making an assumption she shouldn't have made.

"Well, talk to her for me. I'm holding it for her application, but we'll start interviews on Monday either way." He stood. "Oh, and we're losing Mike," he added.

"Which one?"

There were five Mikes on the sales team.

"Mike Bryan," he clarified.

"Two-first-names Mike?" she said.

"He's going to a big corporation to work on one system they use there that he's an admin for, I guess," the VP added, running a hand through his already slicked-back hair.

Two-first-names Mike was the director of sales operations. It was the nickname she'd discovered for him in her second week at the company. The other four Mikes also all had nicknames because if they didn't, no one would be able to get anything done around here.

"Honestly – and keep this between you and me – it's okay. He couldn't keep up with everything we needed anyway, so we were planning on hiring someone in over him as a senior director if we had to. His performance isn't bad, so we didn't want to fire the guy, but we needed someone who could keep up with the changes we need made all the time. His last day is in two weeks, and it was all his call, so that made things easier on us, thankfully. I'll make the announcement in the next all-team meeting, so keep it to yourself until then."

"Okay."

"Oh, and don't forget to check with Talon for me." The VP opened the door. "If she wants it, it's probably hers, but if she's not interested, we need to move on."

***

They'd opted for the movie and snacks first, and then they'd go get a drink and maybe some appetizers after that if they were still hungry. The movie was fine. Emerson didn't pay much attention to it. Talon's hand had been in hers for a large portion of it, and Emerson had loved having Talon's head on her shoulder during one of the scary parts. She never would've taken Talon as a scaredy-cat, but it was one of her many layers, Emerson supposed. Emerson liked *all* of her layers so far.

"Hey, can I talk to you about work for a second?" Emerson asked as they left the theater.

"I guess," Talon said.

"I know you said you didn't think you'd apply for Nick's old job… I just want to make sure that's still the case."

"Why?" Talon asked.

"Because our illustrious VP basically told me they haven't started interviewing yet because they're waiting for you to apply."

"*That's* what he wanted to talk to you about today?"

"Thankfully, yes," Emerson said, taking Talon's hand.

"I'm not applying for it. You can let him know, I guess. It's cool that's he's doing that, though."

"And you're sure, Tal? He pretty much said it's yours if you want it. You'd still have to interview, of course, because there are other internal candidates."

"Who?" Talon asked.

"I can't exactly tell you that," Emerson said, smiling at her.

"Oh, right. Insider information," Talon replied. "One of them will be my new boss, I guess."

"We can keep you with Brock," Emerson replied.

"Is that fair to everyone else?"

"He's the top-performing senior manager; you're the top-performing manager. It makes sense."

"But would you do it if you and I weren't dating?"

"If you told me you were happier and more productive working with Brock – probably." Emerson shrugged a shoulder. "But you can also meet the new person and see how you'd work with them before we decide anything."

"Can we talk about something else?"

Emerson stopped walking, forcing Talon to stop as well.

"Too much work?"

"Yeah. It's a date, Emerson," Talon said.

"You're right. I just didn't get a chance to talk to you about it today. I'm sorry," she replied.

"Don't apologize. I just want to grab a drink with the woman I'm on a date with, not with my boss's boss tonight."

Emerson nodded and moved into Talon's space.

"We can also skip the drink and probably bad-fried appetizers and go back to your place. It's closer." Emerson hovered her lips an inch or so away from Talon's. "I assume you have drinks there should we decide we want them."

Talon closed her eyes, and Emerson wrapped a hand around Talon's waist, pulling her in.

"The bar I like is only five minutes from here," Talon said against Emerson's lips. "They have these… amazing… margaritas. There's a strawberry… lime… one that's…" Emerson ran her hand up under Talon's jacket and shirt and rested it on her lower back. "Really… good."

"You know what else is really good?" Emerson asked, moving her lips to Talon's neck and placing kisses on the skin cooled by the night breeze.

"What?" Talon asked.

"Every time I touch you," Emerson replied. "And I want to touch you, Tal."

Talon's hands moved around Emerson's neck and pulled her in. Emerson continued to press kisses to *Talon's* neck but made them open-mouthed and used her tongue. They were situated between two rows of cars in the parking lot and weren't completely cut off from the rest of the world, but the SUV and truck they were between gave them some cover.

"I want my hands all over you, babe," Emerson said,

moving her free hand to Talon's jeans and undoing the button. "Can I?"

"Here?" Talon asked in a high-pitched voice.

"I was thinking about it, yeah." Emerson unzipped the jeans.

"Oh, wow. I've never…"

"We had sex all over our office," Emerson remarked, sucking on Talon's pulse point.

"I liked it. I thought it was better than the book," a voice said.

"Better than the book? Are you crazy? No movie is ever better than the book," another voice said.

Then, they heard the beep-beep of a car being unlocked with a key fob, and Emerson pulled back quickly from Talon as Talon buttoned and zipped her pants back. Emerson laughed as she took Talon's hand, and they rushed to Emerson's car. Once inside, Emerson leaned over and kissed Talon hard. Her hands were in Talon's hair. Her lips were greedy. Talon's seemed just as greedy. Her hands moved to Emerson's waist and tried to pull her as close as she could get her in the small space with a center console between them.

"Okay. We're adults," Talon said, pulling back and breathing hard. "We don't have to make out in cars anymore. We have apartments."

"Let's go to yours, then," Emerson replied.

"Drinks," Talon said. "I want a strawberry lime margarita with extra sugar on the rim, Emerson."

Emerson laughed and said, "Demanding. Is this your version of my churro?"

"For tonight," Talon said.

Emerson drove them to a bar that was clearly more for tourists than locals. It was brightly lit and had gimmicky drinks and souvenir cups they came in. Their appetizers all seemed to be standard fare, and with the size of the margarita Talon ordered, Emerson thought Talon would need to eat something beyond the popcorn they'd shared in the movie. Emerson ordered three appetizers for them to share, and just as they arrived, her phone beeped. She normally wouldn't look, but Talon was busy grabbing a couple of nachos, so she pulled her phone out and saw it was from her mom.

"It's out," she said more to herself than anyone else.

"What's out?" Talon asked.

"The block party invitation," Emerson said, smiling like a little kid.

"Huh?" Talon asked, shoving a nacho smothered in beans, cheese, guacamole, and sour cream into her mouth.

Emerson laughed again and said, "I even think you're hot when you do *that.*" She pointed.

"What? I'm hungry," Talon defended, shrugging a shoulder. "And what party?"

"The old neighborhood's St. Patrick's Day block party announcement. My mom just texted it to me."

"There's an announcement?"

"Yeah, I told you it's a big deal. We all still go, remember?"

"I remember," Talon said, taking a drink of her margarita through her green-and-red-striped paper straw. "That's, like, a month away."

"They start asking people what they're bringing for the potluck to get everything planned. Normally, I chicken out and just buy cookies from the store or bring a few bags of chips."

"How are your appetizers?" the waiter dressed in an orange-and-purple-striped shirt asked.

"They're good," Talon said, eating another nacho.

Emerson smiled adoringly at her and said, "We're good. Thank you."

The waiter nodded.

"Wait. Can you bring her a water, too?" she asked, looking at Talon, who had already had a third of her giant drink.

"Sure thing," he said and walked off.

"You think I can't handle my booze?" Talon asked with a lifted eyebrow.

"I'm sure you can. I just don't want you to be hungover tomorrow," Emerson replied.

They finished their appetizers, which must have soaked up a lot of the alcohol because Talon seemed fine after they left the bar. Emerson drove them back to Talon's place, parked the car, and took Talon's hand as they walked up the stoop and into the building, where they took the elevator to Talon's floor. Emerson moved into Talon when they hit her front door and held her hips.

"So?" she said.

"So," Talon replied, smiling at her.

"I was hoping we could continue what we started in that parking lot," Emerson said, pressing her forehead to Talon's. "And maybe take it a little slower this time."

"I think I'd really like slow with you," Talon said, closing her eyes.

"Should we see?" Emerson pressed a soft kiss to her lips.

"I want to," Talon said.

Emerson pulled back, took in Talon's now open eyes, and said, "But?"

"But I don't know. I feel like we should wait a little."

"Okay." Emerson nodded. "You want to wait?"

"It's silly. I know we've already done it. I just–"

"Tal, you don't have to explain anything. If you want to wait, we wait." She cupped Talon's cheek.

"I don't *want* to; I want you like crazy," Talon stated.

"But you think we *should* wait?" Emerson asked, smiling as she brushed hair out of Talon's face. "God, you're so beautiful. I look at you all the time, and I think that every time, but there are some moments when I just really look at you and think you're the most beautiful woman I've ever seen."

"Trying to make this harder on me than it already is?" Talon asked, laughing.

"No," Emerson replied, kissing Talon's nose. "I just had to say it. Tal, I like what we're doing here. I'm okay with waiting."

"But not forever, right?" Talon checked.

"No, not forever. I know what it's like to be inside you," Emerson whispered. "And I know what you taste like now."

"Jesus," Talon said, her back thumping against her front door.

Emerson moved with her and kissed her. Talon pulled Emerson into her closer and kissed her back slowly. Hands stayed where they were, as if they both knew that if they wandered, it would be too hard to stop them.

"Good night, Talon," Emerson said, giving her one last quick kiss.

"Good night," Talon replied.

CHAPTER 25

"What are you so worried about?" Paisley asked.

Talon moved the phone from one ear to the other as she walked.

"I'm not worried, exactly."

"Talon, you're sabotaging yourself right now. Why are you doing this? You *like* Emerson."

"Of course, I like her. She's amazing. She loves churros. Did I tell you that?" Talon smiled.

"Yes, and I've made a note of that all-important fact for the future," Paisley said sarcastically.

"Hey, I'm happy here. Be happy for me."

"Tal, I *am* happy for you. You started this conversation, though, by telling me you're worried you're fucking this up. I'm telling you to stop overthinking things and not fuck it up."

"She wanted to stay over," Talon said.

"And why didn't you let her?"

"Because I knew I couldn't keep my hands off her."

"And why is that a problem?" Paisley asked. "You said she tried to fuck you in a parking lot."

"It wasn't like *that*," Talon lied.

"So, her shoving her hand down your pants was just to help you tuck your shirt in?" Paisley joked.

"Obviously not," Talon said. "I know the chemistry is there, and I think the compatibility is there, too. We have fun together, and she's great, Pais."

"Talon, I love you, but this isn't that hard. You like

her. She likes you. If you both want to have sex, you have sex. If you want to wait, you tell her, and you wait."

"I *don't* want to wait," Talon said.

"Then, find a parking lot and let her fuck you," Paisley concluded.

"That actually sounds really good," Talon replied.

"I think you're worried that she's Weston – she's not Weston."

"I don't think she's Weston," Talon said.

"Not exactly, but you did worry that you'd go all-in on the sex part of the relationship and wouldn't give her enough of the other parts. But, Talon, it's like Weston said: she was your first. You were young, Tal. Young people do that sometimes."

"I did it again with Chloe."

"Because you had chemistry with both of them. That's all. Look, you had compatibility with Leigh, but not much chemistry, right?" Paisley recalled.

"Yeah, I guess."

"And with Emerson, you might just have both. I think that's actually what's got you so freaked out."

"What do you mean?" Talon asked her.

"You've never been with someone like this before. You want her, and you're also really crazy about her. You can see a future with her, and you also want to get naked with her constantly. If you had your way, you'd probably lock yourselves in Wes's cabin for a month and just fuck each other's brains out."

"That *also* sounds amazing," Talon said.

"But you'd just as easily sit on the couch with her and watch a movie, wouldn't you?" Paisley asked.

"Yeah," Talon said, smiling at the thought.

"Tal, Leigh was the couch-sitting girlfriend, and Chloe was the locked-in-a-cabin tearing-each-other's-clothes-off girlfriend. Emerson is both, and that scares the shit out of you because that makes it real."

"I'm not scared of real," Talon defended.

"I think you might be, but that's okay. We all are. I mean, look at Aria. She can't even decide if she wants *real* or *right now.* Every week, she's changing her mind on what she wants. Then, look at Wes. I think she has real now, Tal. Annie seems like she gets Wes, and Wes seems to get her. It's new, but I feel like it's going to work out somehow."

"Yeah, me too," Talon said.

"I think you just have to stop putting all this pressure on yourself to have her stay over or not. You just let things happen how they happen. That's a relationship. It's not all sex; it's not all couch-movie-watching. It's a mix of both. Sometimes, it's more of one thing and less of another, and then they reverse. If you don't try to force one thing over the other, I think you'll be happier," Paisley told her.

"Hey," Emerson said.

Talon looked up from where she'd been staring at her shoes.

"Oh, hey," she replied and smiled. "Hey, Pais? I have to go." Talon paused and then added, "Thank you."

"Sure. Have fun." Paisley said that last part in a sing-song voice.

"You didn't have to hang up," Emerson said.

"It was Paisley. We were just wrapping up. What are you doing here?"

"I got out of my meeting early, and my next one pushed to tomorrow, so I thought instead of you bringing me coffee back to the office, I'd drive over here and meet you. I guess we arrived around the same time." Emerson took a step toward her. Then, she froze. "And I want to kiss you, but…"

"We're by the office," Talon said. "Kiss me later?"

Emerson lifted an eyebrow and opened the door for Talon to walk through.

"Later when, exactly?" she asked, joining Talon in the line.

"When are you free?"

"Tonight," Emerson said. "I was supposed to have

dinner with my mom, but she canceled."

"Everything okay?" Talon asked.

"Yeah. She just has to work. I thought about calling my sister, but I'd have to go to her place, and the boys and her husband would be there, obviously. I love them all, but they're a lot to handle."

"Don't you want two of your own?" Talon said, teasing a little.

"Yes, of my *own*. My brother-in-law has a lack of manners and is teaching his boys his awful habits. I wouldn't do that with my kids."

"No?" Talon asked. "So, no elbows on the table or something?"

"Oh, I don't care about elbows on the table. I'm not pretentious. They just have these tablets that they're allowed to have at the dinner table, and they play loud games. My sister tries to get them to put them away, but her husband is staring at his cell phone, watching videos, so it's not like she has a leg to stand on. It's a lot, so I avoid that when I can."

"I'm with you. I don't want my kids to be rude like that," Talon said.

Emerson nodded as they arrived at the counter where she ordered for both of them, remembering Talon's coffee choice after all their trips here.

"So, are you free tonight?" Emerson asked.

"I'm pretty much free every night."

"That's not true. You hang out with your friends a lot," Emerson said.

They walked over to the bar to wait for their drinks.

"Yeah, but you come before a hangout session with my friends," Talon said.

"I do, huh?" Emerson asked.

Talon nodded, and Emerson leaned over close.

"I really want to kiss you right now," she whispered. "I'll have to kiss you a few extra times tonight to make up for it."

"You could come over," Talon suggested.

"To pick you up?"

"Or stay," Talon said. "We could watch a movie or something."

Emerson squinted her eyes a little and said, "Yeah?"

"I think I have popcorn. I can pick some up on the way home, just in case. I have wine, but I don't know what kind. It's like one bottle I got as a gift from someone, but I can get something you like."

"I like *you*," Emerson replied, slipping her fingers into Talon's as their hands dangled between them. "I don't need popcorn or wine, Tal. Bread and water is fine if *you're* there."

"I have water, but I'm not sure about the bread," Talon said, thinking about her pantry.

"I have a meeting until six, unfortunately," Emerson said. "Why don't I just pick up something for us to eat and come straight to your place after?" she asked.

"Okay," Talon replied.

"Emerson, hey," Colby, one of the directors on the operations team, said, waving at Emerson.

Emerson dropped Talon's hand and said, "Sorry."

"It's okay," Talon whispered back.

"Oh, hey, Talon," he said, noticing she was standing there, too.

"Hey, Colby."

"I got that ticket," he said to Emerson, dismissing Talon.

"Oh, good," Emerson said.

Talon could tell, though, that Emerson had no clue what Colby was talking about.

"I can email it to you. We can meet there if you want, or I can pick you up."

Talon's eyebrow lifted on its own, and Emerson seemed to be thinking hard, if Talon was reading the woman's expression correctly.

"For me?" Emerson asked.

"Yeah, I thought you said you'd love to go if you could," he replied.

Then, Emerson must have realized what Colby was talking about because she nodded once and then looked a little surprised.

"I just meant in general, not that I actually could," Emerson said. "You got the ticket for me?"

"Ticket for what?" Talon asked, suddenly *very* curious.

"Basketball. Emerson's a fan," Colby replied.

"You *are*, huh?" Talon asked.

"I can't go, Colby, but thank you. Should I pay you for the ticket or something? I feel bad that you got it for me."

"No, it's cool," he said, looking slightly embarrassed. "I've got a buddy that'll go with me."

"Okay. Sorry about the confusion," Emerson said.

"No problem. Maybe some other time," he said.

"Maybe if the whole team is going as a company event," Emerson replied.

"Yeah, the *whole* team," Talon said, wishing she could glare at Colby but keeping her face neutral instead.

Emerson looked over at her and shook her head with a playful smile.

"Sure," he said.

They all headed outside together. When Colby went to walk back to the office, Talon was grateful Emerson had driven, so they had an excuse not to walk back with him. The tiny coffee shop parking lot was in the back of the building. The moment they were inside and had their drinks in the cup holders, Emerson turned to Talon and pulled her in for a kiss.

"I couldn't wait for tonight," Emerson said.

"Colby got you all hot and bothered?" Talon joked.

Emerson kissed her again, slipping her tongue inside Talon's mouth and placing her hand on Talon's thigh, moving it up and in until she was cupping Talon's sex over her jeans.

"No, *you* get me all hot and bothered. If I'm going to

a basketball game with anyone, it's you, okay?"

"Do I really have to go to a basketball game?" Talon asked.

Emerson laughed, slid a finger teasingly up and back down Talon's center, and then removed her hand.

"God, no. He mentioned basketball once, and all I said is that I like to watch it on TV when it gets to the playoffs. He took that as me being a big-time fan. I don't even like the team he supports."

"He took that as a chance to get into your pants. Colby is like that," Talon said.

"Well, he needs a better gaydar, then," Emerson said, putting the car in drive. "And you were really cute in there, acting all jealous."

"I wasn't jealous. I just don't like that guy. He–"

Emerson's hand went to Talon's thigh and flipped over. Talon stared at it for a second and then slid her own hand into it, entwining their fingers. Just a second ago, Emerson had been very close to making Talon come in the front seat of her car in broad daylight. Now, she just wanted to hold Talon's hand. Talon smiled and brought Emerson's hand to her lips, kissing it.

"Babe?"

"Yeah?"

"What do you want for dinner?" Emerson asked.

CHAPTER 26

When Emerson woke up, the sun was right in her eyes. She covered her eyes with her arm and tried to adjust. Where the hell was she?

"Good morning," Talon said from somewhere behind her.

Emerson shifted her arm and allowed one of her eyes to open. Talon wasn't there, but Emerson did recognize Talon's living room.

"We fell asleep."

"Yup," Talon said. "On my couch, when there is a perfectly good bed in my room."

"That explains why I feel like I need a really thorough stretch," Emerson said.

"Oh, don't tempt me. We have to get to work," Talon replied.

"Shit," Emerson said, sitting up. "I need clothes."

"It's early yet. I'm making coffee. I was going to wake you up in a minute anyway. You have time."

Emerson turned to see Talon standing in her kitchen, pouring coffee in a thermos.

"Is that for me?" she asked, smiling as she stood and reached her arms over her head, trying to grab the ceiling.

"It is," Talon replied. "I thought you could use it for the drive home."

"Next time I stay over, I'm bringing a bag," Emerson said, looking down and realizing she'd slept in her jeans and her shirt from work yesterday. "I must look like shit."

"Nope, you look perfect," Talon told her, coming around the counter and kissing Emerson on the lips quickly. "Do you want to shower here?"

"As much as I would love that – and I would, because

you'd be in there with me – I shouldn't." Emerson wrapped her arms around Talon's neck and pulled her into a long hug. "Thank you for my coffee and for last night."

"We didn't do anything," Talon said, chuckling against Emerson's neck.

"Yes, we did. We watched a movie and talked for hours, and then we passed out together," Emerson said.

"You're thanking me for *that*?"

"I'll thank you for other things later, I'm sure, but last night was great, Tal," Emerson said, pulling back to look at her.

"It was," Talon said. "And can I see you tonight, too?"

"You can," Emerson replied. "But now, I have to go home and change."

"Emerson?"

"Yeah?" Emerson asked as she pulled fully out of the embrace.

"Your place tonight?"

"Sure," Emerson said.

"Can I pack a bag?"

Emerson smiled and said, "Definitely."

Then, she grabbed her coffee, found her phone on the floor, and made it to her car with about an hour to spare before her first meeting. She'd never make it, so while she brushed her teeth, she made a change to her calendar on her phone as it charged. With the meeting pushed back by thirty minutes, she felt she had room to breathe. She also had room to think. Talon would probably just come over here after work, which meant Emerson wouldn't have time to get herself fancy for their date. She realized she didn't need to be fancy for Talon, but she wanted to be.

In the shower, she spent a few extra minutes making sure to take care of certain things she hadn't had a chance to before their first time in the office. Then, she chose her work clothes. Today, she'd wear a light-blue blazer over a short-sleeved button-down with little pale-blue patterns on it. Her jeans and tennis shoes completed the somewhat dressy casual look. Then, she hit the road and arrived at the office just in time to see Talon leaving a conference room wearing that damn skirt. Emerson's jaw nearly dropped. Talon saw her looking and smirked. She'd done this on purpose; there was no doubt.

"Hey, Emerson," Brock said.

"What?"

"Nothing. I just said hi," Brock said, looking at her confused.

"Oh, right. Hi," she replied and cleared her throat.

Emerson walked into her office and sat down, trying to keep her attention on the computer she was opening and not the woman driving her crazy from just outside the room. When she heard a knock, she looked up to see Talon standing in the doorway. Talon closed the door behind her, and Emerson was grateful her officemate was working from home yet again.

"Morning," Talon said.

"You said that to me earlier," Emerson replied.

"I did?" Talon asked, sitting down in the chair across from Emerson's desk. "Oh, I guess I did. It was when you woke up on my couch after we fell asleep together."

"Tal…" Emerson looked out at the people milling about. None of them seemed to be paying any attention. "Babe, you know what that skirt does to me."

"I do," Talon replied. "I was hoping you'd take it off me later." Talon uncrossed her legs and spread them just ever so slightly. "Or, keep it on me at first."

"You're really doing this right now?" Emerson said, feeling her muscles clenching and wetness pooling already. "Fuck."

Talon spread her legs just a few inches more and said, "You can look."

"No, I really can't," Emerson said, looking away again.

"No one is paying any attention to us, Emerson."

"Talon, it's glass. And if I put the whole frost thing on now, people will know something is up."

"I didn't say touch, Emerson. I just said look," Talon replied.

Emerson turned to her and met her dark eyes.

"Shit," Emerson said, knowing she was going to be miserable and hard all day now. "You're so fucking hot."

"Look," Talon said and gave Emerson a couple of more inches.

Emerson looked down and licked her lips.

"You're not…"

"No," Talon said.

"Oh, fuck," Emerson replied.

Talon wasn't wearing any underwear, and she looked shiny. She was wet.

"We can't here," Emerson said.

"I know," Talon replied, closing her legs and standing instantly. She walked to the door and pulled it open. "I'll send that to you right now," she said. "Give me a couple of minutes, okay?"

"Yeah, okay," Emerson said just because it seemed right to say.

Then, Talon turned back to her, winked, and left the office.

***

"Hey, I checked with Pais, and she said this was a pretty good wine. Apparently, it's a cheap alternative to something–"

Emerson cut Talon off with a kiss at her front door, pulling her in and slamming the door behind them.

"Oh, we're starting here," Talon said when Emerson's lips pulled away just for a second.

"Yes, we are. And ending here, too," Emerson replied. "You drove me crazy all day."

Talon laughed, set the wine bottle she'd brought on a small table, and dropped her bag to the floor next to them.

"I did? You mean, me wearing this skirt and nothing

under it while we sat a few feet away from each other surrounded by the people we work with, bothered you?"

Emerson slipped her hand under the skirt and cupped Talon hard. Talon gasped.

"You know it did."

"What are you going to do about it?" Talon teased.

"Fuck you hard against this door."

"Yes," Talon said, pressing her head back against it.

"You want that?"

"You, inside me? Yes. God, I'm so ready, Em."

Emerson smirked and pressed her lips to Talon's again, squeezing Talon and hearing her moan. She ran her fingers through Talon's wetness, gathering what she needed.

"You *are* ready," Emerson said, gasping at how good this felt.

"Fuck me."

"Say please, babe."

"Please. God, please."

Emerson grunted and thrust inside.

"Yes!"

Talon relaxed fully into her arms as Emerson wasn't gentle. She needed to show Talon that she wanted her this much, that Talon was hers, that this was what she'd been missing since the first time they'd done it. She slid her hand from Talon's hip up and under Talon's shirt, grasping her breast over her bra, roughly cupping it, and moving the bra cup away until she could cup her breast more fully. Talon managed to get her own shirt off, which told Emerson she wasn't fucking her hard enough yet.

"More, baby?" she asked against Talon's neck.

"Yes," Talon said.

Emerson moved faster as Talon lifted her breast and moved Emerson's mouth to it.

"Tell me."

"Suck," Talon said.

Emerson sucked the hard nipple into her mouth and moved her thumb to Talon's clit.

"God, I'm going to come," Talon said, pressing Emerson's head to her breast. "Don't stop. Fuck. Emerson, I–"

Talon came. Emerson felt her wetness as it slowly rolled down her hand, so she slowed but didn't stop all the way. When Talon moved Emerson's head to her other breast, removing it from the bra and putting Emerson's mouth there instead, Emerson knew they weren't done with this position.

"More," Talon said.

Emerson gave her more. When Talon could no longer stand, Emerson moved them over to her small, round kitchen table, where she sat Talon after swiping away at the pile of junk mail until it was on the floor. She spread Talon's legs and pressed the woman back until she was lying on the table. Talon's eyes were still dark with lust. Emerson licked her lips as she looked at the two swollen breasts and hard nipples that had been removed from Talon's bra, which was now just beneath them, serving no purpose.

"You are the sexiest woman I have ever seen. And now, I'm going to show you how it makes me feel seeing you like this," Emerson said. "Will you play with your breasts for me?"

"Yes," Talon said, cupping them instantly and massaging them.

"Oh, God," Emerson said. "And…"

"Just ask. I'll do it." Talon tweaked a nipple.

"I like it when you tell me," Emerson said.

"What I want?" Talon licked her lips.

"Yes," Emerson whispered as she watched Talon's hands move against her own breasts.

Talon spread her legs farther and said, "Look at how wet you make me."

Emerson looked down. She knew exactly how wet she made Talon. She could still feel it on her fingers.

"So perfect," Emerson said.

"Do you want to taste it?"

"Yes."

"Suck on your fingers," Talon said, smirking.

It wasn't exactly what Emerson had had in mind, but she'd never turn down the chance to taste Talon's desire for her, so she slipped her fingers into her mouth and closed her eyes at the salty sweetness.

"Good?"

"Yes," Emerson said, slowly pulling them out.

"Unbutton and unzip your jeans."

Emerson did.

"Put your hand in your underwear and touch yourself."

Emerson slid her hand inside her jeans and underwear and closed her eyes at how swollen and wet she was.

"God, it won't take long," she said, starting to stroke herself fast and hard.

"Wait," Talon said.

Emerson opened her eyes, confused.

"Eat me out while you're on your knees doing that," Talon said.

"Yeah?" Emerson asked with her finger still applying a little pressure to her clit.

"Yes. I need your mouth on me; it's been too long."

"Yes, it has," Emerson said, kneeling in front of her and burying her head between Talon's legs under that skirt.

CHAPTER 27

Talon looked down as Emerson sucked and licked. She tried to pull up the skirt so she could see more, but Emerson pulled it completely over her head, giving Talon no view at all. Surprisingly, that only made her *feel* more. Talon closed her eyes and let her head fall back onto the table, not caring that the surface was hard. Emerson's hand moved to Talon's left breast, so Talon removed her own hand and let Emerson play. God, the way Emerson played with it was exactly what Talon had always wanted and needed. It had never been this good before.

With Weston, they'd been exploring and tentative at times. With Chloe, Talon had been more of a giver, and that had been okay for a while. With Leigh, it had happened rarely, even in the beginning, and when it had, it wasn't passionate. It just… was.

Now, as Emerson swirled her tongue around Talon's clit and twisted her nipple, Talon's hips bucked. This was *all* passion. This was Emerson taking her, claiming her, and Talon loved it. She also loved that Emerson liked when Talon teased her and told her what to do. Then, there were Emerson's sounds. In her near orgasmic haze, Talon had almost forgotten that she'd told Emerson to touch herself, and she could hear from the sound of it that Emerson was close, too. Talon pulled up her skirt and met Emerson's open green eyes with her own.

"Come," she ordered.

Emerson closed her eyes, and Talon just watched. Emerson continued to suck on her while her right arm moved up and down. Talon couldn't see what she was doing exactly, but she could see how much Emerson seemed to be enjoying it and how much she needed relief. Emerson sucked harder, and Talon's head went back again. Then, Emerson dipped her tongue inside Talon, moving it in and out at the same pace of the sounds Emerson was making as she was coming herself.

"Oh, fuck!"

Talon's orgasm tore through her in a way it hadn't ever done before, and she felt tears in her eyes as she said Emerson's name over and over. Emerson slowed her pace, but she didn't stop until Talon tapped the hand that was now clenching Talon's breast so hard, it hurt, but she didn't mind at all.

"Again," Emerson said, licking Talon's clit softly.

"Oh, my God," Talon said. "No!" She laughed. "Give me a minute."

Emerson smiled at her, licked her lips, and stood. Her hand was still inside her jeans. Talon could tell her fingers were still moving.

"You need me, baby?" she asked, sitting up.

"Yes," Emerson replied.

Talon reached for Emerson's hips and lowered her jeans for her. She watched Emerson's fingers slowly move around her clit inside her soaked underwear.

"What do you want? Tell me, and it's yours," Talon said, lifting Emerson's shirt as she wrapped her legs around Emerson, using them to pull her sex flush against her, feeling those fingers now and what they were doing for herself.

"Bed," Emerson said. "You, on top of me."

"What am I doing once I'm there?" Talon asked softly, pulling at Emerson's hand until it was out of her underwear.

Emerson grunted.

"I'll take care of you," Talon promised as she smirked up at her. "Rub against me right now."

"Fuck," Emerson said, bucking her hips into Talon, who was wrapped around her.

"You're so fucking wet, Em," Talon replied.

"I need you," Emerson said.

"Bed," Talon said, lowering her legs.

Emerson stopped rubbing against Talon's torso, and Talon could tell she missed the contact. Talon stood, dropped the skirt to the floor, and lost her bra somewhere between the table and the bedroom. Emerson's shirt was in the short hallway. Her bra was probably next to it. Her underwear, though, was still on, and Talon settled between Emerson's legs as Emerson lay on her back on the bed. Talon licked Emerson's inner thighs slowly, teasingly as Emerson squirmed. When Talon licked over the underwear, Emerson bucked, needing more.

"Talon, please," she said.

God, that was hot.

Talon licked again, harder this time.

"Oh, God," Emerson said.

Talon wasn't sure she'd ever felt a clit this hard before. She pulled aside the panel of the underwear and looked at her.

"You're so fucking beautiful," she said, meaning all of Emerson, but staring directly at her clit, which clearly needed Talon's mouth.

So, Talon gave it the attention it needed. Emerson bucked several times as Talon made her come before she tore at the underwear, tossing them aside and climbing on top of Emerson. She stared down at Emerson and used the moment to catch her breath. Emerson's arms were around her neck. She was trying to pull Talon down for a kiss, but Talon just wanted to look at her. Those beautiful green eyes weren't *as* dark as they'd been before, but they still told Talon that Emerson wanted more. She rocked her hips down into Emerson, letting their centers meet and their desire for one another join together.

"Slow," Talon said softly as she leaned down and kissed Emerson.

Emerson understood, and their lips connected and reconnected at the same pace of Talon's hips rolling down into her. Talon moved to kiss Emerson's neck just as slowly, tasting a bit of sweat and remembering what had just happened in the other room. Despite that memory turning her on like crazy, Talon didn't hurry. Emerson's hands grazed Talon's back. Talon felt fingertips caress her naked skin and knew she needed nothing else somehow. This was enough. She could just kiss Emerson's skin like this, and Emerson could run her hands up and down Talon's, and Talon would be completely content. Still, she didn't plan on stopping what she was doing, though.

When she reached between them, spreading her lips enough and angling her body as much as she could to connect their sexes more fully now, Emerson gasped. She was still hard, and so was Talon now. Emerson's eyes opened, and when Talon reconnected their mouths, Emerson moaned. Talon rolled a little faster.

"Yes," Emerson said, moving a hand to Talon's ass but not gripping it.

She just kept it there, encouraging Talon to continue but letting her know that this new pace was fine.

Talon kissed Emerson's neck again, sucking on a bit of skin she hoped could be covered with a shirt or sweater, because she was definitely leaving a mark. When Emerson's other hand moved to join her first one, Talon moved a little faster.

"This feels so good," Emerson said. "God, baby."

Talon smiled against Emerson's collarbone. When her breathing sped up, so did Emerson's, and Talon knew they were both close.

"Like this?" she asked in case Emerson wanted her hand or her mouth again.

"Just like this," Emerson whispered.

Talon could tell Emerson started coming first. The woman's head went back. Her hands gripped Talon's ass hard. Talon moved faster, harder, until she felt her own orgasm begin to take her over. Then, her movements became erratic, and she just tried to hold on.

***

"You're really going to eat that last bite and not share it with me?" Emerson asked her as Talon spooned the last bit of ice cream from the container and stared at it.

"I'm thinking about it," she said.

Emerson laughed and said, "I'll have to buy more. You seem to like it."

"I really, really do," Talon replied, dropping the small spoonful into Emerson's belly button.

Emerson hissed at the cold.

"See? I can share," Talon said as she licked the ice cream from her belly button and sucked at the skin around it until she dropped the spoon into the empty container and left it where it was, moving up Emerson's body to kiss her. She slipped her tongue inside Emerson's mouth, letting Emerson suck on it until she let it go. "Better?"

"Much," Emerson said, smiling up at her.

"I am wiped," Talon stated, rolling off her and lying on her back.

"So, no round four or five? Or is it six?"

"Depends. How do you define a round?"

"Orgasms," Emerson replied, shrugging a naked shoulder.

Talon laughed and said, "Then, I lost count."

Emerson held out her arm. Talon smiled and slid under it, resting her head on Emerson's chest. She ran a finger over Emerson's small breast and played with the nipple a little.

"We ate dessert, but no dinner," Emerson said. "Are you hungry?"

"No, I'm okay," Talon replied, watching as the nipple rose due to her touches. "I love your body."

"You do?"

"You can't tell?" Talon laughed.

"I mean, yeah… But… I don't know."

Talon lifted up to look at her.

"I'm serious: I'm obsessed with it. I love how you have curves and muscles. God, the muscles in your back are so sexy. I love your boobs, too. These nipples are my favorite things." Talon touched the other one.

"My nipples are your favorite things about my body?" Emerson laughed.

"No, I love all of it," Talon replied, smiling at her. "I love this spot right here." She touched the spot beneath Emerson's ear. "It's so soft. I love this one." She pointed to Emerson's collarbone. "God, I love kissing that spot. And this one." She touched Emerson's lips. "I really love kissing those."

Emerson laughed again.

"And I love this one, too," Talon said, slipping her fingers into Emerson's folds, feeling the wetness that was still there.

"Oh, shit," Emerson said, hips bucking.

"Still?"

"I didn't think so," Emerson replied. "You just do something to me."

"I love how wet you get." Talon moved her fingers around. "I can get just what I need at any time to do this." She slipped them inside and watched as Emerson closed her eyes. "I love how soft you are and how strong you are at the same time." Talon moved slowly inside her. "Oh, I love this spot." She pushed in deeper.

"Me too," Emerson said.

"And I love that little freckle on the inside of your right thigh." Talon curled her fingers. "And the way your tongue feels against mine."

"Yeah, that's good," Emerson said as her hips lifted again.

"Already?" Talon asked.

"Yes," Emerson said.

"Your eyes, Em," Talon said.

"What?" Emerson opened them, looking concerned.

"They're my favorite part of your body."

Emerson smiled and cupped Talon's cheek.

"They tell me so much," Talon said, looking into them.

"What are they telling you right now?" Emerson managed out.

"That you like that I said they're my favorite part." Talon curled again. "And that you want to come."

Emerson laughed, but only for a second. Then, she closed those eyes again. Talon watched as Emerson came. Then, she left her fingers inside and lay back against her. When she came to her senses again, her hand was on Emerson's bare stomach, and the alarm was going off. It wasn't hers, though. It was Emerson's.

"Sorry. One sec," Emerson said groggily. "But I need my arm."

Talon rolled onto her side, away from Emerson. The sound stopped. Emerson rolled over into Talon, pressing her front to Talon's back.

"Morning," Emerson said, kissing Talon's bare shoulder.

"Morning," Talon replied, still with her eyes closed.

"I put the snooze on. We have ten minutes to sleep," Emerson explained, tucking her arm into Talon's body and pulling her back against her.

Talon didn't say anything. She just felt Emerson's body against hers, Emerson's warm breath on her neck, and Emerson's leg that had somehow wriggled its way between Talon's and just rested there as if Emerson needed more parts of them to touch. Talon smiled as she thought about how nice this felt. It was scary – Paisley had been right about that – but it was also just so nice.

CHAPTER 28

"So?" Emerson said. "Tonight? Your place?"

"If you want," Talon replied, taking a bite of her chicken sandwich.

"Do *you* want?" Emerson asked.

"Yes." Talon smiled at her through her chewing. "You know I do."

"We've just spent the past two nights at my place. I thought you might want to be at yours."

"My apartment has my stuff, but I don't really care about it like that," Talon replied, eating a fry.

"But your place has the much larger shower," Emerson pointed out.

Talon smiled and said, "Yes, it does."

"And I'd like to shower in it with you tomorrow morning," Emerson said.

"I won't argue with that," Talon replied, looking around the restaurant.

"What's going on?"

"Nothing. Why?"

"You've looked around this place three times since we got here," Emerson said.

"We're in a restaurant where half the office comes to lunch," Talon replied. "I'm just being cautious."

"We can have lunch together, Tal. We've done it a million times by now," Emerson said.

"I know that, but I also don't want people to talk," Talon replied.

"I was going to ask you about that, actually," Emerson said.

"About people talking about us?" Talon asked, taking a drink of her peach iced tea.

"No, about us," Emerson said, leaning forward in her chair and stealing one of Talon's fries.

Talon's expression changed, and Emerson realized what she'd said.

"Oh, no. Nothing like that, babe. Nothing bad," Emerson said quickly.

"Okay. But you know you can't say that without making a girl wonder, right?"

"Yes," Emerson said. "Sorry," she added and stole another fry.

"Well, out with it before *I* run out of fries for you to steal and delay whatever it is you're trying to say," Talon told her.

"The thing we signed for HR," Emerson started.

"The paper?"

"Yes, the agreement that says we're in a consensual relationship," Emerson said.

"What about it?"

"I was wondering how you'd feel about printing a new one and signing it, since the other one is kind of wrinkled from being in your backpack along with our bras and underwear." Emerson smirked. "And I was thinking, we could do that, and then maybe give it to HR."

Talon's expression changed again, but this time, Emerson couldn't read it.

"You want to tell them about us?"

"Just HR. That way, if people *do* start talking, we're kind of ahead of it."

"You were worried before about only having a piece of paper, though," Talon said.

"That was back then," Emerson replied. "We've been doing this for a while now," she added. "At first, I don't know if either of us could tell if this would just be sex or more. But it's obviously more, and I think that means we should tell them."

"What do you think they'll do?" Talon asked.

"I don't know. I've been reading up on situations like ours, though."

"You've been reading up?" Talon asked, smiling wide.

"Yes. *You* slept in this morning; *I* did research."

"You kept me up past one in the morning watching a four-hour movie." Talon laughed.

"It was three hours. We made out for an hour before that," Emerson remarked.

"I remember," Talon said, winking at her.

"Tal, the letter… What are you thinking?"

"It's a big deal, Em."

"I know. That's why we're talking about it."

"I guess I just didn't think you'd want to tell people there this quickly."

"Is that a bad thing?" Emerson asked, worried she'd jumped the gun now.

"No, it's not. You just weren't thrilled by only having a piece of paper for protection. It's you I'm worried about, not me."

"Well, I discovered that typically, when you turn the letter in, HR interviews both parties separately just to make sure it's consensual – mainly, to make sure they can't get sued." Emerson shrugged a shoulder.

"I'm going to get interviewed about us? What would they even ask?" Talon asked her.

"When did we start dating? How long has it been going on? Is this something I coerced you into?"

"I have to tell them when we started?"

"*When*, Talon, but not how. No one needs to know the *how*, babe."

"Well, that's going to be a problem because all of my friends know," Talon stated, eating a fry and picking another up to pass to Emerson. "Here; I at least owe you this."

"You told *all* of your friends how it started with us?" Emerson asked.

"Yeah. Not every single detail, but they do know that you are the sexiest woman in the world, that you've made me come a record number of times, and that we did it all over the office."

Emerson laughed and said, "Talon!"

"We all kind of tell each other everything. Plus, I wanted to brag about you," Talon replied.

"I like that," Emerson said, eating the fry Talon had given her. "So, what do you think?"

"If we tell them we're in a relationship, that means we're *in* a relationship, right?"

"That's the idea," Emerson said.

"No, Em. I mean… You and I haven't talked about that yet. We're dating, but this would mean we're in a relationship, and we haven't had the whole exclusivity conversation yet."

"Should we?"

"I'm asking *you*," Talon said. "Can we just be dating and tell HR? Is that weird?"

"I think it's up to us what we want, Talon." Emerson paused and watched Talon, who looked a little nervous now. "Babe, are you okay?"

"This makes it real," Talon said, leaning back in her chair.

"It's not real now?" Emerson asked, worried.

"No, it is." Talon sighed. "I'm not saying this right."

"I shouldn't have brought this up yet. It's too soon."

"No, that's not what I'm saying," Talon replied.

"It's not exactly private here, either. I should've asked you tonight instead, when we're alone."

"Em, it's okay. I'm not–"

"Hey, guys," Brittany said as she walked over to their table with three other people from the office. "We needed to get out of there, too." She smiled at Emerson and then Talon.

"Hey, Brit," Talon replied.

"This is Evan, and this is Jess," Brittany introduced. "They're two of our newest hires. And you know Colby, obviously."

"Welcome to the company," Emerson said, smiling at the two new guys. "Hey, Colby."

"Hey, Emerson. End of month crunch, and you're out at lunch?"

"Did you mean to rhyme that?" Talon asked him.

"Oh, no," he said, laughing. "I just meant that it's the last day of the month. Shouldn't you both be on calls with prospects or approving deals or something?"

"We're okay," Talon told him. "But thanks for your concern."

"Talon just means that we checked things before we left, and we'll get back to it when we return," Emerson said, giving Talon a glare.

Colby shrugged.

"Well, it looks like you two are about done, so we'll leave you alone," Brittany said. "Just wanted to say hi."

"See you back at the office," Emerson said.

Colby looked at Emerson again before he joined the other three. Emerson waited until they were a safe distance away before returning her attention to Talon.

"You have got to drop it with that guy," she told Talon, smiling playfully at her.

"I told you, I don't like him. What I hate even more is that people know he tries to date women in the office all the time, and no one says anything. You and I have to write a letter."

"My guess is that he's not looking for a relationship with any of them," Emerson commented.

"And that makes it better?" Talon asked.

"No, but, Tal, I'm not trying to get in your pants. I want to be *with* you."

"I know. I want that, too," Talon said.

"So, do we tell HR or not?"

"I'm scared, Emerson," Talon replied.

"Why?"

"Because what if you *do* get in trouble? I've watched guys like Colby act like Colby my whole career. I'm sure you have, too. He's still pissed you didn't go to that game with him and he didn't get to take you to his undoubtedly disgusting apartment with posters on the bedroom walls and one candle that smells like vanilla or lavender or something that he lights whenever he has a girl over to help set the mood. *He* doesn't get in trouble, but you're a woman. And as much as I wish things were different, they just aren't. On top of that, *I'm* a woman."

"Wait. You're a woman?"

"Jokes? You've got jokes now?" Talon shook her head, but her expression told Emerson that they were okay. "If you lost your job, or if they gave you a hard time or overlooked you for a promotion you deserve, I won't be able to live with that, Em."

"I love that you're worried about me, but I'll be okay. I just…" Emerson took a deep breath. "Tal, I think if they know, things will be easier. We won't have to worry as much. I mean, this morning when we were in the kitchen, you called me *babe*."

"You were about to hand me Hot Cheetos, Emerson. You know those give me Nick-flashbacks."

Emerson laughed and said, "You know what I like about us?"

"Sex?"

"That too, but I like that we can have a serious conversation about something that matters, but that you still find a way to make me laugh without taking away from the seriousness of it."

"I do that?" Talon asked, biting into her second to last fry.

"Yes. And you also share your fries with me." Emerson winked.

"You're not getting this last one. I told you to order your own," Talon stated.

Emerson smiled and said, "Tal, it's okay if you're scared, but I just want you to know that I'm ready for it if you are."

"Can I think about it?" Talon asked. "It doesn't mean I'm not all-in with you, Emerson. Letting HR know about us and us being together are two different things."

"So, are we together?" Emerson asked.

"Yeah, we're together."

Emerson smiled, reached over, and stole Talon's last fry.

"Oh, you'll pay for that later," Talon said, laughing.

"I hope so," Emerson replied.

Later that night, as Talon slept, Emerson pulled out her phone and typed. She'd copied the template she found online and inserted their names and some of the pertinent information that HR would need. She wouldn't send it without telling Talon, but she wanted to have it ready for when Talon said it was okay. Then, she put her phone away and looked over at the woman sleeping on her stomach, with her face turned toward Emerson. Emerson smiled softly as she pushed the hair out of Talon's face. Her bare back and just the rise of her ass was visible, with the sheet covering everything else. They'd made love that night and Talon had fallen asleep shortly after. Emerson didn't want to wake her, even though just looking at Talon this way made Emerson want her again. So, she just slipped down beneath the sheet herself, pulled it over Talon more fully, and watched Talon sleep. Before Emerson could fall asleep herself, though, Talon stirred and moved into Emerson.

"I'm cold," she said, half-asleep.

"Come here, love," Emerson said.

Talon rolled onto her side, and Emerson pulled the blanket up over both of them and wrapped her body around Talon's. Talon must not have heard or registered the new term of endearment that had slipped from Emerson's lips, but Emerson sure had, and she knew what it meant. She kissed Talon's bare shoulder.

"Better?"

"Yes," Talon said. "Thank you."

CHAPTER 29

"Invite her," Emerson's sister said.

"Talon?"

"No, Mom," she replied sarcastically and rolled her eyes.

"You are really annoying, you know that? You're married with two children. How are you this immature sometimes?"

"Who's immature?" Emerson's brother asked, taking the box of popcorn from Emerson's lap as he joined them in the theater.

"Hey," Emerson said. "Get your own."

"Can you loan me twenty bucks?" he asked, taking a handful of popcorn and shoving it into his mouth.

"I know movie theaters are expensive, but there's no way a box of popcorn costs twenty bucks," Emerson said.

"No, but I'd need a drink, too. Actually, can you give me, like, forty? I'll get the jumbo box for Matt and me to share and two drinks. Plus, I want some Junior Mints," he said.

"You can just share my popcorn," Emerson said, shaking her head at her youngest brother. "Where *is* Matt?"

"Late, as usual," her sister said, staring down at her phone. "Sometimes, I hate that I'm straight," she said and turned to Emerson. "I bet Talon doesn't pull half the shit my husband pulls because *she's* a woman."

"I don't know that it's a woman thing," Emerson said.

Matt practically skipped up the wide theater stairs and joined them in their row.

"Hey. Sorry, I'm late. I was flirting with the girl at the ticket counter," he said, sitting down next to his brother.

"Matt, Emerson isn't giving us cash, but she's sharing her popcorn," Colton said and handed Matt the popcorn.

"What about drinks?" Matt asked.

Emerson didn't even bother. She picked up the bottle of water she'd bought for herself and held it up for Matt to see.

"Water?" he asked.

"The previews are starting," Fiona said. "Hey, you guys think Emerson should bring Talon to the block party, right?"

"The girlfriend?" Matt asked.

"Yes, the girlfriend," Emerson replied.

"Yeah, totally," Colt said. "I want to meet her. You hardly ever bring anyone home."

"There's a reason for that. You'd probably ask them for money and steal their food, too," Emerson teased and then added, "The whole family will be there, and we just got together."

"You're worried we might embarrass you?" Matt asked in a half-whisper when the lights dimmed.

"Is she, like, rich or something? You're worried we're too wrong-side-of-the-tracks?" Colt asked.

"No, she grew up nearby, actually," Emerson whispered as the first preview played. "Can we not talk about this and just enjoy the movie?"

"Fiona picked it out. I'm sure it's going to be lame," Colt said.

"I'll smack you," their sister said.

Emerson laughed silently. As much as she loved her family – and she did love them – sometimes, nights like this, where they all made the attempt to hang out and have some fun together, were draining on more than just her bank account. When the movie ended, Fiona again suggested she bring Talon to the St. Patrick's Day block party.

"Mom loves that thing. She goes all out. You should really think about it."

"It's just a neighborhood party. It's not a big deal."

"Then, why do you still come every year? Think about it. None of us still live there, but we go to catch up with everyone who still does, and other people return, too. We all drink green beer, and you and I pretend we're Irish while the boys actually are. Plus, I married an Irish guy and have two Irish sons. I want them to experience this and have fun with the family."

"Your husband will spend the whole party on his phone," Emerson said.

"And I'd like to meet your *girlfriend*, so I can find something she does that annoys me. That way, I can constantly point it out to you."

"I'll think about it," Emerson said, laughing. Then, she pulled her sister in for a hug. "Love you. Tell the boys I love them."

"I will. Matt and Colt, if you want a ride, your asses better be in my car in less than five seconds," Fiona yelled to the boys that were looking at something on Matt's phone and laughing.

"Your car has the baby seats in it," Colt said.

"I drove," Matt reminded them.

"I forgot you have a car now. Does it actually run?" Fiona teased.

"It runs less than your mouth does," Matt teased back.

Emerson walked to where she'd parked her own car, and just as she unlocked it, she felt her phone buzz in her pocket. She pulled it out when she got into the car to see a text from Talon.

<u>Talon Mitchell:</u> If your family drives you crazy enough that you want someone to talk to and maybe do other things with tonight, you can come to my place.

Emerson smiled and texted back. Minutes later, she was at Talon's door, holding a carton of ice cream.

"Hi," she said.

"You came prepared," Talon replied.

"I did, actually," Emerson said, looking down at her jeans.

Talon's eyes followed hers, looking confused.

"Do you remember that thing we talked about?" Emerson asked.

"You're wearing it?"

"I stopped by my place and picked up a few things." Emerson dropped the bag she'd packed on the floor next to her. "I hope you were talking about sex when you said *other things*."

"I was mostly just teasing you, but now, I am definitely talking and thinking about sex," Talon said, taking the ice cream in one hand and closing the door behind Emerson with the other. "I can't believe you drove over here wearing it."

"I had this plan," Emerson said.

"Tell me," Talon replied.

Emerson took the ice cream back and dropped it onto the counter. She put her hands on Talon's hips and moved her back against the wall by the door. Talon was wearing sleep shorts and a tank top that left little to the imagination.

"I'd rather *show* you," Emerson said.

She pulled Talon's shorts and underwear down to her ankles, and once Talon had them kicked off, Emerson unbuttoned and unzipped her jeans, lowering them just enough to pull out the toy she'd strapped on when she'd gotten home. Talon removed her own shirt, and Emerson saw her naked girlfriend standing there against the wall, ready for her.

"Yeah?" Emerson said. "Do you need…"

"I'm ready," Talon said. "I was going to get myself off if you couldn't come over; I'm ready."

Emerson moved into her, holding the toy as she slid it through Talon's folds.

"You were going to touch yourself?"

"Yes," Talon said. "Thinking about you."

"We had sex this morning," Emerson said.

"It's not enough."

Emerson pushed inside her.

"God, it's never enough," Talon said.

"I feel the same way," Emerson replied, moving her hips into Talon.

"Oh, this is… so much… better… than…"

"Your own hand," Emerson added for her, pressing both palms to the wall on either side of Talon's head and rocking her hips.

"Yes," Talon replied, pulling Emerson's mouth to hers.

"Does it have a…" Talon paused and reached a hand down between them and then into the harness in search of something.

She found it. Emerson heard the click. Then, she felt the vibration against her clit.

"Oh, fuck," she said, her hips bucking a little faster now.

"Yeah, just like that," Talon said, lifting a leg off the ground.

Emerson reached for it under Talon's thigh and held it up for her as she pushed deeper.

"I know you were worried before," Emerson said as her clit pressed against the bullet vibrator inside the dildo and nearly took her over the edge far too soon. "About wanting too much of this…" Breathing was clearly hard for Emerson right now. "And I think I scared you when I said I wanted a date."

"It's okay. Em, just fuck me right now."

Talon's eyes were closed. Her cheeks were flushed and sexy.

"I want this all the time," Emerson said. "You don't have to worry about…" She paused as she nearly went over again.

"Em, focus," Talon said, holding Emerson's cheeks in her hands. "Fuck me."

Emerson did as she was told and thrust hard. Talon moaned.

"Yes," she said. "That. Again."

Emerson gave it to her again and again until Talon's hands were on her ass, gripping it, begging for more. And she gave her more. Emerson came before Talon did, but her more erratic movements managed to take Talon over the edge right after.

"God, I needed that," Talon said, kissing Emerson's lips. "You are really, really good at this."

Emerson smiled at her and said, "So are you." She lowered her mouth to take Talon's nipple into it and started sucking.

"If you do that, I'm going to need another, and I don't think I can keep standing up."

"Bed?" Emerson asked.

"I'll bring the ice cream," Talon said.

Hours later, they were sated and lying in bed, with the TV playing in the background. Talon had her tank top on and a pair of underwear, which was disappointing, but Emerson had put on clothes, too, so it was fair, she guessed.

"Hey, I know a few days ago we talked about the whole letter thing… And I'm not asking for your decision or anything," Emerson began as Talon turned to her. "It's just that the block party is coming up."

"That St. Patrick's Day thing?" Talon asked.

"Yeah. It's a silly party, but it's a big deal for my family. Truthfully, it's the only time we really were much of a whole family."

"What do you mean?" Talon asked.

"I told you, the boys' father made a big thing about it. He and my mom were together for about six years. So, that was six years of parties where we were all together. The boys had their father, and my sister and I kind of had a stepdad. Her dad and mine were both out of the picture, and my mom's boyfriend wasn't the best dad in the world – I mean, he left, too – but for those years, it was like my mom had a guy she loved, the boys had their dad, and Fiona and I had somewhat of a father figure. After he left, my mom always made a big deal out of it, I think, to make it seem like everything was okay. We all still go because it reminds us of that time."

Talon nodded and said, "So, your whole family will be

there?"

"Yeah," Emerson said.

"You think we're already at meet-the-family stage?"

"It's not like that. It's not some big formal thing, Tal."

"No, but it *is* meeting your mom and your siblings."

"I'm going to meet your friends soon, right?"

"Not exactly the same thing," Talon said.

"You said they were your family."

"Yes, but I *do* have parents and a little brother."

"So, you don't want to go to the party?" Emerson asked.

"Em, we still haven't figured out this whole work thing."

"I have," Emerson replied, shrugging a shoulder.

"The letter?"

"Yeah, the letter."

"And it's that easy? Really? You were so worried about it before."

"I know, but it's different now. We know what this is; what it *can* be. I don't know how easy it's going to be, but I think it'll save us from rumors and people thinking you're sleeping your way to the top or that I'm sexually harassing you, Tal."

Talon looked away for a long moment and said, "I've always been a private person at work. I've never brought a significant other to a work event or party. It's work. I have a personal life and a work life."

"And then I came along?"

Talon turned back to her finally and said, "And I am so happy about that, Em. I never thought I'd get to hold your damn hand, let alone have anything real with you."

"But?"

"But it's an adjustment for me, okay? I had a girlfriend for a year before we did the family thing."

"I'm not Leigh, Talon," Emerson said softly.

"Of course, you're not. You're worse because you're better." Talon turned fully to Emerson and took her hand.

"What does that mean?"

"It means that I feel more for you than I ever did for Leigh or any other woman I've ever dated. I get scared because it feels too good to be true sometimes, and I pinch myself a few times a day when I think that *you're* my girlfriend."

"Babe…"

"It's not that I don't want those things with you," Talon said. "It's just that sometimes, I need a moment to catch up," she added.

"Okay," Emerson said. "I won't ask you to move in with me like I planned tonight, then."

Talon's eyes went wide.

"Babe, I'm kidding." Emerson cupped Talon's cheek. "It's okay. I've never wanted to move this fast with anyone, so maybe I'm going *too* fast."

"I don't know about the party thing yet," Talon said.

"Okay. That's fine. It's a block party; there's no RSVP for a plus one or anything, so you can decide whenever. If you don't go – you don't go, and you can meet them sometime in the very far-off future."

Talon tilted her head.

"What? I'm trying to go slower here," Emerson said.

Talon climbed into her lap and looked down at her.

"You're very patient and tolerant of my little eccentricities."

"I *like* your little eccentricities. They go very well with mine," Emerson said, wrapping her arms around Talon's back. "Why don't I sit back against the pillows, and you sit between my legs? We can find some reality show on TV to make fun of together."

Talon leaned down, kissed her slowly, and said, "Don't doubt how I feel about you, okay?"

Emerson took a deep breath and nodded. She'd needed to hear that and hadn't even realized it until Talon had said it.

CHAPTER 30

As Talon sat at her desk, she thought about the cup of coffee in front of her, which she'd made in her own mug, of course. Emerson had a coffee cup at Talon's place now. They hadn't bought one specifically for her or anything, but she'd used the same one a few times now, so Talon thought of it as Emerson's. It didn't belong to a set. Talon had a standard four-piece set of small black coffee cups that came with the dishes she had bought years ago, but those cups were so tiny, she had been picking up extra-large cups whenever she saw one she liked. She'd accrued quite the eclectic collection over the years. Emerson had chosen one that was blue and had a cartoon elephant on it. Talon smiled as she thought about Emerson telling her how cute the little guy was as she'd held it up in front of her face. Emerson also had a mug at work that she stored next to Talon's in the cabinet no one else used. It might seem strange to some people, but that was big for Talon to share that space.

Talon wasn't sure Leigh had ever had a cup preference. She'd only left a toothbrush over at Talon's place. Emerson already had a toothbrush, her shampoo, and had left a few t-shirts and pants to sleep in. It was scary. Talon hadn't ever gotten to this place with a woman. She supposed she knew that she and Leigh were destined to end. It had taken Leigh actually doing it at the worst possible time for it to happen. But then, just a few short months later, Talon was thinking about her girlfriend's stuff at her apartment, and she was smiling. She looked up when she heard Emerson's voice. It looked like she was leaving an office with nothing in her hand, which likely meant she was on her way to the bathroom. Talon stood a minute later and walked slowly so no one thought she was just following Emerson. She opened the bathroom door and found Emerson standing at the sink, already washing her hands.

"Hey," Emerson said with a smile.

"Hey," Talon replied, smiling back.

Talon nodded toward the three stalls.

"No," Emerson said, indicating that they were empty.

"I missed you this morning," Talon said.

"I had an early meeting and didn't want to wake you," Emerson replied, drying her hands.

"I know. I still missed you," Talon said, walking closer and running a hand through Emerson's short hair.

"Tal…" Emerson said, looking at the closed door behind Talon.

"No one's in here," Talon said, shrugging a shoulder. "Your hair is growing out a little." She pulled a bit at the short brown locks.

"I've been meaning to cut it. It's doing that awkward in-between lengths thing."

"I like it like this," Talon said. "It's just enough for me to hold on to."

"Babe," Emerson said, laughing. "Wait. Do you want me to grow my hair back out how I had it?"

"No, this suits you. The full-on pixie did, too, but I like this length a little better."

"Because you can hold on to it?"

"And run my hands through it," Talon said.

"What's gotten into you?" Emerson asked, placing a tentative hand on Talon's hip.

"Nothing. I just like ya," Talon said, dropping her hand.

"I like you, too," Emerson replied. "But we should go."

"I know," Talon replied. "But you left without kissing me good morning."

"Oh, I *kissed* you good morning; you just slept through it," Emerson argued. "You scrunched your nose a little, though. It was really cute." Emerson smiled.

"Can you come over tonight?" Talon asked.

"Dinner with that prospect," Emerson replied. "I can come over after, but it'll be late. You know how these things go. It's drinks first, then they order a bunch of appetizers for the table, order more drinks, and suddenly, it's three hours later."

"If you want to, you can still come over. I'll be up."

"Oh, you will, huh?" Emerson teased. "I don't know if I'll have enough energy for that tonight, Tal. These guys are fucking exhausting."

"Just to sleep, Em. Come over just to sleep."

Emerson smiled softly. The door opened, and she dropped the hand on Talon's hip and picked up the paper towels she needed to discard.

"And I'm hoping we can close them tonight," Emerson said.

"That would be good. They're a big get," Talon replied, having no idea who Emerson was meeting that night.

Talon worked for the next couple of hours, trying to actually focus on work when all she could think about was those coffee mugs. Then, she had a meeting with a member of her team.

"I'm thinking about applying," the guy said. "I know I'm not a manager here, but I was a manager *before* I came here."

"So, you want to apply for senior and skip over manager entirely?" Talon asked.

"Yeah. I was a manager for two years before I came here. There just weren't any management positions open when I was ready to leave my last place. Is it awkward? I'd be above you if I got it, but I'm supposed to tell my manager when I apply. You have to approve it or something."

"No, it's fine. I just have to add my recommendation in the system," Talon said.

"Cool. I'll apply right now. I have my resume updated already, and today's the deadline."

"Sure," Talon said.

She couldn't tell him no. He was technically qualified, and she didn't want the job anyway, so she'd be happy if it went to someone internally. When she got back to her desk a few minutes later, she already had a notification from the system to approve his application and add her comments. Pulling it up, Talon saw all of the open roles at the company. A new one that must have just popped up caught her eye; director of sales operations. She'd heard rumors that the director was leaving, but she'd missed the all-team meeting because she'd had a dentist appointment. Had they announced he was leaving then?

Talon opened the job description and read through it. It was a stretch since she'd never been a senior manager or worked in sales ops, technically, but she had the years of experience and the systems' knowledge. She returned to approve the application and add her comments for the guy who wanted Nick's job, but as she had lunch in the kitchen, she couldn't get her mind off of the open job.

***

"Thanks for coming over. I just wasn't feeling up to going out," Talon said as she took a bite of her taco.

"I get it; Emerson has plans tonight, so you needed someone to keep you company," Aria replied, teasing her.

"No, I actually wanted to see you. I'm not always with Emerson."

"Close to it, but that's a good thing. I'm just messing with you," Aria said, taking a bite of her own taco. "How's it going?"

"Good." Talon drank her beer.

"Wow! Profound, Tal," Aria said, laughing.

"What? Weston is the writer. It's good." She shrugged a shoulder.

"Yeah?"

"Yeah, she's great. She has a coffee cup here now."

"She brought a coffee cup?" Aria asked.

"No, she just has the one that she uses when she's here. It's basically hers now," Talon explained.

Aria gave her a sideways smile and said, "That's good."

"And she has some other stuff here, too."

"That's not bothering you? I remember with Leigh, you were shocked when she asked you if she could put her toothbrush in your toothbrush holder."

"I was not shocked." Talon laughed. "We'd just been fighting, and out of nowhere, she's asking if she could leave some stuff here. I thought we were about to break up; she thought it was time to leave crap here."

"Is it different with Emerson?"

"Yes," Talon said, smiling. "Which means, I'm more than terrified."

"But you let her leave stuff here," Aria noted.

"I'm taking baby steps," Talon replied, finishing her taco. "Aria, she wants me to sign a letter telling HR about us."

"So?"

"So, that makes it all official."

"It's already official."

"Not to the company."

"Wouldn't you want them to know? That protects both of you, right?"

"Yes, as far as we know. But once people find out, they might think wrong things about us."

"Who gives a shit?" Aria asked, finishing her taco. "I know I don't work in an office, but, Talon, she's your girlfriend. You're obviously crazy about her. Who cares what anyone there thinks or says?"

"It's not just about the letter. She wants me to meet her family, too," Talon said.

"The family? Already?"

"Yeah. There's this party for St. Patrick's Day that they take really seriously, and I get it; she explained it to me. I'd like to go, but she has a sister who's married with two kids and two younger brothers. Plus, her mom will be there, and she's a single mom… You know how *mama bear* single mothers are."

"You think she's not going to like you?" Aria asked.

"I don't know. She and Emerson are really close. If she doesn't like me, that could change Emerson's feelings for me."

"Well, if it does, Emerson's nuts because you're awesome. And she clearly likes you enough to basically risk her career."

Talon finished her beer just as she got a text message.

"Speak of the sexy," Talon said, looking down at her phone. "She's miserable at her work dinner."

"Sext her," Aria suggested.

"What? She's at a work dinner," Talon said, laughing.

"Talon, you two literally fucked for hours in the office. I think you've blurred the lines already."

Talon typed a message, feeling her cheeks flush as she hit send.

"What did you say?"

"I'm not telling *you*," Talon replied, laughing.

Her phone beeped.

Emerson Bagley: You cannot send me stuff like that when I'm with these people.

"Shit. I think she's pissed," Talon said.

Then, another beep came in.

Emerson Bagley: But fuck, Tal. Now, I won't be able to sleep tonight without having my mouth on you.

"Nope. She's all good," Talon said. "And I'm getting laid tonight."

"You're welcome," Aria said, shrugging a shoulder.

"Hey, I'm thinking about doing something at work."

"Is it sex with your girlfriend?"

"No, it's not about Emerson at all," Talon said. "It's about me."

"Okay."

"There's this team on sales called sales operations.

Basically, they're in charge of processes and systems for the sales team. I found out today that the director of that team is leaving."

"And?" Aria wanted to get to the point.

"And that's the stuff I really enjoy doing," Talon said. "I've been helping that team for years now."

"You want the job?"

"I think I do, yeah. I haven't really been thinking about it because Nick left, and everyone just thought I'd apply for his job and get it. Plus, no one leaves on the sales ops team – it's like the best job on a sales team. They don't have quotas; it's not commissioned-based. They just work on projects and requests."

"Well, go for it, Tal."

"It's director level. I'm sure they'll go external for it after the required number of days they have to have it open internally."

"Talon, you've been there for years. You're amazing at your job. If you want this, you should apply for it," Aria told her.

"I'd have to get my resume updated," Talon said.

"Do it now. I'm done eating; I can get out of your hair. As much as I'd like to really meet Emerson when she comes by later, I have a feeling you two will just be making sex eyes at each other, so I'll leave you to it and wish you luck."

"With the job or the sex?"

"Both, obviously," Aria said, standing. "But, Talon, stop selling yourself short. And if you see a future with Emerson, just sign the damn letter already; make sure the girl knows how committed you are. She's got a coffee cup here. Do you have one at her place?"

"No," Talon replied.

"Then, get one. Hell, get a favorite bowl, too. Buy extra shampoo and a toothbrush; leave it over there. Even if you're not ready to meet her family, you're ready for that stuff, and you know it. I think you need to take the next baby step."

CHAPTER 31

Emerson had spent another night at Talon's place. After that awful dinner that went on for hours upon hours, she'd gone to Talon's apartment, and they'd made love before falling asleep. The previous night, Talon had worked later than usual but told Emerson to just go to her place and gave Emerson her key to get in. Emerson had taken a long shower and used Talon's shampoo, even though she had hers right there next to it. She worried a bit that maybe having some of her things over here would be a problem given that Talon had requested patience. She considered taking back some of the clothes she'd left in a drawer and making sure she didn't have anything in Talon's laundry basket to get cleaned. She took a look around Talon's bathroom, and she hadn't left anything except for a new hairbrush she'd bought for this place and her toothbrush.

She would bring everything else with her in a bag and always make sure she left Talon's place the way she found it. Emerson wanted Talon to get where she was, which meant she'd need that patience. She understood, given Talon's experiences, that this relationship was new to her. As Emerson slid the harness over her hips and tightened it around her waist, she thought about how she couldn't wait for Talon to get home. The toy was in place, and Emerson put on a pair of her sweats, wanting to surprise Talon when she arrived. She didn't bother with a bra, put on a t-shirt, and made her way to the kitchen. There, she opened a bottle of wine they'd picked up at a store a few days ago to let it breathe and pulled out a couple of regular glasses since Talon didn't have any wine glasses. Emerson made a note to buy some for her later.

Then, she went into the living room, moving the pillows on the sofa off to the side because she planned to make use of the space in the middle in just a few minutes. When she turned to the coffee table to see if she'd left any of her stuff there, she noticed a stack of papers and some junk mail. Emerson straightened it up and left it in the corner but saw something that stuck out to her. She knew she shouldn't snoop, but it was right there, looking back at her. Talon's resume was on the table. It was up to date. Emerson noticed it even had her most recent end-of-month numbers highlighted in the section regarding her current role. Talon was planning to leave the company.

"Hey," Talon said as she opened the door and closed it behind her.

Emerson quickly dropped the resume and turned around.

"Hey, babe."

"You showered," Talon said. "You look all fresh and sexy, and I look like shit."

"You look perfect," Emerson said, meaning it.

Talon took off her leather jacket, hung it over a chair, and walked over to Emerson.

"You're sweet," Talon said, wrapping her arms around Emerson and kissing her. "Um… babe?"

"Yeah?"

"Are you happy to see me?"

"Yes," Emerson said, looking confused.

Talon looked down.

"Oh, shit," Emerson said. "I forgot."

"You forgot you were wearing that?" Talon asked, her hand cupping the toy.

"Yes," Emerson said. "I wanted to surprise you."

"This is definitely a nice surprise. I was going to take a shower, but maybe I can take one after instead," she said, massaging the toy hard enough that Emerson felt it against her clit.

Emerson's eyes closed. Even if her mind had just been

worried Talon was planning to leave the company, now that she was here and doing this, Emerson was re-focused.

"What's the occasion?" Talon asked her. "For my surprise?"

"Just really wanted to," Emerson said, unbuttoning Talon's shirt. "You wore this today, and you know I have a thing for buttons on your shirts." She pulled the shirt apart. "And I love it when I get to see the bra underneath."

"You can take that off, too," Talon said.

"No, I think I want it on for now. I like it when you tear at it until you can get to your nipples to play."

"And that's what you want right now?"

"I want you in my lap on this couch," Emerson replied. "Oh, that's…"

Talon turned on the vibrator and said, "How ready are you for me?"

"Very. I've been ready all day."

"In the meeting with the IT team about the new security protocols?" Talon asked.

"I was thinking about you riding me on this couch," Emerson said.

Talon shoved Emerson back, removed her own shirt, and undid the button on her jeans. Emerson licked her lips and watched as she unzipped them and kicked them off along with her shoes and socks. Talon then stood in front of Emerson in only her black panties and bra, and Emerson's eyes moved to the side instead of looking at her sexy girlfriend.

"What's wrong?" Talon asked.

"What? Nothing. Come here," Emerson said, holding out her arms.

"You were…" Talon turned her head. "Looking over here."

"No, I'm just ready. You turned the bullet on, Tal. I need you. Come here," she said.

"You saw my resume," Talon said, nodding.

"Yeah, I was just straightening up. Tal, I'm going to

come before you–"

"We should talk," Talon said.

"Talk? I'm literally vibrating," Emerson said.

But Talon just sat down next to her. Emerson sighed, reached inside her pants, and turned off the vibrator.

"Okay. Talk, it is, I guess," she said.

"I'm not leaving," Talon said. "If that's what you're thinking."

"Your resume is up to date as of, like, last week, Tal. I had to update my resume to get this job, but the last time I touched it before that was years ago. You didn't apply for Nick's old job."

"I'm applying for Mike's," Talon said.

"Two-first-names Mike?" Emerson asked.

"Definitely not Amsterdam Mike's," Talon told her, referring to the guy in marketing who was called Amsterdam Mike because he went there one time in college and hadn't stopped talking about it since. "Two-first-names, obviously. Is it too crazy? It's crazy, isn't it? I only printed the thing so I could bring it to the interview to be professional. I printed two copies and left one here because I didn't want anyone at the office to see it accidentally. I had my first interview today."

"What? I didn't know. You didn't tell me."

"Brock approved the application, and I asked him not to say anything to you because this would mean leaving the department, and I doubt I'll make it past today's round of interviews."

"Talon, this is a great opportunity for you," Emerson said, smiling wide. "Babe, this is *the* job for you. You'd be perfect at it."

"It's a director role." Talon shrugged.

"So? Tal, this would be such a good fit for you. Babe, I'm so proud of you for applying."

"I just applied. It's not like I got the job."

"Not yet, but I think you're the best option we've got internally."

"And externally?" Talon asked.

"I'd take an amazing internal candidate over anyone externally, and you are amazing," Emerson said, cupping her cheek. "I'm interviewing candidates for that role once they get to the final round."

"I know," Talon said.

"I shouldn't if you're interviewing. That wouldn't be fair. I'll have to find a way to ask to be removed."

"I was thinking about that, actually," Talon said. "What if we turned that letter into HR, explained the whole interview situation, and go from there. I mean, if I get it, you wouldn't have made the decision, and I'd be a peer then instead of someone who reports to you."

Emerson smiled and said, "You want to tell them?"

Talon nodded shyly and said, "I do, yeah."

"Babe, this is the best news." She kissed Talon. "We can tell them tomorrow if you want. I have the letter written already. We just need to print it and sign it."

"You *were* prepared," Talon said, laughing. Then, she looked down and added, "In more ways than one."

"We should talk more about this," Emerson said.

Talon took Emerson's hand and placed it over her sex, pressing Emerson's palm into her.

"You really want to talk when I'm this wet for you?" she asked.

"You are my actual dream woman," Emerson said, unable to keep it in. "It's like I imagined you to life, Talon."

"Imagine me up an orgasm, then," Talon replied, pressing Emerson's fingers against her clit.

Emerson laughed and said, "How can you go from being all worried you're not going to get the job you were clearly made for, to this?"

"Are we still talking?" Talon asked, reaching inside Emerson's pants and pulling out the toy. "Slide down so I can get these off of you."

Emerson lifted her hips, and Talon pulled the pants until they were at Emerson's knees. Then, Talon stood and removed her own panties. Emerson leaned forward and gripped Talon's hips. She breathed her in for a second and then licked her.

"Mouth first?" Talon asked, running her hand through Emerson's short hair.

"We *are* celebrating, right?"

"I don't have the job yet," Talon said as Emerson licked her again.

"But we're telling them about us. That's worth celebrating to me, baby." She sucked Talon into her mouth.

Talon gasped and lifted her leg, placing it next to Emerson on the couch. A phone buzzed.

"Not mine," Emerson said, returning her mouth to Talon's sex.

"Mine. Don't care," Talon said, gasping as Emerson took her.

When she came minutes later, Emerson leaned back and turned the bullet vibrator on again, watching as Talon maneuvered herself over the toy and then took it inside slowly. Her hands were on Emerson's shoulders, and she rocked. Emerson's hands were on Talon's hips, helping her move at just the right pace. Talon didn't wait long. She removed a breast from the cup of her bra and moved Emerson's mouth to it. Emerson sucked as Talon began to lift herself up slightly and lower herself back down on the toy.

Emerson stopped sucking because she wanted to watch. She leaned back and took in the sight before her. Talon's eyes were closed, and she had her hands on both breasts now. Emerson undid her bra so Talon could let them out of it. Then, she pulled it off for her and looked down at the toy disappearing inside Talon and reappearing. The vibrations were good, but the bullet wasn't in the right position, so it likely wouldn't make her come.

"I'm so close," Talon said.

"You're so hot," Emerson replied, running her hand down Talon's body between her breasts.

Talon came hard, hips bucking as Emerson held on to her. Yeah, Emerson was right: Talon was hot. Talon came down slowly but didn't move to get the toy out of her.

"You're my dream woman, too," Talon said, kissing her.

Emerson smiled into the kiss.

"Shit. Did you come?" Talon asked, realizing Emerson was still vibrating.

"Not yet," she replied.

"I should really take care of that, then," Talon said.

Within a few seconds, Talon was on her knees in front of Emerson. The harness was on the floor, along with Emerson's pants. Talon had Emerson spread in front of her, and her mouth was on Emerson's clit, sucking and driving Emerson crazy. Emerson's hand was on the back of Talon's head.

"God, I love your mouth," Emerson said.

Talon sucked harder, and she came undone. Minutes later, Talon's head was in Emerson's lap again, but this time, Emerson was sitting up, and Talon was lying on her back, staring up at her. They were both still naked, but Emerson was running her hand through Talon's hair, and Talon had her eyes closed.

"Tomorrow, your place?" Talon asked.

"If you want," Emerson replied.

"Yeah, I was thinking maybe I'll stop by the store and pick up a few things to keep over there if you're okay with it."

Emerson smiled and said, "Like what?"

"I don't know. Shampoo. An extra toothbrush. The stuff you have here mainly."

"I think that sounds like a great idea," Emerson said, breathing a sigh of relief.

CHAPTER 32

"You texted me when I was a little busy," Talon said to Weston.

"Your expression tells me that you were busy with Emerson," Weston said. "Whom I still haven't met."

"I'm working on it. Technically, you *did* meet her."

"You, acting like a weirdo when we ran into her at the bar that one time, doesn't count. I didn't even get her name then, and she ran us out of the bar so fast, Aria and I were worried and hung out there for another ten minutes to make sure you were okay," Weston said. "Why are you keeping her from us?"

"I'm not keeping her from you guys. We've just been busy."

"With sex?"

"Yes," Talon said. "Among other things."

"You're happy?" Weston asked, turning to face Talon on her sofa.

"I am, yeah," Talon said, smiling at her best friend. "There's this intense connection between us where I simultaneously want to tear all her clothes off, but I would also just as easily share a bowl of ice cream with her while we watch TV. I've never really had both like that before, and I like it."

"That's awesome, Tal," Weston said.

"It kind of is. We stayed at her place last night, and I left some things there. I bought an extra toothbrush and a hairbrush. I have shampoo and conditioner there now. She doesn't use conditioner because her hair is so short, so I'd been going without whenever I stayed over and showered there. Now, it's like – I don't know – I have *stuff* there. I know it's not a big deal to most people, and people might laugh at me even bringing it up, but it's big for me. Like, if she had a friend over or something, they'd see my stuff and know Emerson has a girlfriend."

"Yeah, they would. Although, I'm sure she'd just tell them that it's her girlfriend's stuff," Weston said.

"We told HR yesterday."

"You did? I thought you wanted to wait."

"Circumstances made it necessary to do it sooner."

Talon thought about this possible new job; how it would mean she was no longer under Emerson at work, and how it would be a better job for her with more money and responsibility that she felt ready for. It was nice to finally have something at work to look forward to.

"Are you okay with that? The company knowing?" Weston asked.

"Yeah, I am. I hated having to answer questions about my private life but doing that meant that Emerson was protected and that we could be together without having to worry about people there finding out. We've been going out in other towns because we were worried someone from work might see us out after hours. I've tried Mexican food in three different cities recently, so if you need a good place in the north, east, or westerly directions, let me know." Talon chuckled mainly to herself. "Now, while everyone doesn't know, if they *did* see us and reported it, HR already knows."

"That's great, Tal. I'm happy for you guys," Weston said as her phone buzzed on her coffee table. "And that's *my* girlfriend."

"You love saying that, don't you?" Talon teased.

"I do, yes. I feel like I earned it. I wanted Annie from the moment I saw her, and now we're together, and it's great. We had a couple of hurdles there, but I think we're safely past them now."

"Do I need to get out of here? Is she on her way over?" Talon asked.

"She is, but you don't have to leave, Tal. The two of you can exist in the same house, and the space-time continuum will be okay."

"You're hilarious," Talon replied sarcastically. "I just didn't know if you guys had plans."

"We're just hanging out. We write together sometimes. I actually re-did my office a little. Want to see?"

"You re-did the weirdest office on the planet?"

"Shut up." Weston stood. "Come on."

Talon followed Weston until they were standing in the open doorway of Weston's office. The room used to only have a small desk against the wall and a small recliner in it. It also had two full dry-erase walls where Weston would outline her novels. Now, Talon could see Annie's influence. There was another desk on an adjacent wall. This one was a bit bigger and had an extra monitor. It also had a potted fake orchid plant on the corner. Behind the desk, there was a bulletin board with pieces of paper and Post-It notes stuck to it.

"You *share* an office now?" Talon asked.

"Yeah, sometimes. It's nice. She doesn't have room in her apartment, so whenever she's here, she uses the office with me. We both have headphones when we need them, but sometimes, we just play music in the background and both write. It works." Weston smiled. "I've never had that with anyone."

Talon turned to her, smiled, and said, "You love her, don't you?"

"I do," Weston said. "And I told her."

"You did?"

"That's what I texted you about the other night while you were *busy*."

"Your text just said that you wanted to hang out. Sorry, Emerson was doing things… and then we…"

"Okay. I get it."

"No, I wasn't going to say *sex*. I mean, we were, at first, when you texted, but then we just lay there on the couch. I don't think we said anything to each other for like an hour. It was weird but not at the same time."

"You love her, too, don't you?" Weston asked.

"I think so," Talon replied, smiling. "I haven't said anything yet, though. I need to go at a slower pace than Emerson with some of this stuff, and I just told HR we're a thing."

"Does she feel the same way?"

"I don't know. I think she might," Talon said. "But I might be jumping ahead. She did ask me to meet her family."

"She did what?" Weston asked.

"At this party thing they always go to."

"Are you going?"

"I haven't decided yet," Talon said.

"When is it?"

"St. Patrick's Day."

"Tal, it's the eighth."

"I know."

"St. Patrick's Day is on the seventeenth. Don't you have to let her know?"

"She said it's an open thing. It's a block party for her old neighborhood. I can show up with a bag of chips for the potluck, and it's fine. What do Irish people like on a potato chip? Barbeque? Sour Cream & Onion? Original? Should I go with Salt & Vinegar, or is that too edgy?"

"She wants you to meet her family, though."

"That's what she said," Talon said, walking into the room and sitting in Weston's recliner. "Hey, who gets this chair when you're both in here? There's still only one."

"Whoever wants it," Weston said, sitting in her desk chair. "And don't change the subject."

"I don't know yet, Wes. I know I've never felt this way before, and I'm really happy in this honeymoon period we have going right now. It's like it's just the two of us, and it's perfect. The more people we let into our bubble, the more possibilities things have of going wrong."

"Annie and I let people into our bubble, and things are fine. We were at the cabin all by ourselves, exchanging Valentine's Day gifts, and we could've stayed there forever, and I think I would have been okay with that, but that's not the real world, Tal. We have friends and family, and they want to see us happy, too."

"I've never had the bubble, Wes. Your dorm room freshman year doesn't exactly count. I just want to enjoy it right now."

"You can still enjoy it and progress in your relationship," Weston said. "You told HR. Has the bubble diminished or popped?"

"Not really, but that was yesterday. Besides, the HR guy we told now kind of looks at me weird."

"He probably didn't know you were a lesbian," Weston said.

"Probably, yeah," Talon replied. "Hey, you told Annie you loved her… Did she say it back?"

"Yes," Weston said, smiling wide. "Thank God. That would have been awkward."

"You say you love her, and she says thank you?" Talon said.

"How do you come back from that? It's not a romantic comedy where there's a cut and another scene a week later. You're standing there in front of them, pouring your heart out, and they give you a thank you."

"I think you just pat them on the shoulder, say, 'Good talk,' and run to the bathroom to cry in the shower," Talon joked.

"I'll have to write that into one of my books," Weston said.

"How's that going?" Talon asked. "We haven't really talked that much lately."

"Everything's signed. Now, the editors have the first book, and I'm dreading getting all of their notes, but it's going to be published, which is insane and awesome."

"Not insane; the book is amazing," Annie said as she

walked into the room. "Hey, Talon." She moved to Weston, leaned down, and kissed her. "Hi, babe."

"Hey," Weston said, smiling up at her.

"You have a key?" Talon asked, wondering if she should give Emerson a key already.

Emerson had borrowed Talon's to get into her place the other day. That seemed to be okay. Emerson hadn't offered Talon *her* key yet. Leigh hadn't given Talon a key until they'd been together for six months, and Talon had rarely used the thing. She and Emerson hadn't been together long enough for key status yet, right? Annie and Weston hadn't been together all that long either, though.

"No, you probably just left the door unlocked," Annie told her, sitting in Weston's lap and wrapping her arms around Weston's shoulders.

"She does that," Weston said.

"Sorry," Talon said.

"You're lucky this is a good neighborhood," Weston teased.

"Are you joining us for dinner?" Annie asked Talon as she ran her hand through Weston's hair.

"Oh, no. I can leave you guys alone," she replied.

"Stay, Talon," Annie said, laughing. "Unless you *have* to go. *I'm* cooking."

"Oh, thank God," Talon teased Weston.

"I'm not *that* bad." Weston laughed.

"Fettuccini with chicken," Annie said, standing up. "You good with that?"

"Invite Emerson," Weston suggested. "We can have a chill double date."

"She's working late tonight," Talon said. "Budgets are due."

"Boring," Weston said.

"I don't miss those meetings," Annie said, having recently left her job as an agent and part-owner of a literary agency.

"I might have to do those now, huh?" Talon said,

realizing it at the same time.

"Budget meetings?"

"Yeah. As a manager, I usually just get the budget handed to me. Sometimes, I don't even get it at all. Now, I might have to sit in those meetings. I guess it's a good thing my girlfriend will be there, too. And she's so hot, I can just stare at her the whole time."

"Hold on. What are you talking about, Tal?" Weston asked.

"I applied for a director job at work," Talon explained. "I had one interview and had no clue how it went – they hadn't said anything. But then I got scheduled for another interview, so I guess it went okay."

"Talon, that's awesome," Weston said.

"I haven't gotten it yet, but that's why we had to tell HR about us: Emerson was interviewing the candidates. She had to recuse herself with me in the mix now."

"I'm going to start on dinner. Congrats, Talon," Annie said, winking at Weston and leaving them alone.

"I don't think I should get the congrats until I get it, assuming I do. I have no idea who else is interviewing," she said.

"Emerson's a director too, right?" Weston recalled.

"Yeah."

"So, you guys would be peers, then?"

"Yes. I'd be on the sales ops team, so I wouldn't be under her at all, which would be really helpful given the fact that I'm in love with her and want to be with her forever if I don't screw it up."

Weston lifted an eyebrow and said, "You've never talked about anyone like that before. Not even Leigh, and you were with her for a year."

"I know. It's big," Talon said.

"If it's so big, why are you taking *baby* steps?"

"Because she's worth me being ready for every one of those steps first. I'm not going to take them before I know they're right and at the right time for both of us."

Weston shrugged a shoulder and said, "That actually makes a lot of sense."

"Wes, where is your strainer?" Annie yelled from the kitchen.

"Think she'll break up with me if I tell her I don't have a strainer?" Weston asked.

"Even *I* have a strainer, Weston," Talon said, laughing.

CHAPTER 33

"Emerson, can I grab you for a minute?" her boss said.

"Sure," Emerson replied, turning abruptly to get to his office instead of her own.

As she did, she glanced over at Talon's desk to see that she'd already gone home for the day. Emerson probably had a text on her phone, indicating as much and suggesting that they spend the night at Talon's place. They'd worked out a routine of sorts. On nights when Talon got done first, Emerson usually met her at her place. On nights when Emerson got off first, Talon would go to her place. Emerson was typically the one working later due to her position, which meant she spent most nights at Talon's place. She didn't mind. She just wanted to be near Talon. They hadn't spent a night apart in a long time now, and Emerson didn't want to, either. She figured if Talon needed some space, she'd tell Emerson, so they'd just keep doing what they were doing until that happened.

"Hey, I've got news," he said when Emerson closed the door behind her.

"Good, I hope," she replied.

"Very good, I think. So, we've got Travis for Nick's old job – I just heard from HR that he formally accepted."

"Oh, good. He was my choice," she said, wondering why she needed to find this out from the VP of Sales since normally, HR would just tell her this information.

"Yeah, that's good, but not why I called you in. We also made a decision on sales ops," he said.

Emerson sat down, bracing herself for bad news just in case.

"Yeah?" she said, swallowing.

"Yeah, it was no contest – Talon got it. I mean, the

project you two worked on is going to save a shit ton of money, and she did that while managing to still have the best numbers."

Emerson wanted to smile, but she held it in. While HR knew that she and Talon were together because Emerson had needed to step away from interviewing to ensure fairness, they'd requested no one else find out until after the decision on the job had been made. So, Emerson just cleared her throat.

"That's great. She's going to be amazing," she said.

"Yeah. That makes her a peer, and since you're new, but not, like, brand-new now, I was hoping you'd take her under your wing and help her get started."

"Oh, sure. I can do that," Emerson said, trying not to agree too quickly.

"Not a problem? I know you're busy. You'll have a new senior manager, too."

"No, I'm good. I can handle it," she said.

"Cool. Well, we've got the offer ready to roll, so we'll have them give her the verbal offer tomorrow, and hopefully, she accepts."

"I'm sure she will," Emerson said, smiling on the inside.

As she drove to Talon's house, she decided to stop and get a nicer bottle of wine and some more ice cream because they'd finished the last carton the other night. When she got to Talon's place, she knocked and waited.

"It's unlocked," Talon yelled from inside.

Emerson pushed open the door and saw Talon sitting at her kitchen table, staring at her laptop.

"Hey," she said without looking up.

"Hi," Emerson replied, closing the door behind her. "Everything okay?"

"Yeah. Why?"

"You haven't looked at me yet," Emerson said, placing the bag from the store on the table.

Talon looked up at her and said, "Sorry."

Emerson leaned down and kissed her quickly.

"What's wrong?"

"Nothing," Talon said. "For the interview process, they had me do an assignment thing where I had to improve a process. I chose our payment system, and I turned everything in, but I just keep thinking about ways I could have done even more. I didn't have much time to work on the part for the interview, but now I just have all these ideas, so I'm in there now, kind of testing a few things. I just got distracted."

Emerson leaned back down from behind Talon and wrapped both arms around Talon's neck.

"You're so cute," she told the woman.

"Sorry, I was rude when you walked in."

"You weren't. I was just concerned," Emerson replied, kissing Talon's neck. "Did you eat?"

"No, I was waiting for you. I don't feel like cooking, though. Can we order something?"

"Yes," Emerson said, standing up. "I got ice cream."

Talon closed her laptop and turned in her chair with a lifted eyebrow.

"Yeah?"

Emerson laughed and said, "Not right now. We're ordering dinner and opening this expensive wine I got. I asked the guy at the store for their best red. I thought about getting champagne first, but I opted for wine instead. I hope that's okay."

"Champagne?" Talon asked, standing up and following Emerson into her small kitchen, where Emerson unpacked the bag.

"Oh, I almost forgot." Emerson pulled out the container of whipped cream and set it next to the bag.

"We haven't tried whipped cream before," Talon said, picking it up and looking at it as if she'd never seen whipped cream in her life.

Emerson took it from her and put it in the fridge and the ice cream in the freezer.

"Babe, sex later."

"But you got ice cream," Talon argued.

Emerson laughed again and said, "Because we're celebrating."

"You haven't told me what we're celebrating yet," Talon reminded her.

Emerson stopped moving and walked to her. She placed her hands on Talon's hips and looked into her eyes.

"I shouldn't be telling you this. You have to look surprised tomorrow."

"Telling me… Tomorrow?" Talon's eyes went wide as she registered Emerson's news. "Wait. I got it?"

Emerson smiled and slowly nodded.

"You got it, babe."

"I did? Really?"

"They told me today. You're getting your verbal offer tomorrow. Then, you'll sign the paperwork. All you have to do is accept."

"I got it," Talon said as if trying to see how it sounded to say it out loud again.

"I am so proud of you, love." Emerson pulled Talon into her. "I was told there was no contest. You were the only one they universally loved."

"Me?" Talon said.

"Yes. How many times will I have to tell you that you're amazing and will be so good at this job?"

"I don't know. A bunch, probably."

"Okay. I'll keep doing it until you finally get it, then." Emerson pressed her forehead to Talon's. "I was also asked to help you get adjusted to the new role."

"You were? Adjusted?" Talon asked, running and hand down the middle of Emerson's chest over her shirt.

"I was. I told him it wouldn't be a problem, so I hope you don't mind spending long hours with me at the office."

"God, that sounds awful," Talon joked, making Emerson laugh. "I mean, you'll be fully clothed, and I won't be able to kiss you, so that's basically just torture."

Emerson smiled at her and kissed her softly.

"Tal?"

"Yeah?" Talon asked.

"Let's order dinner." She kissed her again. "And open the wine."

"And then?"

"Eat and drink said wine."

"When will the ice cream come out of the freezer, Emerson?"

Emerson laughed again and said, "You realize we can just have sex. We don't *have* to include the dessert in it. Do you want the toy tonight?"

Talon kissed Emerson's lips and said, "No, tonight I just want you." She kissed her again. "God, Em."

"What?" Emerson asked, placing her hands into the back pocket of Talon's jeans, pulling Talon into her even more.

"I love you," Talon said.

Emerson had *not* been prepared to hear that tonight. She swallowed hard.

"Oh, shit. You're going to say thank you right now, aren't you? Just know if you do, I'll have to pat you on the shoulder and run into the bathroom to cry in the shower."

"What?" Emerson laughed and cupped Talon's cheek. "What are you talking about?"

"Are you going to thank me for telling you that I love you?"

"No, Tal. I was going to say it back, like, one second after you started talking about crying in the shower."

"You were going to say it back?" Talon asked, looking surprised.

"Yes, I was. Would you like to hear it now?"

Talon nodded quickly. Emerson leaned in, hovering her lips over Talon's and leaving them there, feeling Talon's hot breath against her mouth.

"Babe, I love you."

She felt Talon relax instantly.

"Yeah?"

"Definitely," Emerson said, pulling her in for a slow, perfect kiss.

Talon's arms wrapped around her and pulled her in closer. When the kiss ended naturally, Talon moved in for a hug and held Emerson so tightly, Emerson felt pain in her back, but she wasn't moving until Talon released her from the hug.

"You thought I'd say thank you?"

"I didn't know if it was too soon."

"It's not. I've felt it for a while now," Emerson said, running her hands up and down Talon's back.

"You have?"

"That night when you fell asleep and woke up a little to tell me you were cold."

"And you held me," Talon said, pulling back a little to look at Emerson.

"All night," Emerson said, smiling at her.

"I'm still scared," Talon replied.

"I know," Emerson said. "That's okay."

"I think I want to go to the party," Talon replied.

"The block party?"

"If you still want me to go with you," Talon said.

"I do. Are you sure, though? You don't have to. You kind of took a big step tonight already."

"Can you promise that if your mom hates me, you won't break up with me over it?"

Emerson laughed again and said, "My mom will not hate you."

"You can't know that," Talon said.

"Yes, I can. I talk about you to her all the time. She knows how amazing you are already. Now, she'll just get to see it for herself."

"I was thinking that maybe you could meet my friends," Talon said.

"Name the time and place."

"If I bring the chips and they bring the dip, can they

maybe come to the party? I'd have moral support if your mom starts shooting dagger eyes at me, and you could meet them."

Emerson laughed and said, "I love you."

Talon looked at her seriously and said, "No ice cream tonight. Just you and me."

"Wine?" Emerson asked.

"And dinner. Then, you and me. Slow and all night long," came Talon's reply.

"That sounds like a perfect night to me," Emerson told her.

CHAPTER 34

Seven days ago, Talon had told Emerson that she loved her, and Emerson had said it back. It wasn't something she'd planned. Spending that night at Weston's, watching Annie and Weston act like the world's most perfectly annoying couple, was kind of a big experience for Talon. She'd never seen her best friend with someone she actually thought Weston could end up with. Her girlfriend selection in the past hadn't been the best, and Talon, along with their friends, had commented that Annie might be the one. Hearing Weston whisper that she loved Annie in the kitchen when she thought Talon couldn't hear her, seemed like such a private moment, that Talon thought she should go.

That had her thinking about Emerson. Technically, Emerson had seen Talon at that party, and while Talon hadn't seen her and they hadn't been introduced until days later, they'd been in each other's orbits for longer than Weston and Annie. That was how it felt. Talon was in Emerson's orbit, Emerson was in hers, and it just made sense in a way nothing else ever had to Talon before.

Talon had been certain she'd retire as a sales manager at her company. She'd been fairly certain she'd watch all of her friends find their loves, get married, and have kids if they wanted to. She'd been preparing herself for years to watch them all move away and get on with the next chapter of their lives while she sat at that same desk, approving sales and discounts and attending meetings with high-fives.

When Emerson had come into her life, something had changed in Talon. There was the instant attraction, of course, but because of the complications of wanting to be together and Emerson's job, Talon wanted to find a solution that would allow them their relationship without a complication. She wasn't sure if she would have left the company, but if it had gotten to a point where it would've necessitated a choice between her job and Emerson, Talon would've chosen Emerson easily. It wasn't even a choice, actually; Emerson was her future. She saw things in Talon that Talon hadn't recognized in herself, and that made Talon a better person.

"Okay. You guys need to be on your best behavior today. Wes, talk up your book and how it's about to be published. Make it sound like my best friend is a kick-ass best-selling author."

"But I'm not yet," Weston argued.

"You will be. Right, Annie?"

"*I* think so," Annie said, squeezing Weston's hand and looking all in love.

"I'm asking you as her agent, not her girlfriend. Look like her agent that got her this massive deal."

"*I* did get her a massive deal," Annie said.

"Aria, play up how smart you are, not how rich you are," Talon instructed further.

"Sorry?" Aria said, looking up from her phone.

"Pais, you started your own company. Tell them that."

"You know that actually happened, right?" Paisley said.

"Eleanor, have you recruited any well-known people lately?" Talon asked of her friend who worked at a recruiting agency.

"What? No."

"Okay. Read any good books?"

"Just Weston's," Ellie said.

"Talk about that, then. Scar, talk numbers. You're good at that. Just don't make them boring numbers."

"I don't know how to do that," Scarlet said.

"What's going on here?" Emerson asked.

"Oh, hey," Talon said, turning to see Emerson standing next to her now. "Nothing. This is the gang. Gang, this is Emerson."

"Hi," Weston said.

"Nice to meet you," Annie added.

"Hey," Aria said, returning her gaze to her phone.

"Aria, phone down," Talon said.

"Is she being a drill sergeant to all of you because she's nervous to meet my family?" Emerson asked, taking Talon's hand.

"I am not–"

"Yes!" they all semi-yelled in unison.

"I'm supposed to talk about numbers but not make them boring," Scarlet said, looking confused.

Talon scowled at her, but only half-seriously.

"How about you let your friends just be themselves and talk about whatever they want, and I get you a beer to help calm your nerves?" Emerson asked, rubbing her free hand over Talon's green t-shirt.

Talon felt calmer instantly.

"Does it have to be green? It'll stain my tongue, and I'm meeting your mother," Talon said.

Emerson laughed and said, "No, we can get you a normal beer and probably some food, too." She kissed Talon on the cheek.

"What's that for?"

"Your shirt told me to," Emerson said, patting Talon's stomach.

"I'm not actually Irish. I just bought it to fit in," Talon said.

"Probably shouldn't have. You'll get a lot of cheek kisses today," Emerson replied. "But I love you for trying." She kissed her girlfriend again. "It's nice to meet you guys. Let's get this one taken care of, and we can grab a table."

"Oh, I like her for you," Aria whispered to Talon as they walked.

Paisley gave Talon a wink.

"Just remember, you are awesome. You don't have to make things up about yourself, Tal. Just *be* yourself," Weston said when they were in line at the long buffet table.

"I'm not some soon-to-be-published author. I don't own–"

"No, you're Talon. We already have a writer in our group – we need a Talon. That's you. Emerson needs a Talon, too. That's why we're all here. She's crazy about you, Tal. We can all tell. She's crazy about *you.* She doesn't want a Weston or a Paisley or an Aria – she wants *you.*"

Talon glanced up to where she found Emerson grabbing two beers from a cooler with melting ice. She carried her plate of food with her and walked over.

"I got you this one. Is that okay?" Emerson asked, rubbing her hands together.

"Cold?" Talon asked.

"Ice," Emerson explained.

Talon set her plate down, took both of Emerson's hands in hers, and blew hot air on them. Emerson smiled down at her.

"I hope this is Talon, or else, Talon is going to be pissed," a woman said from beside them.

"Shut up," Emerson said, laughing. "Talon, this is Fiona, my sister."

Talon dropped Emerson's hands and turned to Fiona.

"Oh, hi. Nice to meet you." She held out her hand for Fiona to shake.

Fiona looked at her as if that were ridiculous, laughed and shook it.

"Hi. Your hand is wet," Fiona stated.

"Oh, sorry." Talon wiped her hands on her jeans. "I was–"

"Warming my hands for me," Emerson said, walking behind Talon and wrapping her arms around her waist. "Can you do it again?" she asked.

Talon placed her arms over Emerson's but felt bare in front of Fiona, who was giving her a skeptical once-over.

"She was getting me a beer," Talon said in explanation.

"Mama," a little boy said as he ran up and gripped Fiona's leg.

"Hey, baby. Having fun?" Fiona asked him.

"Daddy let me have chocolate," he said.

"He did, did he?" Fiona asked, rolling her eyes. "How much?"

"Two brownies," he said.

Emerson laughed against Talon's neck, which made Talon feel safe smiling, too.

"Can I go play on the bouncy house?" he asked.

"Where's daddy?"

"He's…" The little boy turned and looked but seemed to be unable to find him.

"I'll take you, then," Fiona said. "Can you get your brother and meet me over there?"

"Yes," he said excitedly.

Then, he ran off.

"Well, I'll have to do more of this meet-the-girlfriend later. I have a bouncy house to supervise, I guess," Fiona said.

"It was nice to–"

"Meet me. Yeah, yeah. Emerson, tell her we're not formal people," Fiona said. "Her posture looks like she's about to burst."

Emerson laughed again as Fiona walked away.

"It's true. You're tense as hell, Tal," Emerson said, moving her hands to Talon's shoulders and massaging them.

"I'm nervous," Talon finally admitted.

"I know, baby. You don't have to be, though. Fiona was easy, right?"

"Fiona looks like a mama-lion, protecting her cubs."

"She has actual cubs to protect. I'm the big sister; *I* protect *her*."

"Fiona told us Talon is here," a young guy said, walking up with another one in tow.

"Colt, Matt, this is Talon. Be nice, or I'll kill both of you," Emerson said, still massaging Talon's shoulders.

"Are you getting ready for a fight? Are we doing the sumo-wrestling thing again this year?" Colt asked.

"I kicked your ass," Matt said, taking a drink of his beer.

"Sumo-wrestling?" Talon asked.

"We dress up in these big suits and–"

"I have no idea if that's happening this year," Emerson interrupted one of her younger brothers. "The boys are in the bouncy house. You should go join them. You're about the same maturity level," she said.

Talon laughed, and Emerson kissed her neck. Talon blushed. Colt and Matt watched.

"Talon, you have a beer yet?" Matt asked.

"Um… yeah. Emerson got me one. I just haven't–"

Emerson handed it to her, but Matt took it instead, removed the top, and passed it back to Talon.

"Thanks," Talon said.

"No problem. Do you bouncy-house?" he asked.

"Oh, that's a good question," Emerson said. "Do you bouncy-house?"

"I don't think I've been in one of those for a long time," Talon replied. "Are adults even allowed?"

"Are adults allowed?" Colt laughed like that was a crazy question.

"We have a slot reserved. No kids; just grown-ups getting their bounce on," Matt added.

"Do *you* get in?" Talon asked, turning her head to Emerson.

"Oh, yeah. And, Tal, this is an even more important question than the whole marriage and kids thing. You have to get in the bouncy house for us to make this work."

Emerson was teasing. Her eyes were alit with glee, and Talon knew this was a joke, but she also took this as a challenge.

"I'm in," Talon said.

Emerson kissed her.

"Gross." Colt laughed.

"I'm going to do it again, so you might want to leave if you don't want to see it," Emerson said.

"We'll catch you guys later," Matt said, pulling Colt along with him.

Emerson moved to stand in front of her, pulled her in gently, and gave her a sweet kiss on the lips.

"You're doing great. Want to put me through the wringer now and get me at that table with your friends?"

"Yes," Talon said. "But first…" She put her arms around Emerson's neck and kissed her. "Just one more of these."

Emerson smiled into the kiss.

***

Hours later, Talon had managed to drink enough water along with her alcohol to hopefully ensure she wouldn't be hungover tomorrow. She'd eaten enough not to be drunk, which was also important. Emerson had been introduced to Talon's friends, and they all seemed to like her. Talon had spent a little more time with Fiona, who was occupied with her own family. Colt and Matt made another appearance for them all to chat but seemed more concerned with picking up girls at this event.

"Okay. Mom's coming over," Emerson said. "She was running one of the raffle booths until now. I asked her to keep her distance until you were warmed up."

"What? You told her I needed to warm up to meet her?" Talon asked, swallowing hard.

"Well, less nervous, but yeah."

"Emerson!"

"Hello," the woman, who looked like an older Emerson, said, standing in front of their picnic table.

"Hey, Mom. This is Talon."

Talon stood up and held out her hand.

"It's nice to meet you," she said nervously.

"I already like her," the woman said, laughing and shaking Talon's hand. "You're nervous, aren't you, sweetie?"

"That obvious?" Talon asked, sitting back down.

"Yes, but I think that's a good thing. It shows you care," Emerson's mom said as she sat across from them.

"I do. I really do," Talon said.

Emerson placed a hand on Talon's thigh under the table.

"Emerson told me you got a promotion at work," the woman said.

"I did. I start next week," Talon replied.

"And that makes you two peers, which means Emerson can't get into any trouble at work," she said.

"HR knows about us, Mom. We're keeping it under wraps a bit for now because it's just easier, but we'll tell our boss soon."

Talon realized maybe for the first time that she and Emerson would have the same boss now.

"I just want you to be okay at work," the woman told Emerson.

"I am. I really like it there. Talon's part of the reason why, obviously, but not just because of our relationship. Working on that project together made a real impact on the company, and I loved doing it."

Talon thought about the day in the office when they'd done no work at all – the day that had started this whole thing that now mattered more to her than anything else – and she smiled.

"You agree?" Emerson's mom asked her.

"I was just thinking about it, yeah," Talon said, leaving out the whole sex part. "I loved working on it with her, too. Emerson is smart and sees things differently than a lot of people I work with. I think I was in a rut when she got here, and working on that project with her pulled me out of it."

Emerson's mom smiled and said, "I think that's one

of the many things people in love can do for and with each other."

"Grandma!" Fiona's oldest son practically crashed into his grandmother.

"Hi there," she said, laughing as she enveloped him into her arms.

Talon watched the display of adoration from the young boy, and before she knew it, her head was on Emerson's shoulder. Emerson kissed the top of her head and wrapped an arm around her waist, pulling Talon in closer. Emerson's mom watched them and smiled.

"Mom, we're next up in the bouncy house. Are you in?"

"You know I'm not," the woman said, laughing. "I'm watching the boys while my grown children bounce in a house together."

"It's big enough for twelve," Emerson said to Talon.

"Okay," Talon replied.

"Me with my siblings is four, and you make five. You have six friends here; that's eleven," Emerson said. "Why don't you ask them to bounce with us?"

"I can already predict the reactions. Wes will be in. Annie will go *because* Wes is in. Paisley will say she has to make a call. Aria will be on a dating app and *too busy*. Scarlet will be too shy but will agree if I ask her to. Ellie will do it because she won't see a reason not to do it."

"Let's mess with all of them and tell them that my family will be super impressed with you and them if they all get in," Emerson said.

"That sounds like fun," Emerson's mom said. "I can glare in their direction or something if you need me to."

Talon laughed and felt relieved. This was a lot easier than she thought it would be.

"Let's do it."

Ten minutes later, Talon had all of her friends, including Annie, their most recent addition, kicking off their shoes and climbing inside the large bouncy house.

"I had a girl I was messaging, Talon. This better be good," Aria said.

"I was just about to leave. I have a client I owe a call to," Paisley said.

"Do I have to do this, Tal?" Scarlet asked.

"God, you really do know all of them," Emerson told Talon as they stood in the corner and watched everyone enter one by one.

"We like to start with simultaneous jumping to build up the biggest bounce," Matt instructed Talon. "So, we count down and then all jump a few times."

"I'm just going to sit in the corner," Aria said.

"No, you're not," Talon said. "Jump, Aria!"

"Ugh. Fine," Aria replied, crossing her arms over her chest like a tantrum-throwing toddler.

"Okay. One. Two. Three," Matt said.

Everyone jumped all at once, and the laughter started immediately. Emerson took Talon's hand as they jumped a few more times, going higher and higher. On the fourth jump, Emerson fell and pulled Talon down on top of her.

"Well, hi," Emerson said. "This is an added bonus."

"Yeah, I think I'll stay here for a while." Talon smiled down at her as the others, still bouncing, lifted them up briefly and then down again. "It kind of feels like we're flying."

"It always feels like that with you," Emerson said, wrapping her arms around Talon's neck.

Talon leaned down and kissed her then, making it nice and slow.

"Hey, Talon? You want to stop making out with my sister during bouncy house time?" Fiona said.

They pulled apart to laugh, but then Talon crashed down entirely on Emerson and let Emerson wrap her up in her arms.

"I love you," Talon said into her ear.

"I love you, too, babe," Emerson replied, kissing Talon's cheek.

EPILOGUE

"Memorial Day road trip," Scarlet said.

"It's an hour and a half," Talon replied, looking into the back seat where Scarlet and Paisley sat.

"So? We have snacks, music, and friends. That's a road trip."

"And I am done," Paisley said, dropping her phone in her lap. "I am officially on vacation for the next three days."

"Congrats," Emerson said from the driver's seat.

"I cannot wait to do absolutely nothing all weekend."

"It's like you've never been to one of these things," Talon said, laughing.

"I will drive the boat while you idiots do the whole tube thing on the back," Paisley said.

"There's a boat?" Emerson asked.

"Weston rents one for the weekend. I don't know why she doesn't just buy one; she has the money," Talon said.

"She's never cared about the money," Paisley said.

"We come here for Labor Day, too. Well, sometimes. We don't do it every year," Scarlet said.

"And it's really okay that *I'm* here?" Emerson asked. "Annie's here, but she's Weston's girlfriend, and this is Weston's place, so–"

"Hi," Talon said. "You're *my* girlfriend, and *we* rented our own cabin near Weston's. We can do whatever we want. Weston isn't in charge here."

"Besides, if any of us actually had girlfriends," Scarlet began. "Or boyfriends," she added for Paisley's sake. "We'd have them here, too, and wouldn't be carpooling with you two."

"Here it is," Talon said. "Take that drive, and we can drop these two at their cabin first."

"Okay," Emerson said, following Talon's finger, which was pointing to the left.

It was the end of May, and if Emerson counted the first time they had sex as their anniversary, that meant they'd been together for three months now. It was probably an insignificant amount of time for a couple who had been together for decades, but it was a big deal to Emerson. This weekend wouldn't exactly put them at their three-month anniversary, but it would get them pretty close, so she'd decided to bring a few things to help them celebrate that she had no plan to tell the others about. She knew this weekend was about the friends all getting together and relaxing, having fun, and spending time together, but she hoped they'd find some time alone, too.

"Hey, what do you think?" Talon asked when she opened the door to the cabin they'd rented for themselves.

"It looks exactly how it did online," Emerson replied, dropping their bags by the door and closing it behind her.

"It's okay, though, right?" Talon checked. "You said you're not much of an outdoorsy person, so I want to make sure this is okay."

"Babe, this is great," Emerson said, looking around the space. "And there's a balcony that gives a great view of the lake. Want to check it out?"

She pulled on Talon's hand through the living room and kitchen, which were fine, but not all that interesting. There was a wood-burning fireplace that they'd sit by later, but Emerson had seen the apparent view in the photos online and wanted to see it in person.

"Wow," Talon said.

"Does Weston have this view, too?" Emerson asked.

"No, her place is really rustic. It faces this direction, but this one is on pillars, so we get the better view. And I have a confession to make now," Talon added.

"A confession?"

"So, we've never really talked about this, but I've always considered our anniversary as the first time we…"

"Went to town on each other in the office?" Emerson finished for her.

"Yeah, that. Anyway, I know it doesn't line up exactly, but I thought since we're here, we could celebrate our three-month anniversary. When I went to rent the cabin for us, this one was a little more expensive than the others, but I thought it would be worth it for this view alone. I mean…"

Emerson smiled at Talon, who was looking out at the lake, which was only feet from where they stood. There was a staircase that led off the balcony down to where there was a canoe that maybe they could use if they wanted to, and they were completely surrounded by trees and the water that had the sun reflecting perfectly off its rippling surface.

"I love you," Emerson said.

Talon turned to her and said, "I love you, too."

Emerson moved into her then and said, "Do you think anyone can see us out here?"

"Huh? I don't know. Why?" Talon looked around.

From what Emerson could see, there were no cabins nearby and no trails that appeared to pop up out of the surrounding woods, either.

"How much time do we have before your friends expect us at Weston's?" Emerson asked, pulling Talon into her.

"Oh," Talon said, looking down at their now connected bodies. "I don't know. But we can be late, if that's what you're thinking."

"Right now," Emerson began, turning Talon until she was facing the water. "I'm thinking about quick." She moved behind her and unbuttoned Talon's jeans, slipping easily inside with the zipper moving down as her hand did. "And later, I'll want slow."

"Fuck," Talon said, leaning back against Emerson.

Emerson found Talon wet but not as wet as she normally was for her.

"Should I stop?" Emerson asked, running her fingers up and down Talon's clit.

"What? No way."

"You're not…"

"Move your hand down," Talon said.

Emerson slid lower to Talon's entrance.

"Jesus," she said at the wetness she found there.

"You wore those tight black pants to work yesterday and were too tired last night. I've been like this since I saw your ass walk out of my office."

Emerson smirked against Talon's neck and kissed her as she stroked. Talon's hand went around Emerson's neck and pulled her in closer.

"I'll make it up to you later, I promise," Emerson said.

"You're making it up to me now," Talon replied, kissing Emerson hard.

"Oh, I have *plans* for us."

"You do? Fuck," Talon said, hips bucking against Emerson's hand.

"This is just the beginning," Emerson replied, biting down a little on Talon's neck.

"Shit. I'm coming," Talon said.

Her hands gripped the railing in front of her as Emerson continued to stroke. When Talon came down, she relaxed fully back into Emerson's embrace.

"I needed that," Talon said.

"We should get going," Emerson muttered against Talon's neck.

"What? No. We can be late. You have *plans*," Talon said.

"Not *that* late," Emerson laughed a little. "My plans are very thorough,"

"Shit. I should have rented this place on a weekend my friends *weren't* here," Talon stated.

"There's always another weekend," Emerson replied.

"I like the sound of that," Talon told her.

"Hey, you two!"

"Shit," Talon said again, quickly redoing her jeans.

Emerson looked down and saw Aria and Annie.

"Oh, hey," Emerson said.

"We figured out how to get over here from Aria and Ellie's cabin," Annie said.

"Joy," Talon replied sarcastically.

Emerson laughed and said, "We'll be right over."

"We're meeting out back," Annie said. "Wes has food all set up and stuff."

"Great." Emerson smiled down at them.

"Talon, your shirt is stuck in your zipper," Aria said, pointing up at Talon. "We'll be back in ten minutes if you don't make it over there."

"She's kidding," Annie said, laughing.

"No, she's not," Talon replied.

Emerson took Talon's hand, and they went to the bathroom, where Emerson washed her hands as Talon attempted to undo her jeans to *return the favor*, as she said. They kissed against the shower door for a few minutes, with Emerson playfully fighting off Talon's hands and Talon finally giving up. Then, they joined Talon's friends in Weston's backyard.

"Took you two long enough," Weston teased.

"It's been eleven minutes," Talon argued. "I needed one minute just to get my shirt unstuck from my zipper."

"Wait. What?" Eleanor said.

"Emerson just had a little fun with Talon on their balcony," Aria said.

"You have a balcony?" Scarlet asked, sitting on the picnic table.

"They just had sex on it, so you might not want to go up there until it rains," Paisley remarked.

"Hey," Talon said, slapping her shoulder playfully and sitting down next to her.

Emerson sat down on Talon's other side, and they all ate lunch together. Emerson hadn't ever had this before. She'd had her family and her responsibilities, so she had very few friends. Shea were one of them, but now that they were moving out of state, Emerson was happy she had Talon's friends and considered them her friends now.

"So, I'm thinking, we eat, then we play some board games over at our cabin," Ellie suggested. "We have the one with all the games this year."

"Oh, Risk," Paisley said.

"Never again," Aria replied, glaring at her.

"You're just mad you lost," Paisley stated.

"You made an alliance with me and then took me out."

"You deserved it for being so naïve," Paisley replied.

"Paisley is the competitive one, I take it?" Emerson asked.

"She has her moments," Talon said, placing a hand on Emerson's thigh.

"When are we taking the boat out?" Scarlet asked.

"Tomorrow," Weston replied. "I thought everyone would want to settle in today."

"Good plan," Emerson said, squeezing Talon's hand on her thigh. "I worked late yesterday, so I could use an early night."

Half the table laughed.

"You're fooling no one with that," Aria said, winking at Emerson. "I'd like to make an announcement, though, if I may."

"If you may?" Paisley said. "Are we really not going to make fun of her for saying that?"

"Have you heard some of the pretentious shit that comes out of *your* mouth?" Ellie said, laughing.

"Anyway," Aria said. "I am going away for a while after this weekend."

"What?" Scarlet spoke.

"Europe. Solo-backpacking trip this time."

"For how long?" Weston asked.

"I'm thinking about a month. I've got some of it worked out, but not all of it yet."

"Why now?" Paisley asked.

"I just need *something*, and I don't know what it is, so I'm going to go there to try to figure it out." Aria sighed. "I'm bored, and… I don't know. I just can't decide if I want to really try to find someone or if I want to keep doing what I'm doing – which I'm bored with, too, but changing and finding someone for real is scary as fuck. I don't know how you guys did it," she said, looking from Weston and Annie to Talon and Emerson. "I think getting away will help me clear my head."

"You sure you should go alone?" Talon asked.

"I need to, but I have friends all over the place. I'll stay with some of them and in good hotels otherwise. I'll be good."

"We'll miss you," Scarlet said.

"I'll miss you guys, too. But this will be good for me, I think."

"Well, then this is the last time we'll all be together for a while. We should celebrate and have as much fun as possible," Weston said.

"I agree," Talon whispered into Emerson's ear, and she was *not* talking about the kind of fun Weston was talking about.

***

Talon stared out over the lake and considered how much had changed in her life just in the past few months. She had a new job that she loved and, it turned out, was pretty good at. She was making more money now, which helped out with the bills, and she was able to put more away for her brother's education. She had amazing friends who still managed to find time to see one another, even though they were all getting busier in their lives, and she had found the perfect girlfriend.

Emerson was her other half, and Talon knew that now. Most importantly, it no longer terrified her. It was just understood. They'd spent the past three months getting to know one another more and spending some time with Talon's family and more time with Emerson's. Talon had even babysat Emerson's nephews when she and Fiona wanted to have a sisters' night, and when they'd gotten back to Emerson's place, they'd found them playing in a pillow-and-blanket fort in Emerson's living room.

"Having fun?" Emerson had asked through her laughter.

"Excuse me. We're busy. We have to fortify this wall over here," Talon had said.

Emerson and Fiona had joined them on the floor and helped by adding the couch cushions. Once the boys were about to fall asleep, Fiona had taken them home, and Emerson had pounced on Talon, tearing the fort down in one fell swoop but making it up to Talon right after.

"What are you doing out here?" Emerson asked later.

Talon turned around to see Emerson standing there, holding a canister of whipped cream in one hand and wearing nothing.

"Holy shit!" Talon exclaimed.

"I bought two of these," Emerson said, shaking it and then spraying some into her mouth. "Interested?"

Talon nodded rapidly and removed her t-shirt before she even made it inside the bedroom.

Printed in Great Britain
by Amazon

56410286R00158